MW01504007

TANGLED LOVE

CHAOTIC REIN
BOOK 1

HALEY JENNER

COPYRIGHT

Trigger / Content Warnings

To anyone who has ever felt shadowed by their dark thoughts.

PROLOGUE

PARKER

I've seen this scene before. A hundred times. Maybe more. You know the one. The rained upon funeral. People gathered in their dark clothes, umbrellas scattered amongst the crowd, shielding them from the dreary weather as they pay their respects. The widower; soul extinguished from his eyes, flanked by his two sons. The boys dressed in the same black attire as their father, loss and anguish cloaking their not-yet-matured faces.

It's different experiencing it first-hand. There's a hollowness to it that swallows you. That engulfs you until you're not sure you're still standing there. You feel as though you're watching from a distance. Watching yourself grieve for the single most important person in your life. You want to comfort yourself and move closer to offer your support, but that would mean being amidst the misery, so you let yourself remain detached. For as long as possible, anyway.

I'm happy about the rain. The bleak and colorless damp thundering down on me. I'd be pissed if Seattle decided to shine one of the few warm days of the year upon us today. No. Rain and gloom are apt. It's what it should be.

Words are spoken, but I let them pass my ears without hearing them. Nothing anyone would say is meaningful enough for me to listen. They'd all be clichés and empty words of how joyous her time with us was. *Was.* That's the word I can't seem to stomach. The word I can't move past without suffocating in my grief. It's painful enough to make my fourteen-year-old self want to die. To crawl into the hole the wooden box is hanging over and move into the abyss with her. Except that would mean leaving Rocco, and I'm not gutless enough to do that.

Her casket begins to lower without further warning, and I choke on my breath. I attempt to swallow it down, wanting to shield everyone from the overwhelming sadness drowning me. I have no choice. I was warned; my father's words still rang in my ears.

Don't embarrass me with theatrics today. Show me your strength. Prove to me you belong in this family. Otherwise, there'll be consequences.

Rocco's hand grabs tightly onto mine, and his whole body shakes with his will not to let his tears spill over, the movement visibly moving my arm. We turn, eyes anchoring, and remain glued to one another as our mother meets the earth. Leaving us in the hell she couldn't have imagined would encase us—a nightmare brought down by her beloved.

Her husband.

Our father.

A man broken down by grief and consumed with hate. He no longer resembles a human being.

No. Now the devil himself would cower against Kane Shay. I force myself to see his side, to understand what happens to a person when something is stolen from them. Forcibly. Brutally.

You lose any good that sat within your soul. It suffocates with your hate.

"PARKER, SWEETHEART, YOU SHOULD EAT SOMETHING."

I glance at Aunt Mira, her soft-spoken voice weak in its delivery. Uncle Marcus charged her with our care today. Ensuring Rocco and I remained dutiful and out of sight, making certain we ate. It angers me. I'm not hungry; the thought of food causes the sick feeling in my stomach to magnify. But I know if I don't, she'll bear the brunt. The blame for my refusing food. Most likely with his fists. I hate him. I hate the ruthless glint in his eyes. The void of emotion that strips away his humanity. Besides anger, of course. He radiates it. I understand why my father charged him with being his second. You want someone that lacks feeling at your side. I watched him at the funeral when I could stomach lifting my eyes from my brother's; all I could see on his face was boredom and irritation at having to be there. Our mother, his sister-in-law, was being laid to rest, and her funeral inconvenienced him. I know he was only there at my father's demand.

"Sure, Aunt Mira," I agree, watching the bunch of her shoulders relax at my compliance. "I'll go find Rocco."

She smiles at me sadly, leaning down to touch her lips to my hair before moving toward the kitchen.

If I'm glad for anything today, it's her. Relief that we still have her. Even if she is nothing more than a shell of a person, I'll take that over whatever else Rocco and I have on offer.

Men and women gather in our living area, hushed tones and commiserated glances thrown at me as I edge past them in search of my brother. It doesn't take me long to locate him, even in this prison our father calls our home.

"Rocco," I call out when I see him.

Lifting a finger to his lips at lightning speed, he instructs me to be quiet, his feet edging him closer to our father's office. I pad on light feet to stand behind him, listening closely to the voices inside.

"We react now, Kane. Take Dominic out."

The malevolence in Marcus' tone shoots a shiver up my spine, and I swallow deeply against how easily he speaks of death, of taking someone's life.

"You don't think they're prepared for that? Be smart, Marcus. No one wants Rein's blood more than I do. He killed my fucking wife."

The pain in my father's voice is obvious but easily drowned out by his hate, making his declaration sound more vengeful than broken.

"So fucking kill him," Marcus argues desperately, and it gives me pause as to why he cares so much. My mother never liked him, and the feeling was mutual. He didn't show an ounce of grief when mom's life was taken, yet he's desperate to exact revenge. It makes no sense, and I can only speculate that his thirst for chaos and blood runs so deep he'll take any opportunity to find it.

Quiet descends, and Rocco looks at me briefly before moving his ear back toward the office. Our father speaks next, the quiet haunt of his tone terrifying. "He blew her fucking face off, Marcus. I couldn't even look at her to say goodbye. He made sure there was nothing left of her beautiful face. So I'm gonna sit on my anger, my vengeance, my revenge, and when the time is right, I will take everything from him. I'm gonna rip his heart from his body as he did mine."

Vomit rushes up my throat, and I bend over in pain. Rocco yanks me upward, his eyes turning a violent shade of black. Our eyes meet, fire storming in his, mine filling with heartache as we try to stomach the words we just heard. The brutality in the way our mother died. He holds my arm and moves us away, but the words follow us. They'll haunt me until the day I die. Until the moment I take my very last breath. I know that. As they flew from my father's mouth, dripping with hate, they engrained themselves in my mind, never to be erased.

He blew her fucking face off. He made sure there was nothing left of her beautiful face.

"What are you two doing?"

Rocco whirls us around at the sound of Marcus' voice, his entire body still vibrating with anger. He can't speak, the violent fury cutting off his ability to communicate. My eyes are brimming with tears, but I swallow my need to cry. Not in front of him. Never will I show weakness to a man so willing to exploit it.

"We're checking if Dad wanted something to eat. Aunt Mira is making us lunch," I blurt out, taking a step back and pulling Rocco with me. "But we heard voices in his office, so we didn't want to interrupt."

Marcus eyes us skeptically, focus honing in on my brother. He reads Rocco's mood, and a wicked smile crosses his face. He knows we heard their conversation, and he's happy we now know the violent end our mother came to.

He wants this version of Rocco he sees to be permanent. The psychotic child no one can reason with. He sees the perfect soldier. A pawn in whatever games he seems to be playing.

Rocco meets his stare, refusing to back down at the devil dancing in Marcus' eyes.

"Go," Marcus finally speaks, flicking his wrist, dismissing us both, and I drag Rocco away.

"ROCCO?" I call into the black of his bedroom.

"What's wrong?" he asks, his voice devoid of emotion. My eyes settle in the direction of his voice, and I make out his silhouette, sitting upright on his bed, knees bent.

"Mind if I crash in your room? I just, what Dad said, I...."

"Yeah, kid," he coughs, shifting on his bed to allow me space.

I wander over, settling alongside him, and by some miracle, I fall asleep, even with the haunting words of my father glowing in the forefront of my mind.

I dream of her. She was beautiful; light hair, a wide smile, and swirling gray eyes. I loved her. *Love her.* Even with her gone, that won't stop. I dream of her laughing and how happy our lives were because of her. But my dreams turn. They twist with the words I wish I hadn't heard, and I see her smile right before a bullet penetrates her skull. Her face is replaced by blood.

"PARKER."

I wake up sweating, my heart racing. Rocco's hands are grasped tightly to my upper arms as he calls my name, pulling me into consciousness. It takes me a moment, my nightmare hits me again, and I cry. I sob heavily, and he pulls me into his chest.

"You heard Dad. We'll get vengeance, Parker. I promise we'll make them pay. We'll fucking destroy them for taking her away from us."

THREE YEARS LATER, my father is shot down in a shower of bullets. A gun trade gone bad. I wish I could say I was sad. But the last three years have been an abyss of pain. Of suffering. Kane Shay made sure of that. He took out his frustration, hate, anger, and grief on us. He beat us and destroyed the light in our souls our mother had placed there. Then, he slowly began training us to hate as he did.

I was relieved by his death, but it fueled something different inside Rocco. He took on my father's vengeance. He took on his hate and let it worsen over time. He let it expand and fester, and without choice, he took me along with him.

ONE

PARKER

My knee cracks as I stand, the effort working my stiff muscles. I've been watching her for days now. Not that she's noticed. I've been discreet, but I sure as shit haven't been hiding. Yet nothing, not even a curious glance in my direction.

Working out her routine was easy enough. Aside from work, she's a homebody. She doesn't have a man or many friends even. But she's also in no way closed off or seemingly disappointed by her lack of social life. She's content. Happy even.

I've been sitting for close to an hour watching her work. Watching her smile. Watching her laugh. Watching the easy happiness in which she lives. I resent her for that. Begrudge how carefree and simple her life must be, how lacking of torment or turmoil it is. That life could've been mine. It should've been mine. But, while she has pranced through her existence with a large smile and happy eyes, I've been fighting against being swallowed up by hell. For eighteen years.

I move closer to the shop window, shoulder leaning casually against a pillar, appearing relaxed to passers-by. If only they knew the truth. If only they could see my mind's eye, working tirelessly behind the scenes as I stand here, nonchalant and indifferent.

From the pictures Rocco showed me, I knew what she looked like before my stakeout began. But seeing her in the flesh, the image didn't do her justice. Not by a long shot.

I've had my fair share of women. Some smoking, others not as much. I've found over the years that hot women are a dime a dozen. Beauty, *real* beauty, the untouchable kind, it's rare. Manufactured for consumers, sure, marketing assholes trying in vain to recreate the unrivaled beauty of someone like her.

Like Codi Rein.

Codi's allure is one hundred percent real. She's flawless. Skin tone like creamed butter; smooth and honeyed. Her hair is naturally highlighted, strands a perfected array of differing shades of blonde. It hits her shoulders, soft waves hanging loosely and dancing around her face. I can't see her eyes from this far away, but I know they're blue, so dark they flash purple. Her body is tight, and I mean tight. Skin pulled firmly over svelte curves.

She's a wet dream come to life, and I get to play with her. Well, that's what I've decided anyway. We had a straightforward plan. Watch her for a bit, learn her routine, and move into the execution phase when the timing is right.

Now though, it seems such a waste. I'm hoping Rocco will be content with me going off-path. Let me have some fun with the sweetness of Codi Rein before her family gets what's coming to them.

I pull the door of the shop open, the warmth of the inside hitting me like a wall. She looks up at the small bell that chimes as I enter, watching my approach.

"Hiya, handsome."

Her smile is so big it breaks her face, stretching her lips in a way that turns them from red to a bruised pink. Her smile is genuine. *Kind.* I pause momentarily, considering that I've never smiled like that. Genuinely. Don't get me wrong; I fake the fuck out of a grin when I need it. But it isn't ever real, not like hers.

Her head tips to the side, my silence making her uncertain, but her smile stays intact, not even the slightest waver in the gesture as she considers me. She's not concerned by my rough appearance. Not in the least. My ink, thick muscles, and bruised and cut skin don't seem to cause her any discomfort. Not in the way it should. She should be nervous. Anxious by my severe disposition. Instead, I see only kindness, intrigue even.

I shake my head, pulling myself back to the moment, forcing myself to remember why I'm here.

I blink slowly, purposefully pushing my tongue out to wet my lips. Her focus drops to my lips, as silently instructed, and I let her gaze run along my mouth, my teeth chewing my bottom lip.

Clearing my throat, I massage the back of my neck, feigning nerves I don't feel.

"Walk past this place every day, and I've never seen you before."

She reluctantly pulls her eyes from my lips, and I mentally fist-bump myself.

Success.

"I've never seen you either, handsome. Worked here for a few years, too." A quiet flirtation dances in her tone as her eyes skirt around the shop before settling back on me.

"Kicking myself I haven't laid eyes on you sooner."

She ducks her head, working to hide the shy smile on her pretty face. When she lifts it again, her pleased embarrassment shows in the shaded blush lightening her creamy complexion.

She lets her eyes track over my body, my bulking biceps visible under my short-sleeved shirt, along the ink decorating my arms down to my hands, now tucked deep into the pockets of my jeans. Her eyes drop to my heavy boots, then back up to my face, absorbed interest peaking as she drags her gaze along the bruise of my eye socket, the generous graze along the line of my jaw.

"That so?" She finally speaks, her palms leaning on the counter as she leans toward me.

I force my fake as fuck grin onto my face, and she buys it, returning the gesture. I don't answer her question; my smile does that for me.

"So, did you come in here to tell me that, or are you buying something?"

I glance around the small store, across the limited clothing displays, and laugh. "I'm not buying anything."

She bites her bottom lip, hiding the pleased smile that crosses her face, and I rock back on my heels as I watch her.

"You got a man?"

She startles at my question, laughing awkwardly. "Umm... Not sure that's a question you dive right into, handsome. You don't even know my name."

I lift my shoulders in dismissal. "Just need to know if I need to kill anyone before I ask your name."

She laughs, her face turning to the side as the sing-song sound echoes into the sparse space. "You don't need to kill anyone."

I wink at her, and she shakes her head, amused by my strange behavior.

I wait another moment, watching her silently. Content that I've planted myself firmly into her intrigue, I turn on my heel, walking on heavy feet to the door of the shop.

"That's it?"

I pause, hand outstretched as I reach to push on the glass. Looking over my shoulder, I wink. "For now."

She coughs out a laugh, shaking her head in disappointment. "You're not even gonna ask me my name?"

Hand on the glass, I push, a small bell chiming overhead. "There's no fun in that, Sugar."

"No fun in what?"

"Knowing too much too soon," I say, walking my feet through the door and letting it close behind me. Without looking back, I walk toward home with a confidence that might be presumptuous. But fuck, this is going to be easy, far simpler than I thought, and a lot more fun too.

THROWING my keys onto the entry table, I scratch a hand down my face.

"We close to locking this down?"

I turn at Rocco's rough statement, irritated at the demand in the sound.

He's shirtless, body rippling with just-used muscle, his skin slick with a thick sheen of sweat. He seems calm, well, Rocco-type calm, and I surmise he's just been boxing, working to relieve the tension that coils tightly in his body. Anger. Everything he does is driven by cold hard fury. Revenge. I get it. I do. I understand his want for blood. For vengeance. It doesn't overtake my body and mind in the way it does him. But I still feel it running through my veins. Shit, our father made sure of that.

I nod, answering his question. His head moves up and down in appreciation, the hard lines around his mouth giving slightly. "Good."

"Listen," I start, and he watches me expectantly, one thick

eyebrow raised. "If you're cool with it, I might play with her for a while. Can't hurt to have some fun first," I shrug.

He doesn't say anything, not straight away, but after a moment's pause, a sick, twisted smile forms along his face.

"There's hope for you after all. She's hot," he states, eyebrows rising this time in playful appreciation.

I cough out a laugh. "Fuck yeah, she's hot. I may as well taste her brand of sweet before she goes to ground."

He nods as I speak, eyes focused elsewhere in contemplative thought. "This'll change our plan. People will see you around, so we won't be able to deny the connection." He pauses, cracking his knuckles to focus his mind. It can't be as brutal or as apparent as we initially wanted.

I cringe internally at whatever brutality Rocco was considering but work to keep my face neutral, not wanting him to doubt my commitment, my thirst for revenge.

"I'll think about it, but I like this idea better. Like the fact that you'll use her up." His face lightens with excitement, his eyes dancing with his psychotic thoughts. "When are you seeing her again?"

Using my thumbs, I push down on my index fingers to hear the crack of my knuckles. "I don't know," I throw out. "I'll show up again tomorrow. Maybe the next day. Not sure yet."

He growls, nostrils flaring as he steps closer. Our height is on par, but he's bigger than me. Easy. The result of countless hours in the gym or the ring.

"This isn't a game, Park. You can have your fun. But not for long. Don't drag this shit out. We've waited long enough."

I push his chest, not intimidated by his festering anger. "You look like Codi Rein; you get every fucker from here to Cali vying for your attention. So I'm gonna play a different game."

He backs off, his eyes skeptical as he waits for me to continue.

"Do I look like the type of guy that walks into some rich bitch shop asking for a date?"

A smile quirks on his lips as he takes in my bruised face, and I shake my head in amusement. "You need to fucking chill, Roc. I told you, I'm in on this. I just thought, playing with her for a bit, we'd get a little something extra. Well, I'd get the extra." I grin, and he shakes his head with an amused sigh. "Trust me when I tell you, Codi Rein, right now, I'm all she's thinking about."

He steps back into my space, his large, inked hand grabbing my jaw roughly. "Ah, that pretty face has to be good for somethin', huh?"

I push him back again. "You're just jealous I pull more pussy than you."

His neck tips back, bringing the flames inked into the side of his neck into full view as he laughs. "Keep telling yourself that, dollface."

I flip him off, moving toward my room, my Xbox calling. Plans to lose myself in hours of mindless blood and violence, a temptation too good to pass up.

"Yo, Parker." I stop when I hear Rocco's voice, glancing over my shoulders to meet his eyes. "You got good inside you, kid. Don't let that fuck with your mind. We have a plan, don't let this bitch's dimples play on your conscience."

He doesn't wait for my response, disappearing down the hall of our loft without another look in my direction.

"Bitch doesn't have fucking dimples," I mumble, irritated by his lack of belief in my ability to pull this off.

I get it. He's the psycho. The brother fueled with rage after living in the hell our dad rained upon us. He definitely suffered worse than me. But that doesn't mean I'm weak. And it sure as shit doesn't mean I don't have the guts to pull this off.

Dominic Rein will feel pain like he can't imagine. He will know what it feels like to have his heart ripped from his chest. He'll know what it's like to try and fight to survive in the cold, harrowing depths of hell.

Only he'll lose.

TWO
CODI

I curse myself again for looking at the glass, trying to catch a glimpse of the handsome stranger plaguing my thoughts. He shouldn't be. I know that. I'm not stupid. I know he's dangerous. If the blackness dancing in his gray, wolf-like eyes wasn't a give-away, the tattoos and bruising most definitely should've been. He was so, ugh, I don't know, magnificent in his menace. Don't get me wrong, he was pretty. So very pretty. Dark lashes surround his predatory eyes, and dirty blonde hair is styled in a way that makes it obvious he takes pride in his appearance. Shaved short along the sides, longer on top, his fringe tickling his forehead. His body was tall and broad but lean enough to down-play his bulk. Almost every visible inch of skin was decorated with colorful ink; down his arms, on his hands, and up his neck. I wanted a closer look. I've never seen anything quite like it. Don't get me wrong, associates of my father have tattoos, but not like this. Not so artfully placed on their bodies.

My eyes hit the glass again, and I growl in frustration at myself. This is ridiculous. I have no clue why my thoughts are wholly derailed by this man. I'm smarter than this, Jesus; he didn't even ask my name. He didn't ask or say much of anything. He just kinda stood there, staring. It wasn't creepy, though. More confusing and a little intriguing.

"Excuse me?" I turn my head, plastering on a smile for the customer standing before me. "Would you have this in a smaller size?"

I glance at the black mini-dress held in her hands and rid my mind of the dangerous stranger. Pushing away from the counter, I walk toward her, hands reaching for the dress. "Let me check."

She smiles her thanks, moving back toward the fitting rooms. Having handed her the next size down, the door chimes in its sing-song declaration that someone has entered the store, and I move in that direction to greet my customer.

My feet stumble when I see him, an awkward stagger before I catch myself, smoothing my skirt to hide my embarrassment. His arms are crossed over his broad chest, eyes scanning the immediate space in search of me. He smirks at my misstep, not amused, more pleased at the reaction he seemed to have caused.

"Hello, Bob."

A fleeting glance of shock cloaks his features before he schools it, letting his indifference once again stare out. "Bob?"

I shrug. "You wouldn't give me your name, so I picked one for myself."

He tries hard to camouflage the smile once again twitching at his mouth. "And Bob was the best you came up with?"

Again, I shrug. "Humanized you a little."

He turns his face to laugh, and the threat in the sound taunts me. A delicate rose is tattooed along the column of his neck. "Sugar, trust me, best you consider me for the monster I am."

I'm taken aback by his words. At his belief in the words he just spoke.

"I don't see a monster when I look at you. I see danger, sure. But no monster."

"You're not looking hard enough."

I blink at him slowly, trying to read his intention. He's here. A purposeful act to see me again, but he's what, warning me off?

"Agree to disagree," I dismiss him, moving to a display of clothes to readjust unnecessarily.

"Parker."

His voice is coated with a rough gravel, and I gift myself a moment to turn back and look at him properly. His bruising has subsided in the few days since I first saw him, his eye socket and jaw now tarnished with a faint yellow hue.

"Sorry?" I ask.

"My name. It's Parker."

"Hmmm," I nod thoughtfully. "Suits you better than Bob."

We share a smile, and I high-five myself internally, happy I brought a genuine grin to his face. Sure, he's smiled a few times, but there always seems to be a falseness behind it. An act. A portrayal of someone he's trying to be.

"Looking to buy something this time," he states, and I raise an eyebrow in shock. "For a girl," he continues, and my happiness dissipates, disappointment filtering inside me at reading his signals so wrong.

I school my features, plastering on the smile I've been trained to offer, and his eyes settle on my face, his brow furrowing as he focuses on my mouth. "Don't do that."

My smile falters. "Sorry?"

"Your smile was fake. Don't smile at me like that. I only want your real ones."

I cough out my embarrassment, uncertain at his strange statement. He looks much the same. Pushed off-guard by his own demand.

His head twists and turns, his eyes scanning over the space of my workplace. "You wear shit from here?"

I don't answer. Not purposefully. Confusion has consumed my mind, and I struggle with piecing words together.

After moments of silence, his intense stare falls back on me, and he raises an eyebrow.

Readjusting my blouse, I clear my throat. "Sorry, what?"

"You do that a lot. Apologize unnecessarily. You should stop that. I asked if you shop here yourself?"

I stutter. "Umm... No. I, ah, sometimes." I nod blankly. "They have cute dresses occasionally, but mostly I feel more comfortable in jeans and a t-shirt."

He assesses my outfit; my tight-fitting pencil skirt and white blouse.

"Dress code," I fill in unnecessarily with a shrug.

The girl I'd been helping moments before Parker's untimely arrival steps into the space and freezes awkwardly.

"Better?" I direct my full attention to her, turning my back on Parker.

She glances at Parker, then back to me. "Much. I'll take it."

I gesture at the counter, and she moves toward it without looking at us again.

"Look around for your girlfriend, and I'll be with you in a moment."

"She's not my girlfriend," he speaks to my back. My feet falter again, and I miss a step, recovering it quickly. "Not yet, anyway."

Serving the customer, I work my hardest to ignore the penetrating stare of the dangerous man suffocating my workspace. My cheeks feel flushed, and my hands shake.

Waiting for the young girl to leave the store, I push out a

place the dress carefully back in the box, press the card delicately on top, and replace the lid, grinning the entire time.

I STAND IN MY UNDERWEAR, staring at the dress draped across my bed.

I should definitely meet him. He invited me. I like him. *I think.* I don't really *know* him. But do you really know anyone before you start dating them?

It's too risky. Too dangerous. He is too risky. Too dangerous. Good God, the man is menace personified. Storming eyes, inked skin, and ripped muscles. Not to mention the bruising and the cuts. He vibrates threat, daring anyone to challenge him.

"Reason you're standing in only your underwear, biting your nail all the while staring at a scrap of red material?"

I turn at Camryn's voice, smiling at her in greeting. Her shoulder is propped against my doorframe, scrubs covering her body, feet bare.

"That guy came back into the shop," I explain. "It was odd. *Again.* I thought I'd read his signals wrong. He came in to buy something for a girl. It turns out that girl was me. This dress was waiting on the counter, gift-wrapped." I arch an eyebrow. "When I came back from lunch. He left me a note asking me to meet him tonight at Ruin."

"How the fuck did he get into the shop if you were at lunch?" She pushes off the doorframe, walking into my room to drop onto my bed. "Cute dress."

I nod. "I'm refusing to think about how he managed to break into the shop without actually breaking in."

She nods offhandedly. "Still don't know why you work in

that rich-bitch shop. You're too smart to be serving people for a living."

I frown at her. "Ryn. I like it. It's stress-free."

"So, you like him, he bought you a dress *and* invited you out, but you're second-guessing?"

My hands fall to my hips. "You're right. I should go."

"You should go," she agrees. "As long as you feel safe around him."

I sigh, moving to sit next to her. "I shouldn't feel safe. There's definitely something dark working behind his eyes, but he doesn't scare me."

She looks a million miles away, and I know better than to reach out and touch her, so I wait for her to come back to me. She does, eventually, forcing a pained smile onto her face before standing up. "Instincts are usually pretty spot on."

She watches me for a beat, forcing away her demons before smiling affectionately at me. "I'm done staring at your tits. I'm going to eat something incredibly unhealthy and pass out."

She stops at my door, hand on the frame as she glances back. "Be safe, ok? Text or call me and let me know what you're doing."

"You could come, you know," I call out to her retreating form.

"HA!" she barks out. "Good one."

THREE

PARKER

"If you see a blonde walk through these doors in a red dress, you buzz me. Immediately. Got it?"

The security guard nods with bored indifference, and I step into his space. "You know who pays you? Me." I point heavily to my chest. "So fucking listen to what I'm telling you before I break your face."

He holds his hands up in surrender, nodding vigorously. "I got it, Parker. Blonde. Red dress. Call you. Immediately."

I nod, shoulders relaxing as I take a step back. "She's really fucking cute. You'll wanna fuck her, don't let yourself think about that. I'll know, and I'll cut off your dick. Got it?"

His eyes widen, and he nods, turning to the gathering crowd. Stalking back through the club, I push past people without care, working to get back to my office to take a breath. Closing myself into the small space, I crack my knuckles, irritated at the tension I feel at the uncertainty of tonight.

What the fuck do I do if she doesn't show? I'm still caught on how I'm supposed to cement myself into her life. For someone who isn't afraid to let her feelings show on her face, she's really fucking hard to read. She seems to contradict herself at any given opportunity.

She's shy, coy almost when it comes to our interactions, but in the same way, her diffidence shows on her face. Her quiet and easy flirtation stuns me in its openness.

She's unsure, I'd almost bet somewhat inexperienced, but she'll watch me candidly, her interest in me not camouflaged.

If I play this wrong, she's gone. That I'm sure of. That happens, and Rocco spirals. That happens, and I lose out on the time I plan on spending with her. I know that's dangerous to think about. But I'm intrigued.

My cell buzzes in my pocket, and I reach in to retrieve it.

TY

She's here

Tucking my phone back into my jeans, I rub my hands on my pants, cracking my neck from side to side. Yanking the door open, I stalk back through the club, pushing people out of my way without issue.

I see her as soon as my feet hit the bottom floor of the two-leveled building. She'd be impossible to miss. She's wearing the dress, fitted so perfectly to her figure you'd think it was painted onto her skin. The red material blazes against her ivory skin, her back on show. The naked skin taunts every man in the club, two dimples pushed into the sway of her lower back like a target, raging and at the ready.

The dress hits about three inches below her ass, the shape of her slender legs emphasized by the red stilettos her feet sit within.

Her shoulder-length hair is down, pinned severely back on the right side, messy waves falling along the other.

She leans across the bar, offering her ear to Fin, my bartender. The move arches her back, offering the mass of men watching her the gift of the bend in her spine, the line clear and defined.

Her neck tips back at something Fin says, an accomplished grin shining on his face as he watches her. Another dickhead approaches her side, his hand touching her bare back, and my hands clench into fists unconsciously. I shake them out. She pleases me, immediately stepping from his touch and shaking her head in rejection. He moves in again, and she holds her hands up, waving them in a negative gesture, refusing his advances. Having seen enough, I move forward just as the wanker touches her again. She glances away from the douche, seeking help from anywhere she can find it.

Grabbing his shoulder, I yank him backward, throwing him to the ground. Glowering down at him, I look at the security guard hovering nearby. "Get him the fuck outta my club."

Turning back to Codi, her focus is still distracted, her body angled away as she searches the growing crowd. Finally, turning back, her eyes hit mine, and a slow blink of relief relaxes her posture.

I'm stunned by her beauty. She's wearing makeup thicker than I've seen the few times I've laid eyes on her in person. Her deep blue eyes are rimmed heavily in black, intensifying the color of her iris to almost purple. Her perfectly crafted lips are painted nude, currently tipped upward in the delicate beginnings of a smile.

I want so badly to kiss her, and I hate myself for it. Kissing isn't something I crave. Typically, it's a means to an end. Women love making out. It gets them wet. Which is my end goal. To fuck them. But right now, staring at Codi's pillowed mouth, I'd give my next breath, most likely my last, to taste her. I pull my eyes away from her luscious mouth and thoughts that should not be planting themselves in my mind.

Her ear, the one not covered by her hair, is encased from lobe to tip in an intricate cuff, and I lean closer, my lips a breath away. "Nice dress."

Her teeth catch her bottom lip, and she laughs softly, dragging the soft cushion through her bite. "Yeah, someone happened to gain access to my *locked* place of work to leave it for me."

I raise my eyebrows in appreciation. "Impressive."

She glances to the side. "Or concerning."

Tilting my head, I instruct her to follow me. She does this without argument, and I am more than fascinated by the lack of games she seems to be playing. Her interest in me is genuine, and she feels no need to hide it. It's liberating.

She follows my lead up the stairs to the VIP area on the second floor, and I force myself not to look back and watch her ascent. Dropping my guard, even for a second, letting her see the biting need I feel to consume her, isn't an option. Yeah, I want to fuck her. *Bad.* I want to dirty her pretty little perfection of a life. I want to introduce her to the addiction a hard and filthy fuck can cause. My want might be hardwired, but I need her to swallow my indifference. Detached. That's who I am. All that she'll get.

Reaching the top, I freeze briefly at the sight of Rocco. He lifts his beer in salute in my direction, eyes hardening almost immediately as Codi comes into view.

Moving to the seating farthest away from him, I wait for Codi to slide along the small rounded booth before following her in. I focus my complete attention on her and her alone, working to rid Rocco's looming presence from my psyche, unsure of what the fuck he's playing at.

"Codi." She leans in closer, and I let my fake as fuck grin grow on my face.

"It's better. I'll give you that."

She leans back slightly, looking uncertain. "What?"

"Than Bob. I prefer Cody to Bob."

She pulls a hand to her face, covering her mouth as she giggles into it.

Women giggling usually pisses me off. The forced need to feel for it to sound attractive. Their inability to really let loose, afraid they'll embarrass themselves. Not Codi, no, like the rest of her, the giggle is real. A sound that escapes her stomach, her whole body shaking with the freeness in her laugh. Sitting here, listening to her laughter, I want to make her do it again.

"No," she sighs cheerfully. "It's my name. *I'm* Codi."

"Your parents gave you a boy's name?"

She shrugs, smiling in a way that makes me know this isn't the first time she's heard something to that effect.

"My sister's name is Camryn."

I nod, pursing my lips in thought. "Codi. I like it. Gotta last name Codi?"

"Rein. Codi Rein."

I swallow the tremor of anger that flashes through me at hearing her last name, turning away to signal a server. Ordering our drinks, I work to suppress the volatile temper wanting to spill from inside me, the quaking fury that wants to grab her by the throat and make her listen to what her father took from me.

I sit silently, eyes averted while we wait for our drinks. She stares at my profile but doesn't fidget or attempt conversation. She waits quietly while I repress my overwhelming need to fight.

Our drinks arrive, and I exhale heavily, turning back toward her and holding up my glass. "Nice to meet you, Codi Rein."

She clinks her glass against mine, taking a small sip as she watches me down my gin and tonic in a single swallow. She eyes me cautiously, but I don't see her fear even as I saturate in my rage. It's not there. Instead, I see only curiosity, definitely a small sliver of caution, but it's not significant.

As our eyes remain anchored, she gives away to her caution, a beautiful smile spanning her face. Is it possible for someone to be this attractive? Or am I amplifying it in my head because she's forbidden? Is it possible that her beauty is on par with every bitch in this club, and because she's poisonous for my soul, my self-destructive fuck of a mind is deceiving me?

I blink purposefully, working to rid the haze of exaggerated lust. It doesn't work. Worse, her beauty hits me painfully when my eyes refocus on her face.

I want to strangle her. I want to wrap my inked hand around the creamy column of her neck but not to hurt her. No. I want to feel her fluttering pulse under my fingertips. I want to cut off her air supply only to exemplify her orgasm and make her come *harder*.

I want to sink my teeth into her skin, only to mark her flawless skin a rainbow of blue, purple, and red. Imprint my bite marks all over her body like tattoos, marking her as mine.

I want to tear her open, fuck her so hard and deep she'll struggle to remember a time when her body and her pleasure didn't belong to me.

"So, how do you reserve a VIP booth in Ruin?"

My thoughts are fucking with my head. I shouldn't be so lost in her. But, unfortunately, my control is slipping, and we've yet to share a proper conversation. Worse, I haven't fucking *touched* her. This was a bad idea but fucked if I'm ready to admit defeat before I've had my fun.

I lift my hand to the waiter, signaling my want for another

drink, waiting for him to acknowledge my request with a quick drop of his chin before turning back to Codi.

"You own it."

She looks a little taken aback by my words, but the shock is pleasant, not disbelieving. "You own the club?"

"My brother and I." I indicate toward Rocco.

She swallows visibly. "The guy that's been death-staring me since I walked up those stairs? He's your brother?"

Once again, Codi Rein shocks me. She clued into Rocco's animosity but didn't let herself be frightened away by it. She ignored it.

"That's Rocco," I state. "He's a little intense."

She watches him for a few drawn-out seconds, meeting his glare head-on before focusing back on me. "Just a bit."

I smile. For real this time, and the ease with which the gesture came over me shocks me.

"Give me a sec." I push out of the booth, approaching Rocco with an irritated glare.

"Fuck you playing at?"

He shrugs indifferently. "Don't know what you're talking about."

"You need to go," I spit, kicking my foot against the table and tipping his drink.

He stands, stepping into my space.

"Rocco, for fuck's sake, how am I gonna play this right with you scaring her away. We're on the same fucking team here."

His eyes bore into mine, the devil dancing in his pupils, and I fight against the urge to step back.

"Remember that," he warns, stare darting to Codi and then back to me. Pushing my chest, he moves past me, his large frame jogging down the stairs without another glance in our direction.

I walk to the balcony rail, bracing my hands along the bar and growling into the pounding music of the club.

"You didn't have to do that on my account."

I twist my neck to bring her into view. "I didn't do shit for you." Pushing away from the edge, I move back to my seat, retrieving my glass to down it in one gulp as I signal for another. Codi doesn't follow me, remaining at the balcony edge, looking down on the partygoers with eager interest.

She stands like that for several minutes, my eyes cutting like a laser into her back. She either doesn't seem to notice. Or doesn't seem to care.

A new song starts, and as she watches the throes of people below, her hips move unconsciously. Her ass swings seductively side-to-side, and I pinch the bridge of my nose for wanting her as much as I do.

This was not supposed to happen this way. She was supposed to be crazed by her need for *me*. She was supposed to be lost in her need to touch *me*. Not the other way around.

I watch her ass move, scanning my eyes over the small number of people scattered along the balcony with us, their focus on her perky ass and the scrap of material covering it.

Growling, I stand, moving away from my desperate need to claim her. I jog down the stairs without a word, not letting myself care to see if she noticed. I move toward the bar in haste, waving Fin over. He doesn't dawdle, pouring my drink without instruction. Moving closer to the first bitch I see, I chance a look at the balcony to find Codi's confused stare pinned on me.

I smile. Sardonically. My arm moves along the tiny waist of the girl standing beside me. She takes the invitation with fervor, leaning into my body and introducing herself. I play along, nodding like I give a shit.

Looking back to Codi, I frown when I don't see her. Pushing

the random chick away, I whirl around in search of her, catching a flash of red as she beelines for the exit. I skirt between the crowd, rushing toward her.

I grab her arm when I reach her. She startles momentarily before realizing it's me.

"Where are you going?"

She looks to the ground, pulling in a steadying breath, building her confidence to meet my stare. "Listen, Parker. I honestly don't understand what's happening here. You're sending a whole"—she lifts her hands emphasizing her point, only to drop them again— "range of mixed signals that I am *nowhere* near equipped to decipher. I'm sorry, but I'm out of my depth here. I think it's best that we forget we ever met."

Panic ceases my body, but not for the right reasons. I should be afraid of Rocco, of what my failing at the task will do to his psychotic nature. But I'm more fearful of her walking out of here and me not being able to see her again.

"You're out when I say you're out," I growl.

She laughs, but it's a nervous sound, not the giggle I've discovered I enjoy hearing. "I don't even know what that means. I... Goodbye, Parker."

Her eyes blink over at me, taking a snapshot of the moment before she shakes her head and disappears through the swarm of people. I should go after her. Chase her down and force her to stay, but I just discovered how *not* to win Codi Rein's affection.

"Fuck happened?"

I clench my teeth in irritation, turning to face my brother. "Nothing, man. Something came up with her sister. She needed to bail. I offered to drive her home, but she refused."

He eyes me skeptically, and I meet his stare head-on. Eventually, he buys it, stepping back. "Gonna head off. I have some shit to take care of. Stay. Close up."

Walking back to my office, I slam my door shut. "FUCK!"

Dragging a palm down my face, I move to my desk, standing over it, breathing heavily. Using the palm of my hand, I slide it across my desk in force, throwing the entire contents to the floor in frustration. Dropping heavily into my chair, I rip at my hair, doubting my ability to pull this back on track. We had a fucking plan. A solid strategy for taking Rein down, and I let emotion get involved. I need a new method of attack. A new approach. Codi Rein *will* be mine. She'll be putty in my fucking hands right before I rip her life away, before her doting father's fucking eyes.

FOUR

CODI

The rain drizzles down lightly as I turn the corner to Blaq. I stuff my hands into the pockets of my jacket, ducking my head against the cool air of the afternoon. I skirt around the foot traffic, moving with a want to get home as soon as possible. It's freezing, I have a cold, and I want to be tucked into my bed, not pushing through downtown Seattle. For my cell, no less. I leave it at work on occasion. Not on purpose. I'm forgetful. It's an awful trait. But I need my phone. I've been without it since I left work sick on Monday and haven't contacted my dad since before then. If I don't call him soon, he'll panic, and a panicked Dominic Rein is something I don't need to deal with.

Glancing up from the path as I near the door, I come to an abrupt halt. I haven't seen him for an entire week. Not since I left him scowling after me on the ground floor of Ruin. That night was a complete disaster. I know I'm inexperienced, but if that's the way relationships work, I'll happily remain in my naivety.

He wrenches the door of Blaq open with greater force than necessary as he enters the shop. Sticking my entire body against the brick wall fifteen or so feet away, I attempt to remain invisible as I wait for him to reappear. Tucking my hair into the collar of my jacket, I disguise myself as best as possible, wanting to remain inconspicuous against his potentially searching eyes.

He exits the shop only a few minutes later, hands braced against the back of his skull in frustration. I see his lips move at the shout of his loud cussing, startling a few people walking close by. I'd bet money that he most likely growled in their direction at their disapproving looks if their scurrying feet are anything to go by. He glances up and down the street, turning to kick the wall by the door before walking in the opposite direction to my hiding spot.

I watch his retreat with a mixture of eager interest and confusion. Parker Shay turning up at my place of work was not something I'd considered a possibility. I was pretty confident we were done. Not that we'd even started anything noteworthy, I can't imagine why he'd be seeking me out, especially after last Friday night.

Unsticking myself from the brick, I take the few steps needed to reach Blaq, pulling the door open more gently than he had. Pia glances up from the counter, a small smile of greeting playing on her lips.

"You look like shit."

I walk toward her, clearing the scratch in my throat. "Feel like it."

"So listen, this guy, Parker, keeps coming by. Hot as all hell. Scary in the same way."

I frown unconsciously. "He's been by more than just now?"

Pulling my cell from the counter drawer, she hands it over, nodding her head. "Yeah, at least four times. Look, he's scaring the customers, not that he's rude or anything. I told him you'd be back on Monday. Hope that's okay."

Stuffing my cell into my jeans, I consider what Pia's told me. "Did he say what he wanted?"

She shakes her head. "Nah. Just comes in, asks whether you're working, asks when you'll be back in."

"Did he leave a number or something?"

"Nope," she sighs, no longer interested in the conversation. "Look, he'll be in on Monday. You can ask him what he wants then."

"Yeah, okay, thanks," I mumble to her retreating back.

CROUCHED DOWN BY THE COUNTER, I restock the bags and tissue paper, trying to create some order within the shelving. This is what happens when Pia is left in charge for a week. Everything turns to crap. She's the owner's daughter. A spoiled kid who hates working here as much as I hate her being here. She messes with everything. The racks, counter, and storeroom are all a complete disaster when I come back. Not to mention all the shit that goes missing, conveniently, all her size too. I don't know why she bothers stealing and denying it, her mom wouldn't charge her anyway.

Being down with a cold is torture because not only do I feel like death, I know what I have to look forward to on my return.

The door chimes and I rearrange the last of the bags, straightening them before standing. Readjusting my skirt and blouse, I plant a smile on my face, looking up to say hello. My smile falters almost immediately, and I swallow deeply against the nerves in my throat.

He watches me quietly, taking a few steps to bring himself

closer. He looks good—no bruises or cuts on his face today. Instead, a fine shadow of unshaven hair decorates his jawline. He's dressed simply. Dark jeans, heavy boots, a white tee, and a leather jacket.

"Walk past this place every day. I've never seen you before."

I let my eyes meet his familiar gray stare, a slight grin playing at my lips.

He's starting over. Or at least attempting to.

"Worked here for a few years now, can't say I've seen you before." I can't recall exactly what I said last time. I know I flirted. I smiled big. I made my interest known.

Not this time. No. This time, I'm hesitant. No hint of intimacy dancing in the words. He's disappointed by this, his eyes closing briefly in regret before he opens them again.

"Kicking myself I haven't laid eyes on you sooner."

I watch him candidly. Looking for the animosity that seemed to overtake him in the club, but it's not there. In all honesty, he seems a little lost. Unsure, not of himself, more of me.

"That so?"

He doesn't answer. Much like last time, but instead of the false grin he offered me the first time we met, he smiles genuinely. Maybe stupidly, this pleases me. Parker Shay is dark. Anger and loss ricochet from his demeanor. I like that I can make him smile.

"So, you come in here to tell me that, or are you buying something?"

He scratches his neck, shifting on his feet. "I'm not buying anything."

I raise an eyebrow, and he mimics the gesture.

"You got a man?"

This one catches me off guard. Again, making me laugh

awkwardly. "Not sure that's a question you dive right into, handsome. You don't even know my name."

He steps closer, bringing him flush against the counter I'm standing behind. He's so close I can smell him; a subtle spiced scent, and I lean a little closer. "Just need to know if I need to kill anyone before I ask your name."

I laugh on cue, and his smile becomes wider, pleased with the reaction.

"You don't need to kill anyone."

He chews his bottom lip, and my focus drops to his mouth. Disappointment overtakes me at the realization that he didn't attempt to touch or kiss me in the short time at the club.

Leaning toward me, my body automatically retreats. He winks, reaching out to grab a pen and paper. He scribbles a number on it, pushing it toward me and taking a step back.

"That's it?"

He takes another step backward, his hands buried in his pockets. "All those eyes on you in the club... I'm not used to feeling jealous, and it caught me off-guard. I acted like a dick. I shouldn't have treated you the way I did. Hoping whatever was maybe growing between us isn't lost completely."

There's sincerity in his tone that seems out of place on such a severe man. But it's real, and he considers me for only a moment longer, letting his words sink in before walking backward. Reaching the door, he stops. "What's your name, Sugar?"

Elbows on the counter, I lean over it. "Codi Rein."

He nods, turning to place a hand on the glass door. "Codi Rein. I like it."

He pushes on the door, the small entry bell chiming with the move. "You've got my number, Codi Rein. Hoping like hell you use it."

He leaves without another word, and I stand upright, glancing at the scribbled-on piece of paper. Picking it up, I laugh loudly, looking back at the door in time to catch his wink before he's gone from sight.

Bob 206-555-5555

FIVE

PARKER

I've been checking my cell religiously, waiting for Codi to reach out. It's been hours since I left her work, tail between my legs, almost ready to beg her to give me another shot. I watched the war behind her eyes, the hesitancy initially, the thawing of her doubt, and finally, intrigue and interest.

But her radio silence has spiked my frustration. I thought I'd broken through. Enough for her to text.

My fists hit the punching bag in a quick succession of powerful jabs. The irritation lacing my frame subsides with each connect but peaks again almost immediately.

Rocco's been breathing down my neck all week, asking for updates. He's accepted the fact that Codi's been sick well enough, but if something doesn't change soon, he'll know. I need her to call me. Text me. Fucking anything.

My body drips with sweat. My closed fists pound relentlessly against the leather, loud cracking sounds echoing through our home gym with each hit. Over and over again. Paired only with the exertion in my grunts.

"Yo." Rocco appears before me, hands reaching out to steady the bag. I drop my fists, relaxing my stance, breathing heavily on a chin lift.

"How do you do this without music?"

I laugh with a breathless smile. "I like hearing the crack of the bag."

He pushes the bag at me, and I grab hold to stop it from hitting me. "Sounds psychotic." He smiles. "I should try it."

I push the bag back, and he grabs hold, keeping it still. "Aunt Mira called. She wants us over for dinner. I told her we'd be there."

My hands clench into fists again. "Is *he* gonna be there?"

Rocco shrugs without care. "Say so, dollface. You need to push your hate for Marcus down, man. It doesn't help anyone, especially not Mira."

There's a softness in Rocco's tone that I don't hear often. In fact, I only hear it when he speaks about, or to, Mira. The one person in our lives who, since Mom died, has shown us love. Any good we still hold inside, any compassion, any affection, she's worked damn hard to put it there. All the while living in the depths of hell with someone who resembles more of the devil than anyone else I've ever met.

My cell beeps, and I turn away from the unfamiliar look of intense warmth in Rocco's stare.

"You get me?" he snaps at my avoidance, and I collect my cell, turning to back to him.

"Yeah, I got you," I spit, not looking up.

Unlocking my screen, I flick through to messages, smiling when I see the text sitting unread.

CODI

Alright, Bob. Coffee. Starbucks. 7th Ave. 5:30 pm.

I should be irritated that she's all but ordered me around through a blunt text, but I'm too fucking relieved she's actually reached out. Five goddamn hours after I betrayed everything inside of me by apologizing. By walking into her place of work with my tail between my legs.

Any other girl, I'd bet money on the fact she was letting me stew and punishing me for being a dick. But I can't believe that with Codi. Even the few short interactions I've had with her prove mind games aren't her style.

So, my relief is warranted. It's justifiable. Because she almost decided against me. Codi Rein just about cut me out before I'd even had a chance to get a foot in.

"Should I be concerned about that idiotic grin on your face?"

Rocco's sharp inflection pulls my attention, and I scowl at him. "Say, what?"

"You look a little too fucking happy to be hearing from the bitch."

I choke down the violence at his insult. More irritated by my reaction to him calling her a bitch. Codi Rein isn't deserving of our hate. Her dad, for sure. But not her. No way she's aware of the evil inside her family. She's too good. Her soul, it's too fucking clean.

"I'm happy she's feeling better so I can get in front of her again. Pretty hard to win someone's affection when you can't fucking see them."

He watches me cautiously—something he's been doing a hell of a lot lately. The lack of faith is obvious. Not quite distrust. But close enough to piss me off. He takes a moment longer to nod, forcing himself to believe my words. There's no lie in them, though. There might be a little more to it than I vocalized, but he sure as shit doesn't need to know that. His doubts and lack of

confidence don't need to be overblown because I'm also interested in just spending time with her.

"Been thinking about how to play this now you're
connecting yourself to her." The seriousness in his tone cuts
evenly through the room, and I swallow thickly. "We'll make it
look like a robbery gone sour. Take some cash, trash the store,
shoot her in a way that makes it look like her death wasn't
intentional."

My heart rate quickens, and it has nothing to do with the
punches I'd been throwing at the suspended bag only moments
before. The sweat covering my body suddenly feels cold, like the
looming sense of death is whispering along my skin, threatening
me. Taunting me with the hell it will rain down if I dare to dip
my toes into its merciless depths.

I stand silently, unable to speak. Afraid if I do that, he'll hear
the hesitancy in my tone, the niggling doubt I can't seem to move
past whenever I think of Codi Rein.

"If we wanted to, we could do this as a two birds, one gun
type scenario."

I wait quietly for him to continue, and he seems a million
miles away as he considers what he's about to say.

"We rob the store, kill the girl, and plant the cash and gun on
Marcus somehow. Police will surely look into our family, but we
were young enough that they might not think we'd carry Dad's
vendetta against Rein. Marcus would, though."

Kill the girl. I push the thought from my mind, focusing on
the rest of his plan.

"We give Mom her peace and save Mira in the same breath.
We rid that parasite from our lives once and for all. Two lives,
one bullet."

A life without Marcus. *Mira's* life without Marcus. I'd give
my last breath for her to have that. Fuck, living every day

knowing he's locked away. It'd be freeing the last demons from our lives.

"Let's do it. Let's make sure the evil motherfucker goes down in flames."

He lifts his fist, and I tap mine against it, our eyes anchored with the fired promise of taking Marcus down.

"You should've taken her chicken soup or something." He steps away, and with a clear mind, I laugh loudly.

"Yeah, that's not at all creepy, rocking up to her home, an address she hasn't given me," I retort, grabbing the nearest towel to wipe the sweat from my neck.

He rolls his eyes, turning to walk back toward the hall and his room. "I'll tell Marcus and Mira you have a date."

"Kiss Mira for me. Tell her I'll call her for lunch soon."

He turns away without anything further, and I look back to my cell, an impermissible feeling of excitement in my veins.

I ARRIVED at Starbucks earlier than she suggested. I let myself believe it's to prove to her I'm invested—an apology for poor behavior. But in reality, my eagerness got the better of me. I was itching to leave the loft, and it was either throw punches at the leather again or get out. So here I am, half an hour before she's supposed to show, knee bouncing with what, nervous fucking energy? I've never been made to feel nervous by a woman before. But sitting here, I'm unconvinced as to how much of *me* to show, afraid as all fuck the monster inside of me will scare her off.

"Thinking pretty hard there, Parker Shay."

My leg stops its incessant movement, and I glance up in time to see Codi slide into the seat beside me. Not across from me. Beside me. I can smell her this way. She smells sweet. Like candy. A Jolly Rancher, maybe. It's fucking intoxicating. Bracing my elbows on the table, I lean closer, inhaling *her,* a small smile drifting onto my lips.

"Hey, Sugar."

Her smile breaks open, pleased at the endearment, and I make note to use it more often. Especially if that megawatt smile is my reward.

"You're early," she exclaims, a little surprised.

Lifting an eyebrow, I shift my chair closer to hers. "So are you."

She moves her head side to side in this adorable as fuck gesture while she thinks. "I thought if I got here first, I'd be able to calm my nerves, but then I walked in, and you were already here. Not going to lie, I stood near the door for almost five minutes, trying to build up the courage to approach."

I enjoy her honesty. Her lack of need to fabricate the truth to make her sound, I don't know, *cooler.* She's one hundred percent comfortable with herself, and I like that. I envy it. Like the genuineness of her smile. I feel a constant need to pretend, to show a false image of who I am. To protect myself or others, I'm not quite sure.

"Gonna grab us coffee. What do you want?"

She purses her teasingly crafted lips, moving them to the side in thought. "Caramel latte, three sugars. Please," she finishes with a smile, dropping her chin into her palm.

I blink quickly in shock. Holy fucking gross. I turn to walk toward the barista but stop after a step, looking over my shoulder. "Really fucking glad you reached out."

Her amused smile softens, her cheekbones shading, and she bites her lower lip, nodding delicately. "Me too."

Placing her coffee directly in front of her, I lean down,

inhaling the addictive sweet scent of her skin. "Sugar with a shot of coffee."

She giggles. The sound shocking me again in its appeal. Like honey, tender and smooth. It's so happy, so natural, so fucking *sweet*.

Glancing at my cup, dwarfed in size against my inked palm, she leans closer. "Flat white. No sugar. Not so hardcore you drink it black." She shivers in repulsion at the thought. "But no need for an added sweetener like sugar or syrup." Her perfectly shaped eyebrow raises in question, challenging me to disagree.

"Long macchiato, no need for sweetener, sugar, sweet enough all on my lonesome." I wink, and she barks out a quiet laugh. "Just wait till you taste me," I add, leaning in to run my lips along her ear as I whisper my words.

She pulls away, her hair falling around her face as she ducks it away, hiding her reaction.

Clearing her throat, she takes a sip of coffee before finally looking at me again. A red stain still decorates her face, and she smiles tightly.

"So, Parker Shay, tell me about yourself."

I watch her silently, drinking from my cup, my mind suddenly a mess of irritation and uncertainty.

I'm pissed she's more in control of this situation, of *us*, than I am. Women don't order me around. They don't avoid me for days to *gift* me a small window of their precious time when and how they see fit. They sure as shit don't demand I give them more of me than they have of themselves, especially when I haven't fucked even them. Shit, I've barely touched her. I couldn't tell you what her lips tasted like. Codi Rein shouldn't be dictating this relationship. This is my game. My vengeance. My rules. Yet, every second that passes, in and out of her presence, my control is slipping. How the fuck she managed to take the upper hand without me even knowing it is driving me to insanity.

Sitting back in my seat, I place my mug on the table, hands cupping the back of my head. Her eyes watch the movement, her focus scanning the bulge of my biceps under my dark Henley.

"I'd prefer to know about you." I wait until her eyes meet mine before I speak again, the sound of my voice cracking in its animosity. I'm pissed off. At myself. At her. And it's shown. In my voice, the tone, and no doubt, the irritated glare on my face.

Her features morph from intrigued interest to a guarded contemplation. Her eyes don't break away from mine as she considers me, and I know I should apologize. I've reverted to ulti-mate dick. But, honestly, I'm too afraid to say anything, fearing any further movement or sound will push her in the direction I least want. *Away.*

"I think I'll go," she speaks after a loaded pause, moving to stand, and panic rises in my throat.

I grab onto her hand. "Wait." The dejected sound in the sigh of my voice is almost humiliating in its desperation. She looks at my large tattooed palm covering her ivory skin and pulls her hand away.

"*Please.*" Once again, I'm mortified by my plea, by the fear in my tone, but it gives her pause, her eyes flicking to mine to read my intention. Whatever she sees must be enough to convince her to stay, her body dropping back into her seat. I imagine the worry in my voice is also portrayed enough in my eyes, giving her reason to sit back down. To listen to whatever my argument is to convince her to give me *another* chance.

I entwine my hand with hers, interlocking our fingers, all the while watching the movement. It's strange to find comfort in holding someone's hand. To find strength in the smallest of inti-macies. But I do. As the contrast of my inked and her clean skin connect more forcefully, Codi squeezing my hand in reassurance, I feel nothing but a sense of calm filtering through my veins.

"I've built some pretty high walls over the years. I've spent even more time reinforcing them. Learned that's my greatest form of defense against a world I was born into."

Her face softens, the hand not holding mine coming to rest on top of our knotted ones. She rubs her thumb along the top of my wrist, watching me expectantly to continue.

I sigh, moving in as close as possible, dropping my free hand to her knee, and squeezing. "I'm asking you not to give up on me. I don't know what's growing between us, Codi, but I like you."

She smiles affectionately. "I like you, too," she admits softly.

"Opening up to people isn't something I'm used to. Just gotta," I pause, rethinking my words. "I'm *asking* that you give me time."

She scans my face, her deep blue eyes blinking delicately. "I've got time."

"Glad to hear it, Sugar."

"Look, Parker, I'm not trying to discover all your dark secrets, but if we're going to explore this, I'd like to get to know you. If you're not comfortable telling me something, say so. But... you gotta give me a little of *something*."

"Parker Shay," I state. "No middle name. Friends call me Bob." I smile, winking at the playfulness dancing in her eyes. "I'm thirty-two. My birthday is in August. I have one sibling, an older brother, Rocco. He's intense, a little psychotic even. As you've witnessed." She watches me with rapt attention, taking in every empty detail I feed her with eager interest.

"Rocco is my only living blood relative, and that isn't something I'm comfortable talking about yet. I've recently discovered that my favorite color is red. I'm moody. A lot of shit pisses me off. On the regular. I box to relieve my frustrations, but I'm hoping if we work out, I'll find another way to blow off steam." I wink, and she blushes, the line in her throat exaggerated by her deep swallow.

"I'm self-employed. I co-own Ruin with my brother."

I drop my eyes to our entwined hands. "I like the contrast of my inked skin against the fresh ivory of yours." I drop my voice. "I really fucking dig your laugh. The sweet smell of your skin sidetracks my thoughts on the regular. Finally, I'm *really* looking forward to the moment my lips touch yours."

There's barely a breath between us; my lips ajar, breathing in the fan of her soft, stuttered breaths. She leans in, almost touching her mouth to mine, her eyes closing briefly before pulling back. Lustful eyes look to where her lips almost touched before she moves right back.

"Codi Rein," she starts, her voice thicker than usual, and I shift in my seat, the deep longing scratching her vocal cords turning me on more than I'd care to admit. "I also don't have a middle name," she continues, oblivious to my raging hard-on. "Friends call me Sugar," she smiles shyly. "I'm twenty-five. My birthday is in February. I, too, have one sibling. An older sister, Camryn. She's a nurse and by all outward appearances seems pissed off at the world, but she has a good heart."

I imagine I'm looking at her in a similar way she was me when I was dropping my bio, drinking in everything she's saying with solid interest. Most facts I already know, but hearing her voice tell them to me, makes me want to learn more.

"My favorite color is a multitude." She glances down at my ink, a finger coming up to drag along the rainbow of colors decorating my hand. "I'm naïve. Unintentionally. I'm just a little inexperienced with life as a whole. I don't exercise, and I devour sugar like it's oxygen. Comments like you just made make me happy but also make me blush."

I squeeze her knee, and color floods her cheeks. "So does that." She ducks her face to hide her smile, and I like that way too fucking much. "I work at Blaq and have for years. It's stress-free, and I love it. I don't swear, but I have no issue hearing other people do it."

I watch her expectantly, wanting her to give me what I want, and she laughs quietly, leaning in closer. "I, too, like the contrast of our skin. Your smile, your real one"—she clarifies on an arched brow— "while not common, makes me want to do a victory dance when I see it. It's more of a sneaky smirk. It's playful. I've inhaled the way you smell more times than I'd be comfortable admitting, and I thoroughly enjoy the way you look."

She meets my eyes, staring at me for a long enough moment that I think she's finished, but she takes a breath to speak, her voice soft as she finishes. "But what I like most is that even though you aim to intimidate the hell out of me, for some unknown reason, I see kindness in your eyes. It's not something you show many people, so it feels good that you shine it my way."

My intention was always to make her feel cautious of me. Maybe to stop me from feeling like such a monster when it comes time to strip her life away, so I'm a little caught off guard by the way she views me. I never meant to show her something I didn't think I had inside. I never meant to misrepresent myself so forcefully. Yeah, I want her interested. Just not invested.

SIX

CODI

"Your stalker's out front," Pia states with an eye roll, strolling behind the counter to drop her purse.

I glance at her, confused. "Sorry?"

"Your stalker, you know, the hot, scary-looking dude that was creeping up the shop a week or so back."

I glance at the shop window, searching for any sign of him. "Parker?"

She looks at me, puzzled, evidently having moved past our conversation seconds before. "What?"

I shake my head, dismissing her. "Nothing. I'm going to lunch."

I break the threshold, my eyes scanning the vicinity for Parker.

"Looking for me?" His breath tickles my ear, and I shiver, the whisper of his words skating the whole way down my body.

I haven't seen him since the coffee shop almost a week ago. Our work hours aren't exactly complimentary, and he's been short-staffed, working every overnight shift at Ruin.

I turn, smiling wide and stopping myself from my want to launch myself at him. "I thought you'd still be sleeping."

He shrugs, his large hand coming up to twist a lock of my hair between his fingers before tucking it behind my ear. "Rocco came back last night from wherever the fuck he was, so he's picking up the slack now."

Smiling up at him, I'm surprised at how pleased I am to see him. We've been speaking via text message. He's still virtually a stranger, yet I've been craving the chance to see him. To be given an opportunity to smell him, to touch him.

"I don't listen to music when I work out."

My smile falters slightly, and I blink up at him, confused. "Sorry?"

"Random fact to know me better, I don't listen to music when I work out."

I can't stop the smile that repositions itself on my face. "That's odd." I scrunch my nose up. "So, it's just white noise floating around you?"

He shrugs, moving to clasp my hand in his. "I prefer to hear the sounds of my workout. My labored breathing, the crack of my knuckles against a punching bag."

"I don't work out," I reply with a lift of my shoulders. "Random fact about me."

Parker pulls my arm around his waist, moving his to drape across my shoulders. I lift my hand, the one not wrapped around his waist, to hold his hand hanging over my body, and he leans into me, sniffing my hair.

"I missed you," I confess. "Is that weird? Considering we barely know one another."

I tip my head to meet his eyes, and he pushes his bottom lip out with a quick shake of his head. But he doesn't tell me he's missed me back, which hurts more than I expected.

We've walked a dozen silent steps before he speaks, clearing his throat awkwardly as he does. "I like that you've been thinking about me."

I glance down at my shoes to hide how happy his declaration makes me.

"Been thinking about you too," he admits, easing my anxiety. "Mostly been thinking that I've seen you a few times now, and I still haven't tasted your lips."

My feet halt their movement, and he turns toward me. I glance along the street, searching, and I smile wide when I find it. Grabbing his hand, I pull him behind me, and he follows without argument. Moving into the entrance of an alleyway, I plaster my back against the wall, my bottom lip caught between my teeth, looking up at him through my lashes. He steps into my body without a need for an invitation. Every hard plane of his large frame pushes heavily against every soft curve of mine. It's intoxicating. It electrifies every nerve in my body. Parker Shay is beautiful. Menacing and attractive in a way that makes him unattainable. Yet, he stands here, pressed against my body and focused solely on my lips.

My body. My lips.

My hands move on their own accord, up the solid press of his chest, wrapping my arms around his neck, bringing his face closer to mine. A large palm hits the wall beside my head, the other gripping my jaw tightly.

I could swear in the single moment before his lips touch mine that my heart stops beating. It pauses in my chest, and I stutter around a missed breath. His lips twitch, amused at his effect on me, just as his mouth reaches mine.

Electrified. Invigorated. Inflamed.

I don't know exactly how I feel as Parker's lips open against mine. I'm certain that nothing I've ever felt in the past has come close to the spark that hits me when his tongue pushes into my mouth. It's gentle without being soft. Hard, without being obtrusive. It's devastating and skilled in a way that tells me he's done it plenty of times. But I don't care—quite the opposite. I'm grateful to the women that have come before me. Because Parker Shay has just slain me with the beginning of a simple kiss. A quick, rhythmic slice of his tongue against mine, and I'm confident that never in my life will another man feel this good.

I meet his fraught need with my own desperation. I kiss him in a way that shows him that I've been dreaming about tasting *his* lips. I make sure he knows I hate that he hasn't kissed me until now. It depressed me. It wounded my ego. It made me needy. It made me crazy with want.

I tell him this through my kiss. He gets it. He groans in understanding. He growls his agreement. My soft unrestrained moans vibrate against his talented tongue.

The thick bulge in his jeans grows with every brush of our tongues, with every caress of our lips. It pushes into my stomach relentlessly, persistently, daring me to ignore its presence.

Discounting his swollen arousal would be futile.

I may be inexperienced, but I'm still a woman. A hot-blooded female that has finally found someone to spike a need that up until now has lain relatively dormant. I'm a woman with desires that enjoys kissing and touching enough to know she'd enjoy more. *Much, much more.* Specifically, a more with Parker Shay.

Parker's hand flexes at my jaw, his hips thrusting forward, demanding I feel him, and I whimper into his mouth, my tongue ceasing its dance with him to open on the pathetically needy sound.

He slowly drags my bottom lip between his teeth, letting go to wrap his lips over the same spot in a gentle kiss.

He walks me back to Blaq with little conversation, his eyes staring ahead. Arriving back, he pulls me flush into his body, hugging me tightly. I look up as he looks down, his lips touching mine. He kisses me much like before, deep and hungry. I'm too caught up in the feeling of his mouth to care we're in the middle of the street, surrounded by people.

Pulling back, he steps from our embrace, the corner of his mouth teasing up in the telltale sign of his smirk. "Second fact for the day, you don't need to pull me into an alleyway to kiss me." His smirk widens into a grin, and I can't help but return it. "Happy for every fucker in this city to know you're mine. And I'll touch and kiss my woman wherever and whenever the fuck I want."

"Noted," I whisper.

He winks, turning to walk away before glancing over his shoulder. "Text me your address, Sugar. I'll pick you up at eight."

SEVEN

PARKER

I scratch my naked chest absentmindedly, my body leaning against the open fridge door as I survey its contents. It's near lunchtime, and my eyes are still blurry from sleep, which I just woke from, like the fucking dead.

I'm exhausted. Shit, I didn't breach the threshold of the loft until after the sun had risen this morning, barely having enough energy to shed my clothes before falling face-first onto my bed. Where I'd stayed, passed out, until only fifteen minutes ago.

"Coffee or a shake?"

I twist my head at Rocco's voice, stepping from the crisp air of the fridge and closing the door.

"Kill for coffee, but I'll go the shake."

I drag my feet from the kitchen, dropping onto the first stool along the kitchen island, elbows to the cool marble, pushing into the sockets of my eyes with the hard press of my palms.

"Got in late last night," Rocco states, pulling bits and pieces from the fridge.

"Hmmm... try fucking early morning."

He glances back at me, nodding. He's dressed presentably; dark jeans, dark Henley, boots still on his feet. "Just got in or headed out?" I ask.

He chops and cuts a range of veggies and fruits into the blender, turning it on and watching me as the screeching sound of my breakfast ricochets through our loft. It stops, and he turns to the cupboard, reaching for our protein and scooping heavy spoonfuls in before turning it on briefly once again.

Pouring us each a shake, he moves closer, handing me mine and taking a deep swallow of his. "I just got in. I had breakfast with Aunt Mira."

I look over him for a drawn-out second. "You've been spending a lot of time with her lately. Everything cool?"

He tips his head this way and that. "Yeah. Finally, setting our plan into motion, I've been thinking about Mom a lot. Mira's the only one who remembers her. She can tell me things about her. It helps with the fucking train wreck that is my brain."

I smile solemnly before my mouth twists in obvious distaste. "Was Marcus there too?"

He grunts angrily around another large swallow of his shake, emptying the glass. "Been on a bender for a few days," he discloses. "Rocked up smelling of some other bitch's perfume, red lipstick staining his shirt. The dickhead doesn't even try to hide it. I made her pack some shit and put her in a hotel for the next few nights. I don't want her around him when he's coming down off whatever the fuck he's been on."

I shake my head furiously. "Why the fuck does she stay? Shit, she knows she'd be welcome here. We'd protect her."

"Tried, man, but I get her fears. Marcus is fucking unhinged. She's not just protecting herself. She's trying to protect us as well."

I cough around the revulsion coursing through my body. "Like to see him try and come at me. Fucking coward."

"That's the problem, dollface. He wouldn't come *at* you. He'd come from behind. This way, we can all keep him in line."

I shrug him off. I want nothing more than to put that psycho in the ground. Take his breath from his body for all the hurt he's caused Mira. I feel weak not being able to protect her. Not that he tends to use his fists on her anymore, not since Rocco and I grew stronger than him. Still. The guy is scum.

"Why were you at the club so late?" Rocco breaks into my angry thoughts, and I sigh heavily.

"Speaking of the fucking devil, Ruin was his choice of hell last night." I smile sarcastically, irritation and rage bubbling over my skin at the mere thought of the fuckwit. "He rocked up with a group of underage fucking girls, feeding them booze and God knows what else. They weren't with it, though."

The flare of Rocco's nostrils gives away the bristling storm swirling within him. He's silent, and it's eerie, so I fill the void with the sound of my voice. "A fight had broken out before I even knew he was there. He was throwing his weight around, kicking a group outta the VIP lounge upstairs."

Biting his bottom lip to hold back the tirade of expletives he's dying to let loose, Rocco shakes his head. "What did you do?"

I shrug. "He went head to head with me as soon as I came into view. Asshole. In the end, I had to threaten to call the cops to get him to leave. Thankful he did so without his schoolyard groupies in tow."

"Glad I moved Mira today. He'll be fuming over you making him look the fool."

I nod my agreement, pissed off we're forced to hide Mira to protect her stubborn ass. "The new bartender is fucking stupid, I fired her on the spot, so I was working the bar until we closed. I stayed a little after that to finish some of the paperwork I was supposed to spend the night doing."

Guilt flashes over Rocco's features, knowing he's leaving me to run the bar solo most of the time. "I'll take tonight. Is the bar tended, or will I need to cover?"

I shrug. "Fin thinks he's got a cousin that can handle the consistency of the crowd. I told him to bring him in tonight. I'll let you decide how competent he is."

He nods. "Fucking hate staff."

"Amen, brother. So, how was Mira?"

Rocco smiles affectionately, starting his retreat from the kitchen. "Come here. She gave me some shit I wanna show you."

I follow him into the living room, dropping onto the couch beside him. Sliding his hand into a small brown paper bag, he pulls out a small pile of faded photos, and I glance at them in interest.

"They're of Mom and Mira when they were kids. Teenagers. Before Kane. Before Marcus. Before us."

I sit up straighter, reaching out a hand to look as he passes them to me individually.

Mom stares out at me, her smile commandeering her entire face, unfiltered happiness shining from her. "Shit, she can't be more than sixteen here," I say, more to myself than to Rocco, my finger brushing along the line of her smile.

She was so beautiful, with a tan covering her skin and long blonde hair falling over her shoulders in messy waves. Large gray eyes, much like mine and Rocco's, stare out at me from the faded photo. I can pretend, almost, that she is looking at me. Only me. Her wide, infectious smile was directed at me like it once used to do.

I swallow against the sudden onset of emotion choking me as Rocco passes me another photo of Mom and Mira.

"Shit," I laugh. "Look at how goofy they were."

Rocco laughs, leaning over to look at the picture again. Mom and Mira are standing together, arms draped over one another's shoulders, foreheads pressed together in a laugh.

"They looked so alike when they were younger. I only see the similarity in certain facial expressions nowadays."

I nod as he passes me another photo, letting myself get lost in my mother's face again. My heart feels heavy in my chest, and the feeling of loss I work so hard to suppress rears its ugly head, and I swallow the ache sliding up my throat, attempting to suffocate me.

We flick through photo after photo, watching her smile, laugh, and let the wound in our chests, so barely contained, reopen and bleed inside.

"Fuck. I miss her."

I don't even think he's realized he's spoken, but I move a hand to grab hold of his shoulder, squeezing. He sniffs, his head tipping back, and hands me the last one in the bunch. "We should frame this one."

I take it from him and understand the sudden show of emotion. Mom is sitting on a couch, Rocco climbing over her back, laughing. Her hands are grasped around my middle, tickling me, my face alight with laughter. It's *her* smile, though, staring directly at the camera, so fucking *happy* in that single moment with the two of us.

I clear my throat, my neck twisting to look at Rocco. My eyes sting with the tears I've held so long at bay, and I nod. "Yeah," I exhale heavily. "I'll grab a frame when I'm out today."

We sit silently for nearly an hour, flicking through some of the few things we have left of our mother; memories and photographs.

Placing the pictures on the coffee table, Rocco stands, his

eyes red-rimmed, the fire in his eyes dancing dangerously. "Gonna clean up the kitchen, then head into work. I'll text Fin and tell him to bring his cousin in early, check him out before we open."

"Good idea," I offer distractedly, eyes still focused on my mother.

I feel his stare for a moment longer before he walks away. I stay on the couch for an indefinite amount of time, letting myself recall every tiny detail of her face, working to bring her back to life. At least in my mind. I close my eyes and remember her smiling, laughing, and loving me. She did that fiercely, love us. Fuck, there was never any doubt in my juvenile brain that she fucking adored Rocco and me. She made sure we knew we were her world. *Us.* Nothing more, nothing less. I often wonder how different we'd be if she hadn't been taken from us. If her life hadn't been stolen away without consideration for the collateral damage that would follow. I try to imagine what it would be like to live without this fire in my heart, this fire for revenge. This *hate.*

What would Rocco be like? Shit, he's consumed with rage, with the unrelenting need for vengeance. What if he didn't need that? He's spent his life playing parent while wrestling with the maniac inside his head, fueled only by the need for retaliation.

I'll never know. *He* likely won't ever know. But maybe, with any luck, our plan for atonement will bring him a sliver of peace. However small. He deserves that much. *We* deserve it.

Our strategy for payback is right. It's justified. I know that deep in my soul. Staring into the same eyes as mine, so similar they could be hers, so faded and discolored in a photograph, I feel it. I might have my doubts, but she deserved more.

My. Mom. Deserved. *More.*

Collecting the pictures into a small neat pile, I move toward my bedroom, tucking them safely into my drawers, buried safely under my boxers and socks. Changing into a pair of gym shorts, I wrap my hands, eager fury running through my veins. This is what I needed. A reminder. An emotional slug right to my face, impossible to ignore. A not-so-subtle whisper recalling the reason behind this plan. Codi Rein is sweet, sure, but other than a sweet piece, who is she to me, really?

No one.

She's fucking no one.

My mother was someone. My reason for living. The person who gave me a heart and showed it how to beat. The person who taught me what love was. The most important person in my life, alongside Rocco. The lifeline that was ripped from me.

Codi Rein will be their penance. I'll rob her from them, the way they took her from me, and I'll show them what real pain is. What misery feels like. What hopelessness is. I'll rip their goddamn blackened hearts from their chests before their eyes and crush them in my palm. They'll see their blood and tears run over my tattooed hand as I extinguish their souls, and I'll smile doing it. Really fucking big.

Then we'll have our peace.

We'll have our revenge.

MY CELL BUZZES in my pocket as I walk toward Codi's apartment block, my heavy footsteps echoing along the quiet street. My mind feels clearer than it has in weeks. A renewed sense of purpose seems to have washed over me, and I feel invigorated with my determination.

Rocco's name lights on my screen, and I slide my thumb across it, drawing it to my ear.

"Yo."

"Checking in. Seeing how you were holding up after today. Seeing those pictures was heavy."

I swallow. "I'm good, man. Better than. I'm glad we have them. Fired the monster inside me. Made me more determined."

I can see the smile on his face, evident in the elated sound of his voice. "Good. Real fucking glad to hear it, brother."

I reach Codi's apartment, stepping past it and turning my back. "I'm ready, Rocco. I'm ready to send them to hell."

"Calm down, dollface. Enjoy yourself for a bit first. No harm in tasting what the bitch has to offer before we take the next step."

I nod, even though he can't see me. "So, listen," I cough out. "Don't think I say it enough, *if ever,* I appreciate you, man. Always got my back, and I —"

"Parker, don't sweat it. You don't thank me for being here. You've got my back just as much as I have yours."

"Nah," I laugh. "There isn't anything in this world I could do to pay you back for all the shit you've taken to protect me."

Silence hits me for a moment, and we remain that way for a second before Rocco clears his throat. "Do it again. No hesitation."

"We'll get it, Roc. Our peace. Hers. We'll make sure of it."

"Damn. Fucking. Straight. Listen, I'm gonna get back to it. I'll catch you later."

He hangs up without waiting for a reply, and I push out a deep breath, cracking my neck and rolling my shoulders before shoving my cell in my pocket and turning around.

I stop at Codi's anxious face, her eyes moving over me nervously. "Didn't mean to eavesdrop. Heard your voice."

"How much did you hear?"

She shakes her head vigorously. "Not much. Nothing. Barely anything."

Her cheeks shade at her rambling, and I take a tentative step closer. She doesn't recoil from my advance, and I breathe a sigh of relief. Not afraid means maybe she didn't hear anything of value. Anything that could derail our plan.

By the time I've reached her, her cheeks still shine but with an entirely different emotion. Her tongue peeks out, wetting her brightly painted lips, and I smirk down at her. It's fake. My worry about what she heard still plays in my mind. She reads the falseness of the smirk, her eyes narrowing slightly, and I don't give her another second to second-guess me. I lean down, dragging my nose along the line of her jaw.

"Smell good. Always so *sweet*."

She releases a shaky breath, and I grin to myself. *Success*. I plant a soft, drawn-out kiss along her jawline, pulling back marginally to find her lips. They're delicately agape, her eyes closed, and I don't hesitate in dragging my tongue along her top lip. She chases my tongue with hers, and I give in to my need to taste her—Rocco's right. I need to enjoy her while I can.

I push her against the doorjamb, standing within the open frame as the door closes against my back. Any of her neighbors could see us, caught halfway between the inside and outside of her apartment. She doesn't seem to mind, pulling me into her as I assault her lips. She gives as good as she gets, her tongue moving desperately against mine, soft, needy cries breaking into my throat.

She pulls away first, the back of her head hitting the door-frame, and I smile down at her.

"I like the way you say hello."

I stare at her briefly, eyes hooded, bottom lip caught between her teeth, and hair purposefully messy. *Fuck*. My gaze slides down her body; she's completely covered, long-sleeved, fitted gray top tucked into her black high-waisted jeans. There's a cut of material open across her cleavage, showcasing the decent swell of her tits, but that's it. Still, she's sexy as all fuck.

I step back, stopping myself from pushing this further and fucking her for all her neighbors to see.

"Random fact," I start, and she smiles expectantly. "I don't like people listening to my business. Don't eavesdrop on me again."

Her smile falters, and she nods with fast and shaky movements. "Of course. I'm sorry. Honestly, it wasn't my intention."

She's intimidated by the stern throw of my voice, but she needs to be. Caution is imperative. My whole plan could have gone up in flames in a single moment back there.

She swallows heavily and attempts to move back into the apartment, uncomfortable with the intensity of my scrutiny.

"You didn't tell me yours."

"Huh?" she squeaks.

"Random fact. You didn't tell me yours."

She looks momentarily stunned. Whiplashed at how easily I move between moods. She'll get used to it.

"Oh. Umm... I'm allergic to peanuts."

I didn't know that. Everything Rocco has dug up on her, and her family so far has been concrete. Nothing she discloses has come as a surprise. I'm lucky I haven't kissed her after eating heaped spoons of peanut butter. That could've ended badly. Or quicker than I planned.

"Hmm... guess I shouldn't eat peanut butter before I taste your lips then."

"That would be appreciated," she laughs, finally settling from the uncertainty filling her eyes only moments prior.

"Let me grab my shoes and bag. I'm ready to go."

I follow her into the apartment, my eyes focused on her retreating ass, sculpted perfectly in her tight jeans.

"Yeah, totally not ready to die, just saying."

"What?" I cough out a little too loudly.

She looks at me, her eyes dancing with puzzled amusement. "Joke, Parker. Peanut butter, I just said, I wasn't ready to die. Like, don't eat it before you kiss me." She tips her head side-to-side. "It was a lame joke."

I force a laugh, heightening her embarrassment, and I scold myself internally. "Let's go," I declare, changing the subject. "I'm starved." I let my eyes travel over the shapely figure, letting her read my double innuendo.

Sliding her feet into a pair of shimmery black pumps, she rolls her eyes, color scattering over her cheekbones as she nods.

"DINNER WAS AMAZING."

I squeeze her hand before letting it go and reaching into my pockets for the key to the loft. "Sugar, we had pizza."

"Don't curse at me like that. Pizza is God. And definitely the way into my heart."

Pushing the door open, I let her in ahead of me. "Interested in something other than your heart right about now."

She whirls around on high-heeled feet. "Parker," she scolds joyfully, whacking my arm with her purse. I shrug. It's true. Best she knows it.

"Get you a drink?"

"Water would be good," she answers, eyes skirting over the loft in intrigue.

"My rooms that way," I point in its direction. "Rocco's that way," I point in the opposite. "Living room, kitchen, gym." My finger follows my instruction, pointing to each space as I recite them, and she follows my lead toward the kitchen.

"Bathroom?" She arches an eyebrow.

"No main bathroom. Rocco and I each have an en-suite. You'll locate mine that way."

Placing her purse on the kitchen counter, she nods, turning toward my room. I fix our drinks, tempted to follow her path, but she's back before I consider the thought much further.

She takes the water I offer, smiling in thanks before moving to the couch. "I like your place." She admires, eyes drinking into every possible detail. Finally, her eyes meet mine as I sit beside her.

"I like you," I offer quietly, taking her glass and placing it next to mine on the table in front of us.

She swallows audibly, and my hand cups her jaw, holding it tightly as I lower my mouth to hers. She lets me kiss her. Softly. First, her top lip. Then her bottom. Her eyelashes flutter, eyes closing as my lips caress hers, a smooth, almost inaudible moan escaping her parted lips.

I tease my tongue along the groove of her upper lip, and like clockwork, hers tips out to follow it.

My body pushes hers into the couch, and she goes willingly, her legs moving open to let me fit between her thighs. Her arms wrap around my neck, pulling me more forcefully onto her body, her mouth opening to allow my tongue entry. I grind my hips against the apex of her thighs, her soft, needy moans vibrating into my mouth as I kiss her.

My cock is hard, straining heavily against my jeans, and I push against her firmly, letting her feel what she does to my body. She gasps, her mouth falling open, neck tipping back, and I take the opportunity to break our kiss, trailing my lips along her jaw, down her neck, tasting her skin.

She moans and whimpers, her hips pushing against mine, feeling me. My large palm finds her chest, nipples straining through her thin bra, barely hiding the heaviness of her tits.

Fuck. Codi Rein is an accelerant to my fire. Making me mad with the need to claim her body.

I pinch a nipple, and she arches into my touch, her lips seeking mine again. My hand travels farther down her body, fingers finding the button of her jeans. I pop it open quickly, and our kiss breaks, her head falling back, and before I can open my eyes, she moves to sit up fast.

Too fucking fast.

Her forehead connects heavily with my nose.

"Motherfuck," I spit out, hand flying to my nose, eyes watering.

Her surprised gasp hits me. I attempt to move off her while she rolls and arches, kneeing me right in the balls as she pushes me off.

I fall from the couch on a yell, one hand clutching my junk, the other on my nose. My back slams against the coffee table, our drinks soaking the back of my shirt.

She mumbles something about working tomorrow, mixing it with a rushed apology. But I'm too caught up in pain to listen. I'm not sure what hurts more; my nose or my balls.

Fuck.

What. The. Fuck. Just. Happened.

Motherfucker.

My front door slams shut, and my eyes shoot open, glancing around the loft, no longer containing Codi Rein. I pull my hand from my nose, blood pooled in my palm, and I tip my head back on a growl, working to stop blood from dropping anywhere else.

"Fuck, man."

I groan at the sound of Rocco's voice. "How much did you see?"

I don't look at him, eyes trained on the ceiling, but his voice travels through the loft, moving with his body toward the kitchen. "Heard an almighty grunt, pained, not sexual, came out to check and saw the knee to junk and then her fleeing the scene. She barely made time to grab her shoes."

Standing over me, he hands me a bag of frozen veggies. "Ice your balls."

I struggle up, moving to sit on the couch, and do as he says, lodging the ice-cold packet against the ache of my nutsack. He hands me a dishtowel, ice packed inside. "Hold this against your nose."

"One second, she was moaning, arching into me, totally fucking into it. Next, she's causing me grievous bodily harm. What. The. Fuck." My voice is muffled, nasal from the hit, and I hear Rocco's breath of laughter. "Shut the fuck up."

"You guys fucked yet?"

I shake my head, my head spinning from the movement.

"Probably moving too fast. You know what some chicks are like. They hold out so they don't seem like they're sluts. I don't give a shit if a girl gives it up the first time I meet her, man. I don't know where they pulled this *wait a certain number of dates* shit. All that does is piss me off."

I grunt in agreement. I hate games. Fucking despise women holding out on me for no other reason than trying to keep me interested. Wanna know what keeps me interested? Knowing how their pussy fucking tastes, not wondering. Knowing they're not a fucking dud lay, that they openly participate in our fucking. That's what keeps me the fuck interested.

I don't know what Codi Rein is playing at, but I'm not interested in being her puppet.

Later that night, showered, balls a little less tender than they were a few hours ago, I grab my cell, searching for her name and hitting call before I can second guess myself. The shrill ring of her phone echoes in my apartment, and I stalk through it, locating her purse still sitting on our kitchen island where she had left it earlier.

I scowl at it, pulling my cell from my ear and ending the call. Bitch ran out of here *so* fast she didn't think to grab her purse. What the actual fuck?

Nose still tender, I head to bed, trying to decipher what the fuck is going on in Codi's brain. Maybe Rocco was right. Maybe I was moving too fast for her. Did it necessitate a hit to my junk and a black eye? Fuck no. But perhaps she isn't playing a game. Maybe she was genuinely panicked with us moving too fast. A conversation needs to be had. Save me another black eye.

EIGHT

CODI

A stream of light hits my face, and I open one eye, glancing around the room, hoping that the world had opened wide overnight and swallowed me whole. Unfortunately, my room looks very much the same. I open my other eye, considering the possibility that I've entered an alternate universe—one where I didn't just humiliate myself beyond belief.

God, I'm such a loser.

I never considered my virginal status as an issue. Even now, I don't think it is a problem per se. The fact that I'm keeping it from Parker could be wrong. *Maybe.* Or definitely.

But what if it scares him away? Jesus. I'd be a fumbling mess. Definitely not what he's used to and hardly attractive.

Last night started with so much promise. Until it didn't. My God, what Parker must think of me. I throw an arm over my eyes, shielding myself from the mortification of the evening before, without success. The events replay in my mind; the heavy make-out session, the expert way in which his large palms caressed my body. I was so turned on.

Until I wasn't, no, that's not right. I was still incredibly turned on, but as soon as his hand unbuttoned my jeans, I freaked.

Understatement of the century.

Definitely likely.

And the head-butt.

"Ugh!" I massage my eye sockets with my palms.

"Sounds like you're strangling a defenseless puppy in here."

I startle, pushing up onto my elbows and glaring at Camryn. "Should I be concerned that you know what that sounds like?"

She shrugs, strolling into my room and settling in bed beside me. "Hypothetical."

I roll onto my side, pulling my comforter over my head, groaning loudly.

She pulls it down enough to see my eyes. "What happened?"

"Oh, Ryn," I sigh, throwing the blanket off and rolling onto my back. "It was a disaster. Everything was amazing until our make-out session started morphing into something more. I freaked." I cover my face with my hands, shaking my head.

Silence meets my ears, and I turn my head, peeking from behind my fingers. Camryn swallows thickly, her eyes shut forcefully to block out the images in her mind. "Did he force it?"

I sit upright. "Oh, God no." I curse myself for not thinking about my words before I spoke them. I grasp her hand in mine, squeezing tight. "Ryn, I promise, no. I should've chosen my words more carefully."

She offers me a tight smile, her default to the shadows that slice into her soul. "What happened?" she scratches out.

I stay sitting upright, wanting to keep my eyes on hers. "We had dinner. We talked, and we laughed. It was amazing. Ryn, really, beyond perfect. We kissed a lot. It was phenomenal." My voice sounds breathy, my thoughts back to the feel of his lips on mine, the skillful drag of his tongue against mine.

"A lot of heavy touching," I continue. "Then his hand started at my pants. I freaked."

She eyes me suspiciously, a smirk pulling at the side of her mouth. "Describe freaked."

I blink, holding my eyes closed. "I sat up so fast I head-butted him. My forehead connected with his nose. *Hard.* If that didn't startle him enough, I attempted to move, awkwardly rolling off the couch, kneeing him in the—" I wave my hand in the air, indicating what I can't bring myself to vocalize. Finally opening my eyes, I look at my sister, expecting sympathy. Understanding of my mortification, even. I should've known better. Camryn's hand covers her mouth, barely containing her wide grin, her eyes dancing with her imminent laughter.

"You head-butted him. In the nose. Kneed him in the balls, and then what?" she mumbles behind her palm.

I smash my hand against my forehead, groaning. "I ran. I got up, grabbed my shoes, mumbled something about having to work today, and left."

A loud laugh bubbles from her throat once or twice before it cackles heavily into the air. "Oh, my God. Fuck, Codi. Did he follow you?"

I chew on my thumbnail, shaking my head. "He was still clutching his, you know—" I wave my hand again, indicating his nether regions, and Camryn folds in on herself, her laughter now hysterical as tears stream from her eyes.

I give her a moment. Only a few seconds before I push her. "Ryn," I whine. "It's not funny."

"On the contrary, sister. It's fucking hilarious."

She's right. Humiliating, sure. But still, beyond amusing. I fall back onto the bed, my laughter mixing heavily with

Camryn's. Every time the sound dies off, it starts back up with more fervor. We're gasping for air, clutching our stomachs at the pain our excessive laughter causes in our abdomen.

Finally, she exhales heavily, wiping at her eyes. "Fuck me. Has he texted? Called?"

I shrug, my eyes wide as I turn toward her. "I left my purse and cell in his loft. I'm lucky I grabbed my shoes."

Ryn matches my wide stare for the briefest of seconds before her laughter overtakes her again.

Her laughter didn't die down, so I left her to it, marinating in my mortification, Ryn's incessant cackle taunting me from every corner of our apartment.

Bitch.

Sipping coffee laden with sugar (of course), I glare at my bedroom door. Her laughter had died down to a sporadic chuckle every thirty seconds or so.

Wandering from my room, she smiles at me widely. "I'm sorry," she almost laughs again. "I've just been recreating it in my head. It's brilliant. On so many levels."

"I've showered, dressed, and made coffee in the time it's taken you to stop."

She glances at my appearance, her eyes skating my body before her bottom lip pushes out in thought. "Huh. Haven't laughed so hard in a really long time."

Her off-handed comment ceases my scowl immediately, and I return her grin with one of my own. "Glad to be of service. Now come, sit," I urge. "I need your advice."

Sliding onto a bar stool, she grabs my coffee and takes a large sip. "Oh, sugar, how I love thee."

I pour another mug, heaping sugar into the dark liquid before adding cream. "What do I do?"

Ryn watches me over the rim of her mug, taking a sip before placing it back on the counter.

"Does he know?"

"I'm a virgin?" I clarify, and she nods. "No."

She tips her head side to side, thinking. "Was he moving for sex or just wanting to touch you?"

"I don't know," I state, dropping my elbows to the bench and massaging my temples.

"Are you ready for sex? I know your virginity is intact, but you're not completely *untouched*?"

"I've done some. Not a lot, though."

"You need to tell him, babe, for your sake and his. He's a thirty-year-old man. Kneeing him in the balls whenever he attempts to touch you will wear thin. *Fast.*"

I groan outwardly, but it's stuck in a laugh, the sound coming off as frustrated and strangled. Exactly how I feel.

"I can see it moving that way with him. I *wanted* him to touch me. I just panicked. What if he's creeped out that I'm a twenty-five-year-old virgin?"

She drains the remainder of her coffee, sliding the empty mug toward the sink. "Could go either way. Some dudes freak. Some dudes take it as an accomplishment. Look," she adds. "You could give him a little of something," she offers. "Use your hand, your mouth. Something to tide him over while you work out what you want. *But* only if it's what you want to do. Babe, don't let yourself feel rushed into anything." She reaches out to grab my hand. "Promise me."

"I promise."

I finish my coffee in silence, Ryn staying to keep me company. The quiet of the morning was refreshingly peaceful, considering I could overanalyze what Parker will think of me after last night. But I guess it's out of my hands. So be it if he decides I'm a complete loon and no longer wants to see me.

Our apartment intercom buzzer sounds, and we glance at the intercom, then back to one another. Shrugging, Ryn leans over, pressing the button. "Yello."

"Codi in? It's Parker."

My eyes feel like saucers in my face, and I glance nervously at my sister's wide grin.

"Hey. Hey. Come on up. Take the elevator. Don't want you to strain any injuries you may've endured recently."

"Ryn," I screech when I'm confident her hand has released the intercom.

She shimmies off her chair. "Try not to cause him physical injury this time. My abdominal muscles have had enough of a workout."

I dance awkwardly in the kitchen, turning toward the door, then scurrying back into the kitchen, wondering what I'm supposed to say.

His loud knock echoes through the apartment, and I swallow the bile rising in my throat. Exhaling heavily, I move toward the door.

He's leaning casually against the doorjamb, his head tipped down, my purse held in his hand. His head lifts slowly when the door opens, an amused smirk decorating his mouth.

"Oh my God, Parker." I move forward, my hands reaching for his face and the slight discoloration of the bruise forming at his right eye socket. "I'm so, so sorry."

"Random fact, I've never been assaulted by a woman. Especially one that I was making feel pretty damn good only seconds prior."

His face is a twisted mix of shock and amusement, and I

walk forward into his body, dropping my face into his hard chest. "I'm an idiot. I'm sorry."

His large arms come around my body, his feet shuffling forward to move us into my apartment.

"Fun fact about me?" I muffle into his shirt. "I've never physically assaulted anyone. In my life. Accidentally or intentionally."

He laughs, kicking the door closed behind him. "Listen, Sugar. I get that it probably escalated faster than you felt comfortable. Future..." he pauses, pushing me back marginally, using a knuckle to lift my chin, allowing him access to my eyes. "Words are good. Far preferable to a knee to the junk."

I groan loudly. "I'm so embarrassed."

He throws my purse onto the first available surface he sees. "No need for that. I'm finding I'm enjoying your brand of different."

Relief floods my body, and I know I should use this moment to come clean. To admit why I freaked so badly. But I like the way he's looking at me. I like the genuine smile and the lack of judgment he's offering me. I don't want that to change. Not right now.

"Gonna taste your lips, Sugar. That cool? Or will it earn me another head-butt?"

I narrow my eyes at his teasing. "How long will you hold that against me? Just so I'm aware..."

A smugness crosses his face, a fuck-you-gonna-do-about-it smirk twisting his lips in an incredibly sexy way, a large hand grabbing my jaw tightly.

"Because—" I start, but he cuts me off, his mouth crashing down on mine and cutting off not only my meek argument but any thought in my lust-clogged brain.

My words break off on a heady moan, his skilled tongue stroking against mine.

Like everything else about Parker Shay, his kisses are authoritative. Dominating. The way he holds me so forcefully in place. He takes ultimate control. And as inexperienced as I am, I know this is how I always want to be kissed. I want him in complete control of my body. He'll take pleasure from me unapologetically while giving me mine.

His free hand finds my ass, pulling me aggressively against his solid frame. Against the swelling length tucked into his jeans.

He groans. Or growls. Or does both. The sound is rough, desperate, and laced with unrivaled need, exactly like the kiss. I echo his sound with a moan, my hands clutching at his chest, working on getting closer.

Pulling back, his teeth bite my bottom lip before letting go. Panting heavily, he scowls down at me, seemingly irritated by the effect of our kiss. His gray eyes darken in their craving, the carnal desire evident in the way they glow. Cavernous in their moonlit shadows, demanding my allegiance.

His hand remains tightly gripped at my jaw, his heavy breathing grazing my skin in a hot current of need. I chase his kiss, attempting to drive my face forward, my need to feel his mouth against mine almost too much.

Parker Shay is addictive. We're barely acquainted. Still virtually strangers, but when I'm caught in his proximity, I cannot refute my overwhelming need. Everything about him is fueling an obsession that no longer feels healthy. His kiss. His dominance. The thunder of his temperament. Parker Shay is quickly becoming a habit. A fixation I'm happy to find dependence on.

He may not feel healthy for my soul. He's definitely dangerous to my well-being. But he feels *good*. Better than. He feels like a dream I never knew I wanted. He may not feel safe, but all I can yield is that he feels *right*.

He snarls at my attempt to move, but the sound isn't hateful. It's hot. It's heated. It's as needy as the whimper that escapes my mouth.

His lips roughly caress my bottom lip. Then my top. He strokes his tongue against my top lip. Then my bottom. He bites me, his lips following the sting in a harsh touch to ease the pain. Finally, he closes his mouth over mine, giving me what I need. He kisses me severely, his firm grasp on my jaw not easing through his attack.

Stepping from my space, his lips are the last of his body to disconnect. He's one hundred percent immodest in readjusting himself in his dark jeans, his eyes fluttering closed in the movement.

"Kissing shouldn't be that satisfying on its own. You're fucking with my head, Sugar."

He tips his tongue out, dragging it across the wetness of his lips, an indecent grin tipping the right side of his mouth upward. Looking me over, his eyes drag along my work attire savagely. The lewd graze of his eyes complementing the salacious slide of his smile.

"You're working today." He sounds disappointed by his statement, his thoughts clearly having wandered to alternate ways in which we could spend our day.

I nod, not trusting myself to speak, not the words or the sound of my voice.

"I'm working the next few nights, so I won't see you. Text me, yeah?" Again, it's a statement, not a question, not a request, and I find myself nodding before he's finished speaking.

"I kiss you again, and I'll most likely find myself with a

matching bruise under my left eye socket." He winks, turning to take the few steps to my front door. "I'll hear from you."

I smile like a goof, remaining mute for fear of *sounding* like a crazy person if I speak. Instead, I stay rooted to the spot, waving my goodbye, downright giddy that I didn't scare him away. Not with the head-butt. Not with a knee to balls.

Parker Shay might just be as addicted to me as I am to him.

The door clicks over, Parker no longer in view, and I fist pump the air, turning on my heel, my stupid grin remaining firmly fixed on my face for the rest of the day.

NINE

PARKER

I stand, extending my hand.

"Appreciate your time, Parker."

I nod my reassurance. "I'm a gin man. You promise me something good, and you'll always have my audience."

Eli barks out a laugh, moving toward my office door. "I'll organize some samples over the next week. Trial it over a few nights. Let me know how it's received."

I nod again, flicking my hand up in farewell as he exits my office without anything further. That's why I always make time for Eli. No bullshit. No fabricated sales pitch. He won't come to me unless he knows I'll be interested in purchasing. He doesn't waste my time. I respect that.

Dropping into my chair, I rub a hand on my face, yawning loudly. *Fuck.* I've been going non-stop for going on twenty-four hours. Rocco did a no-show last night, so after only three hours of sleep, I was back here from nine pm until now, nearing eight in the evening.

I'm fucking shattered.

I'm hungry.

I need a stiff fucking drink.

And I want Codi.

I don't let myself read into that last one. I barely let myself admit its truth in the first place. I convince myself I'm horny, which isn't a lie. Far from it. I need inside her like I need fucking oxygen.

The way she kisses me. The sexy little moans that spill from her sinful lips. Shit, my cock's been rock solid for six days. Six fucking days. I won't even let myself jerk off. Fuck that. It wouldn't satisfy me. Not the way I need it to. Not in the way Codi would.

Fuck, you'd think after my last effort, I'd be scared off. Jesus, the force with which her face collided with my nose. I'm lucky she didn't break it. Shit, the bruise has only just subsided.

She's hijacking my thoughts and steamrolling every aspect of my life. And I've spent next to no time with her. I've *barely* touched her. Save tasting her sweet lips. I wouldn't mind a taste of the rest of her, though. I know this makes me the biggest dick on earth. I'm working through a plot to terminate this girl. To take her life. And I'm determined to fuck her before I do that. I could pretend it's just another facet of my revenge plan. Gain her ultimate trust by making her give me access to her body. But I'd be lying, and I'm man enough to admit that. She turns me on. She's beautiful. Like no other. She's sweet. Like sugar. She feels good to touch, and so far, I've only been given surface access. Fuck, I'm dying to touch her naked skin. To taste it. To dirty her perfect complexion with the rough splash of colors from mine.

This isn't a long-term arrangement. It can't be. It's a play. A sequence of events that need to play out for Rocco and me to find our peace. That doesn't mean I can't enjoy myself before being guaranteed a one-way ticket to hell.

Tipping my head back, I give in to the need to close my eyes. I need to go home. I need to sleep for at least fourteen hours. And I sure as shit need to stop letting Codi Rein seize my capacity of thought.

I close my eyes, letting myself drift off into the land of sleep for a few minutes, to tide me over until I can crash out tonight.

I startle awake at the sharp sound of my office phone. I sit up, rubbing a hand down my face roughly. Clearing my throat, I retrieve the phone from the cradle. "Parker."

"Boss. Blondie's back. Took her to the VIP area and planted her at your table."

I sit up straighter. "Blondie? You mean Codi?"

"Don't know her name, the same chick you were here with a little while back, red dress."

"Get a waitress to get her a drink. I'll be up in a minute."

I replace the phone, grabbing for my cell to check any missed calls or texts from Codi, but there's nothing.

I stand abruptly, readjusting my clothes and sliding my cell into my pocket. I move fast through the club, bounding up the stairs, eager to see her. Mike, my security guard, nods at my approach, and I slow, clapping my hand on his shoulder as I pass.

Codi's face opens into a wide smile when she sees me, and I return it automatically. Maybe it's unhealthy, but I'm really fucking pleased to see her.

Sliding into the booth, I pull in beside her, my arm stretching along the back of the seat, fingers ghosting over her naked shoulder. I give into my need to touch and smell her, dropping my nose into the smooth expanse of her neck and inhaling deeply.

"Miss me, Sugar?"

She's dressed like sin. As always. Legs painted in acid wash jeans, a thin strip of her upper abdomen naked to the eye. Her shoulders are bare, and a black tube top covers her gorgeous tits.

Sin. Temptation. A siren of seduction, and she's fucking oblivious.

Codi arches her neckline, offering me greater access to the candy-scented skin. I take the opportunity eagerly, brushing my lips against her pulse point, feathering kisses up and down her skin.

She moans softly. "Mmm-hmm. Miss me?"

I pull back, eyes falling to her parted lips. Lips begging for my mouth. I refrain, lifting a hand and dragging my thumb across the soft cushion. "In a way that's dangerous."

Her tempting lips move into the hint of a smile, the gesture showing confusion and not joy. I won't let her read further into the insight of my psyche, my words giving away more than they should. Finally giving into my need to kiss her, my large palm cups her jaw, and I pull her face to mine. She comes willingly, moving without resistance, more than eager to be at the mercy of my touch.

Her mouth opens to welcome my tongue, and relief coats my entire nervous system. Calming me and unraveling the unfulfilled need coiling my body. Codi Rein is a sensory overload I'm willing to overdose on. Her taste. Her smell. Her touch. Her physicality. I've been dying for another taste, another touch of her, and the deliverance I feel on contact is soul-destroying. I've become addicted to her in a way that isn't conducive to my end goal. It concerns me, just not enough to stop.

I shouldn't need this as much as I do.

I shouldn't crave her the way I do.

I shouldn't want her. Not to the point of obsession.

But I do. And no motherfucker is going to ruin that. Not even my evil fucker of a conscience.

Our kiss verges on obscene. It's intimate in the way it flaunts our violent need. So lewd, it should be private. But we let

TEN

CODI

I kick my heels off with a complete lack of grace, flicking them in opposite directions across my apartment. Dumping my clutch on the entry table, I pace the living area. My entire body bounces with nervous energy, my thumbnail caught anxiously between my teeth.

"OhmyGod. OhmyGod. OhmyGod," I chant, marching back and forth.

"Camryn?" I pause my incessant movement, yelling into the space of our apartment. "Ryn?" I repeat, moving toward her bedroom.

I make the most hideously desperate whine of a sound when I find her room empty.

"Crap."

Turning fast on my heel, I move quickly toward my clutch, throwing the contents in search of my cell. In my rush, I drop it. Twice.

"Crap. Crap. Crap. Crap. Crap."

He hasn't contacted me, and even though I shouldn't expect more, disappointment leaks through my body.

He'd know by now I bailed. Ran from the club in haste. God, it wasn't the plan. Touching him had felt good. That's not even the right word. Incredible. Unreal. Amazing.

Parker Shay isn't a man you bring to his knees. But stroking him in a darkened corner of his club, I was powerful. The rough sounds scratching from his throat. *God.* I clench my thighs, every nerve ending in my sex sending fire through my veins. I've never felt more turned on in my life. It's without question the first time I've ever wanted anything *more* from a man. Sexually, anyway. I felt ready. I felt energized by my need, by my want.

I had every intention of following him into his office.

Until I didn't.

The closer I got to the bathroom, I realized what was about to happen.

Parker was taking me somewhere private.

To fuck me.

I was about to lose my virginity.

In a nightclub.

And Parker remains unaware of my virginal state.

It felt wrong. I couldn't catch him off guard like that. I didn't feel right. But after what we had just done, I couldn't bring myself to blindside him in the middle of his workplace. Because as little as I know of him, this conversation will be tumultuous. I'm sure of it.

Camryn was right. I should've been upfront from the beginning. I could've screwed any chance of him and me exploring this relationship further.

I'm an idiot.

Granted, I didn't know I'd want to go that far with him. But, still, my dishonesty is why I'm in this mess.

CODI

Funny story. I have this friend that's
bailed on the guy she's seeing twice
now at some REALLY crucial moments.
Without explanation. Any insight on
whether you think this guy will give her
ANOTHER shot? Asking for said
friend......

My thumb dances over the send arrow before I find the balls
to hit it. The text reads delivered, and an overwhelming sense of
panic overcomes me. That was stupid. Immature. I just
completely devalued what we just shared.

My text goes from delivered to read, but nothing else. No
response. No three little dots indicating an imminent reply.

He's mad.

Understandably.

Trudging through my apartment, I feel deflated by my
behavior. I'm disappointed in how childish I'm acting. I feel like
a stupid little girl. Not a twenty-five-year-old woman.

Dropping my cell on my bed, I amble into my bathroom,
stripping my clothes and leaving them strewn across my carpet. I
adjust the spray of water in my shower, waiting for it to run hot
enough to almost hurt.

I feel almost regretful washing the dried remnants of his
orgasm from my hand, bitter that that single moment of
touching him may be the only opportunity I had. I want more.
Severely.

I wash quickly, a wall of cool air hitting me forcefully as I
step from the blistering steam of the shower. A fine sheen of
sweat covers my reddened skin, the freshness of the air sliding
me in a mugginess as I wrap my body in the thick material of my
towel.

Padding back into my room, I run my towel over my skin,

drying the excess dampness from my body before discarding it on the ground and climbing into bed.

Reaching for my cell, hopeful anticipation crawls over me but deflates immediately, the blank screen taunting me.

Falling backward, I groan loudly, unlocking the screen, my *read* message still open, still unanswered.

CODI

I'm so sorry

He reads the text as quickly as it's sent, offering me hope that he's sitting in his open messages, wanting to reach out. I count five thick, drawn-in breaths, the heavy inhales of air deafening in the vast space of my bedroom. I choke on my fifth breath, the three dots dancing as he types.

The thumbs-up emoji. That's it. An emoji. Who even gives a thumbs-up nowadays? It's detached. Sarcastic. And hurtful.

I begin typing another apology. Then delete it. I ask to see him again, but I delete that before sending it.

CODI

I've never had sex before

CODI

I ran so I didn't blindside you.

It seemed the only way to respond. With honesty. I could've begged for him to see me in person and talk it out. But there'd be no guarantee he'd agree to it. Maybe it's less awkward this way. If he never wants to see me again, maybe I've saved myself from the humiliation of him telling me that in person.

PARKER

Rephrase. Wanna make sure I'm not misinterpreting.

Not unexpected. My virginity is shocking. I'm on the fast track to thirty, and I'm *untouched*. I understand Parker's need for reassurance.

CODI

I'm a virgin

I wait, staring at my cell for over an hour, without a response from Parker.

Nothing.

Not even an indication he considered replying.

I'd be lying if I said I hadn't been holding out the slightest sliver of hope. I'd been enjoying getting to know him. He's stoic and morose. But I saw something more behind the walls he seems to reinforce so heavily. Someone altruistic. Someone loving, if only in his specific way. It was there. I wanted more of it.

I consider texting him again. Apologizing, but for what? For not having lost my virginity before now? For not having met a man that set my skin on fire as he does? No. I won't apologize for that. Sure, I kept information from him that I probably should've been more upfront with, but I've said sorry for that.

If Parker Shay is no longer interested in me because my hymen is still intact, I have to believe I'm better off without him. I'm not scared of it, and nor should he. He's one of the scariest-looking men I've ever met, yet a small membrane intimates him.

As I toss and turn in my bed, I convince myself it is better this way. Imagine the conversation in person, considering this one went so damn well. How humiliating. Would he have just stared at me in silence until I left? At least I would've seen his face, though, and been able to read into his inner thoughts. Now all I have is a thumbs-up emoji and a demand for a paraphrased sentence.

ELEVEN

PARKER

No matter how many times I read her text, the words don't change.

I'm a virgin.

A virgin.

What. The. Fuck.

The woman I'm working to seduce with the ultimate goal of killing is a virgin. Hymen intact, untouched, *pure*, type virgin. No cock has broken that threshold. Fuck, no wonder she was so skilled at stroking my cock. That's what she does—hand jobs.

The evil snare of her cunt isn't even real because she has no fucking idea about sex. Jesus.

I stare at the text again, willing the words to change. For this situation not to have just taken a complete nosedive into an abyss that sends me farther into the depths of hell.

Can I take her virginity, knowing I'll be the only guy she experiences? Yes, because as wrong as it fucking sounds, I don't want some other dirtbag touching her. She deserves someone to make her feel good. Not just take. I could do that. I'd give her that until it's time for Rocco and me to find our revenge.

But even that seems unjustified. Every moment I spend with her, the more I begin to realize she doesn't deserve our hate. Our vengeance isn't warranted, not with her as a pawn.

"You've been spinning your cell in your hand for the last hour. What's going on?"

I pause the incessant spinning of my phone, keeping it upright, held tightly between my thumb and forefinger, Codi's text still tempting me. I don't look toward Rocco. I don't need the judgment, the lack of belief in his eyes. Not right now.

"Started to think we've picked the wrong person. Codi doesn't deserve this shit, man."

An irritated bark of laughter coughs into the dark space of our loft, and I hear his knuckles crack in frustration. Without glancing in his direction, I can see him. Perfectly. His large, bulging frame quaking with the anger coiled in his veins, hands closing over the other and pushing until the biting crack of his bones echoes through our loft. He'd be shaking his head, disgusted by the words that have just fallen from my mouth.

"She's good, Rocco. She's got no clue about the shit her dad does. It doesn't touch her, never has done. She's clean. In every sense of the word. Our animosity toward her isn't warranted."

His feet move closer, his heavy footsteps thumping loudly against the polished concrete of our home.

"Codi Rein doesn't need to be deserving of our hate. That's the point, Parker. She's not who we're trying to hurt. Killing her hurts that piece of shit Dominic."

I throw my cell onto the couch, massaging my eyes with my palms. "I know that. But why should she have to die because her dad's an evil motherfucker? It's not right."

Rocco's silence is as heavy as his frame, as consuming as his presence in a room. I've pissed him off. Actually, pissed off is an adorable counterpart to what Rocco would be feeling right now. His cyclonic temper would be preparing to wipe me out right now. But like always, he'll refrain, never letting me bear even the slightest hint of his fury.

"You think Mom dying was right?"

The pain in his voice stops me, and I drop my head. "Of course not. Don't make it out like that. All I'm saying is, we do this, we kill Codi, we're no better than him, stripping away the good in the world."

"I told you not to get caught up in this bitch."

I finally look at him, scowling at his insult about Codi. "I'm. Not. Fucking. Caught. Up. I'm just saying maybe we take him out. He orchestrated it. Let's kill Dominic and be done with it."

"An eye for an eye, Parker. We want him hurting. We want him living in the pain we have for almost twenty fucking years."

Just like that, my anger spikes again, and I know Rocco's right. Dominic Rein deserves to live in hell. Just as we have. He deserves to have his heart stripped from his body. Just like we did.

Relieved that he can see the anger dancing behind my eyes again, Rocco steps closer, kicking my foot to grab my attention. "What's going on?"

"She's a virgin."

The thick barrel of laughter runs out of Rocco's mouth, and I want to punch him in the face.

"A virgin? Fuck. That's tough. You'd probably be into that. Too delicate for my tastes." He shrugs, moving away.

"Take it as a positive sign. This may be your way to redemption. Into the pearly gates of heaven. The sacrificial blood of a virgin." He laughs again. "Dripped all over your cock."

"You're funny. Really fucking funny," I growl out, but it's

said around a smile. Because it was fucking hilarious. His laughter booms through our loft, and I stand, searching for anything to throw at his retreating back.

I throw a cushion, the first thing within reach, and miss him by a mile. Shaking his head at my pathetic attempt, he keeps walking. "Pick that up. You know I don't like shit thrown everywhere."

I flip him off, throwing myself back on the couch.

PARKER

Did you feel pressured by me? Is that why you ran?

She begins typing immediately, and I groan outwardly at her response.

CODI

No. I wanted it. WANT it. Want you. I was afraid you wouldn't want me.

She honestly has no fucking clue. Zero. My need is now on fucking steroids. Bursting as a result of long-term abuse. Codi Rein has just handed me the greatest fucking gift I could ever want to receive from her. And she thinks it would turn me off.

Good. Fucking. God.

I SIT on the edge of her bed, watching her chest rise and fall in sleep. Her naked chest. Tits completely bare for my greedy eyes. Seriously not helping the painfully hard cock that's been stuffed within my jeans for weeks now.

She's not an attractive sleeper, which is a little surprising. Maybe I've fallen into the generalist belief that women this good-looking are perfect in every aspect of their lives. It's refreshing seeing her with flaws. Her arms are stretched wide at her side, mouth anything but *delicately* agape. More zombielike. She doesn't snore, though. *Plus.* I guess.

I reach for her cell, discarded on her nightstand, unlocking it. Her last text to me brightens her screen, and maybe I feel a little guilty about not replying. She passed out, stressing over my lack of reply.

Honestly, as much as it turned me on, I wasn't sure I'd be seeing her again after that initial text came through. Too many complications. This wasn't what I signed up for. Taking her life is hectic enough. Her virginity as well. Nah. It didn't sit right. I mean, I wanted it. *Fuck,* do I want it.

Selfishly, I'm most concerned about myself. I know I'm a self-serving asshole, but taking her virginity will mean more to me than it should. Knowing no one else has touched her. Knowing I'll be the first to feel the deepest, warmest parts of her body. Claiming her will spike an irrational sense of possession. She'll be mine. In more ways than one. Because in the end, I'll be her first, her only. Most concerning, these thoughts feel good. More than. They've fueled something within me that I definitely shouldn't feel. Something satisfying. Something that has flooded my veins. Something that has begun to soothe the flames of hate dancing around my heart.

Then she stripped away the final thread of willpower I was violently clutching onto.

No. I wanted it. WANT it. Want you. I was afraid you wouldn't want me.

Pure.

One hundred percent.

She was afraid her untouched state would turn me off, would scare me off.

Jesus. This girl. She might kill me before I do her. Before I knew it, I was picking the lock of her apartment, creeping into her room, and staring at her naked chest.

I've never wanted anything more than I do right now. Just to touch her.

Reaching out, I glide my knuckle across the underside of her generous-sized tit, watching her nipple harden, even in sleep. She stirs but doesn't wake. Pulling my hand back, I suck my thumb into my mouth, wetting it before circling it over her stiff nipple. First, the right. Then the left.

Her lips smack, rolling together in an ardently tender moan. I do it again. She offers me a similar sound, and I adjust my position on her bed, offering my swelling cock room.

Pinching her rigid nipple between my fingers, I flick the peak. Hard. Codi's back arches, her mouth falling open on a desperate swallow of air. I pause, wanting more, and she gives it to me, her hand diving under the sheet haphazardly covering her body. I watch the sheet dance as her hand works her body.

She moans.

She whimpers.

And still, I need more.

Throwing off her sheet, her naked body in complete view, I watch her hand move where I long to. Her fingers rub softly over her clit, bringing her the much-needed relief I should be giving her.

Leaning down, I suck a nipple into my mouth, my tongue swirling over it heavily. Her breathing stutters, her neck arching on a broken groan.

Watching her through hooded eyes, I pay similar attention to her other nipple, watching as her eyes begin fluttering open.

I bite down when her eyes meet mine, only to see hers close over again.

"Parker."

Sitting up, I drop my gaze to her hand. She freezes, her arm moving away, and I reach out fast to grab it. "Keep going," I demand, but my voice cracks, the rough whip breaking with how badly I want to see her come. "Keep going," I repeat, clearing my throat.

She hesitates, her hand no longer pulling away but still frozen against the naked skin of her pussy.

Sliding my eyes to hers, her cushy bottom lip caught between her teeth, I watch the uncertainty flicker in her pupils.

"My cock's been hard for you from the moment I saw you. Your message turned it to granite. I've never wanted something, *someone"* —I correct— "so bad in my life. My need for you went from a solid want to a level of desperate I've never felt before."

The uncertainty dies in her eyes as she blinks softly. A moment passes, I couldn't tell you how long, but our eyes catch, and we stay like that, staring at one another, barely breathing.

She moves first. Well, her hand does. Or maybe it's her thighs. Either way, her legs fall open, gifting me a full view of her cunt, and her hand starts its torturously slow movement.

I inhale deeply through my nostrils, rubbing a hand down my face. Bracing a hand on the far side of her hip, I push myself over her body, hovering above her.

"There'll come a time, you'll hate me. More than you thought possible. That moment, remember you wanted this as much as I did."

I look into her eyes then, drawing them away from her hand. She looks puzzled but nods softly in the darkened light of her bedroom.

"I'm gonna eat you now."

Her body locks rock solid. Her hand pulls from her heat and grabs onto my arm. "Umm... I ... Ah."

"Never had someone taste your pussy?"

She swallows audibly, her head shaking in quick, vigorous movements.

"Fuck me," I whisper. "Does that mean you've never tasted cock?"

Again, the short, sharp shake of her head.

"Sugar, you might just kill me." I smile, and she laughs.

My cock may never forgive me for killing this girl.

Dropping my lips to the soft skin of her stomach, I trail them downward, scattering soft touches all the way down.

The first long stroke of my tongue shoots a spasm through her entire body, her thighs falling open wide. Coming up on her elbows, she watches me, blue eyes almost indigo as a fire of lust burns inside them.

Keeping her purple flames locked with mine, I stroke upward again. A thick, wet caress of my tongue, and she almost chokes on her breath. "Oh. God." Palms on the delicate skin of her thighs, my thumbs slide down her slit, pushing her open for me, exposing her slick, pink flesh.

Relaxing the force of my tongue, I ghost my touch over her tightly coiled clit. I barely touch it, but she bucks her hips frantically as though I've sucked it hard. Flattening my tongue, I drink her up. Stroking. Teasing. Playing her body into a desperate, sex-starved realization. Lapping along her untouched pussy, I'm crazed with a need to make her feel good. To give her this. Reign the overwhelming feeling of pleasure over her sweet heat.

Codi's hands fly to her tits, her back hitting the mattress, hips rising to meet the eager caress of my tongue more forcefully. I growl into her throbbing flesh, my cock leaking into my boxers with how fucking hot Codi Rein fucking my face feels. My desirous eyes glue themselves to her hands. On her tits. Her brightly painted fingers tweaking her nipples in perfect timing to my tongue hitting her clit.

I suck her. Push my tongue inside her. I devour every shudder, every heady moan, every stuttered breath. And when she begins pulsing against my greedy mouth, I slide two thick fingers inside her, hooking them to grant me access to her crest. The deep part of her body that'll bring her to where I need her. Screaming my name and coming; on my hand, all over my mouth. Dripping so heavily with her orgasm to allow my cock a slippery and welcoming entrance.

She comes the way I want her to. Loud and hard. Her entire back lifts off the bed, her ass pushing into the mattress before she falls back down violently.

Her hands fly into her blond hair, pulling at the roots. *"Holy."* She breathes. *"Crap."*

Coming up on my knees, I watch her eyes flicker open, blazing purple under heavy lids.

Dragging my hand across my chin, I wipe her climax from my skin. She smiles at the move, her body shuddering in post-orgasmic quakes.

"That was *so* good," she smokes out, the tremulous sound exaggerated by her thick breathing.

I move up, dropping over her body once again. The entire length of me is glued to her naked skin. Her legs wrap tightly around my waist, pulling me harder against her in the most non-virginistic way. It's an unconscious move. Her body wants and craves more. She hasn't even been fucked yet, and Codi Rein's body is already showing what she's capable of. How eager, how insatiable she'll be.

Arching her neck, she moves her mouth up to meet mine, tongue sliding out to lick my lips. Desperately. Messily. I thrust my hips forward, fitting the thick swell of my jeans against her damp center. Her heat soaks my jeans, and I push forward again, *harder*. Her eyes roll backward, her body bucking against me.

Breaking the drag of her tongue against mine, I come up high on my knees, a hand snaking over my shoulder to pull my shirt from my body.

She groans loudly, her covetous hands moving fast to touch me. To glide hungrily down my naked chest and torso. Her fingertips graze the waist of my jeans, dipping inside to trace the ink disappearing underneath the material.

Reaching into my pocket, I grab the condoms I stuffed inside before I bailed from my loft in a hurry to get to her.

Presumptuous? Maybe. Do I give a shit? No. I'm fucking ecstatic that I came prepared. As if she has condoms on hand. Imagine getting to this point to have to stop.

Fuck. That.

No. I may be a self-assured prick, but I'm a self-assured prick that's about to fuck *Codi Rein*. I'm about to pluck the sweetest cherry and keep it all for my fucking self.

Throwing the wrappers on the bed, I unbuckle my belt and unbutton my jeans, watching her teeth bite into her bottom lip and her glorious fucking tits heaving with the nervous energy of her breath. Nervous but damn excited. Her hips undulating to bring her in contact with the bulge in my jeans.

I keep her eyes, and reach into my boxers, pulling them down simultaneously. My cock now free; Codi's breath stutters, and her fiery eyes widen.

Swallowing deeply, she stretches her hand out tentatively, brushing a thumb over the cum beading at my head. She circles the wetness around my tip, and my eyes roll backward, the timid touch tightening my balls.

"You're big," she states, more to herself than to me, but I

smile, all the same, tensing the muscle to make it jerk against her hand.

She laughs.

The fucking bells.

Pulling her hand back in amused surprise, I grab a condom and hand it to her. Her eyes turn like saucers, "I... uh... I've never—"

"Sugar," I cut her off. "Open it."

Licking her lips nervously, she nods, reaching to take it from my hands. Concentrating on the small foiled square, she tears the wrapping, discarding it as she pulls the rubber out.

She glances at my cock—staring angrily at her—then back to me under dark lashes.

"Pinch the top," I grate out, my hands moving to her hips, pulling her farther up my body. "Glide it down."

She does as I say, a slight furrow of focus in her brow, fat bottom lip caught at the corner with her teeth. My cock jerks instinctively at her touch, her small palm skating down my length, rolling the condom over as she goes.

Fully sheathed, she drops her hand slowly, skimming her fingertips on the underside of my balls as she does.

"This isn't gonna feel the best for you, Sugar."

She blinks and looks up at me quietly before offering a quick nod.

"Gonna feel fucking phenomenal for me." I smirk, and she coughs out a laugh. "I'll be as gentle as I can be. I'll make it feel as good as I can."

She raises her hips again, silently begging me to go for it, and I give myself a breath to look at her and take in this moment.

Codi, sprawled naked below me, legs draped around my waist, dripping cunt trembling with the need for my dick. I've never seen anything more perfect. Something so fucking tempting. So severely *mine*. No one has ever seen her this way. No one except me ever will. That spikes something heavy inside of me. Something dark. Something twisted. Something so supremely fucked up, and I've never felt this fucking happy.

Grabbing hold of my base, I yank her up toward me, bending to tease my head against her clit, earning me a desperate whimper, a body shudder, and her delicious pink nipples to harden. I repeat the action and am gifted a response, not at all different.

"Parker," she begs, the sound a tortured breath of need and want.

Pushing my head inside her slick, snug opening, I growl. Loudly. Inching forward, her constricting heat suffocates my cock in the most excruciatingly satisfying way, and I groan out something to that effect, the sound drawn straight from the rough edge in my throat.

A pained gasp breaks from Codi's mouth, and I glance up from where my body is entering hers to meet her eyes. They're closed tightly, her teeth biting her bottom lip painfully. So hard, she's probably tasting blood. Using a thumb, I pull her lip from the sharp bite of her teeth, and her eyes fly open.

"Breathe, baby."

She lets out a stuttered breath, lifting her hips ever-so-slightly, and I grab her hand. She squeezes tight, nodding her reassurance, and I push forward again, feeling the resistance of her virginity pushing back. Clenching my hand in hers, I power on, breaking through on a loud and tortured groan. Codi's face is twisted in pain, a soft, agonized whimper pushing from her lips. She blinks, her mouth opening wide as she breathes through the ache.

Fully sheathed, my eyes roll back into my skull. Her virgin pussy squeezes me tight enough that it suffocates the entire length of my dick. *Jesus*. Virgins, who would've thought? Fucking heaven.

"Gotta move, baby."

"Mmm-hmm." Her hips arch backward, away from mine. They push into the mattress, working to find relief from the pain throbbing inside her.

"Sugar, don't pull away from me," I coax, sliding out of her body tortuously slow. She strangles me the entire way, her muscles contracting with every inch I pull from her. I drive in faster, not hard, not powerfully, just an accelerated momentum of my hips to hit deep inside her.

I grind against her, stretching her, my pelvis connected tightly to hers. The movement stimulates her clit, and she shudders at the gratifying roll of pleasure. At the same time, she winces against the pain of her body widening for me.

I pull back again, much as I did before. *Slowly*. Relishing in the way she chokes my dick.

"Could get used to this," I grit out, watching myself drag from her body. She tightens her fingers around mine in response, and I look back at her face, a satisfied smirk playing on my lips.

She offers me a grin, her lips falling apart with a muted gasp as I drive forward. I roll my hips, mixing with my thrusts, stretching her to accommodate my size. The pain of my initial intrusion subsides, and her body begins arching upward, meeting mine with every forward movement. She moans on every gyration of my pelvis. She whimpers on each drawback of my dick.

Leaning down, I suck a perfectly pink nipple into my mouth, circling my tongue over the hard point.

She likes that.

Really fucking likes it because her back bows, and pushes her tits farther into my face.

I like that. Really fucking like it. So I do it again.

"Parker," she moans.

"Baby," I growl, moving my mouth to hers, and she doesn't hesitate to draw me into a kiss.

Our bodies move in sync.

Pull. Push. Roll.

It's like heaven. Better than. It's as though Eros and Aphrodite have kissed me on the end of my dick, enveloping me in their power and desire.

Fuck. Sex has never felt this good.

"Gonna come," I ground into her mouth, and she cries out softly, her hand tightening in mine, her kiss deepening.

I should be embarrassed by how quickly I've come. But I'm too blissed out to care, and she hasn't got anything to compare it to. Next time will be better for her, longer, and more satisfying.

One final thrust and I push forcefully into her, making her gasp in pain, but I'm too far gone to care. My cock pulses once, twice, three times, emptying into the condom covering me. The only regret I have is that I'm not blowing into her bare and filling her with hot spurts of cum, to have it fall from deep within her body tomorrow, reminding her I was here.

Moving my mouth to her neck, I kiss the soft skin. I pepper kisses down to her collarbone, tasting the dampened column of her neck.

Pulling back, I scan her eyes, working to read how she's feeling, and she smiles softly at me, a lot of emotion shining on her face.

"Hiya, handsome."

I drop my face down to kiss her lips. "Okay, Sugar?"

She nods, leaning up to kiss my lips. "Little sore but feeling good. Really good," she corrects.

I touch my lips to hers again before pulling myself from her body. Lips open, she grimaces almost silently, and I groan. It's simultaneous and such starkly different sounds we both laugh. Our eyes connect. It's intimate. Almost too much, but it feels strangely fitting. Something between us shifts, and I swallow deeply against the unfamiliar feeling.

Breaking the moment, I cough to clear my throat. Standing, I move into her bathroom, discarding the condom in the trash and turning on her shower. Wandering back into her room, she looks up, her legs closed and bent at the knees. She's every man's wet dream. Coy, a little unsure but still hot-as-sin. Reaching the side of her bed, I lean down, scooping her into my arms without speaking. She startles slightly, a small surprised yelp falling from her lips unintentionally. Winking down at her, I turn, walking her back into the bathroom, not stopping until we've entered the spray of warmth from her shower.

As much as I hate to, I place her gently back on her feet, palm to her chest, as I nudge her backward into the cascade of water. Codi pulls me with her, and I go willingly. She kisses my mouth and chest and then looks up at me through wet lashes.

"Just so you know, I'm glad I shared that with you."

I open my mouth to speak, but she lifts a finger to my lips, shaking her head. "You don't need to say anything back. I just wanted you to know."

She turns without another word, tipping her face into the spray. The back of her head meets my chest, and I lean down to kiss her neck, feeling a dangerous sense of connection. I feel something so detached from hate or animosity I should be nervous. Instead, I shut my brain down. I push away anything beyond the feeling of satisfaction and happiness and wind my arms around her waist.

"Glad you shared it with me, too, Sugar."

TWELVE

CODI

It's not pain, more of an ache. A dull ache. A leaden throb between my thighs that feels almost nice, especially knowing how it got there. Tangled around him in the dark of my room, covered only in the soft cotton of my bed sheets, I feel different. I feel restless in the most fabulous way. I feel energized by the intimacy we just shared.

"Why?" he asks quietly into the room, his large palm sliding up and down the naked skin of my hip.

"Hmmm." My neck tips up so I can bring him into focus, and he drops his chin, eyes searching mine in the lamplight.

"Abstaining from sex for so long. Why?"

I contemplate his question, nuzzling myself back into his neck and kissing it before pulling back. "It wasn't some clichéd reason of never finding the right man or wanting to be swept off my feet," I assure him, and he barks out a laugh. I smile against his inked skin. "I guess I was always a little afraid."

His hand pauses its slide over my skin. "Explain."

I sigh, ending the sound with an airy cough of laughter. He's different. That I'm certain about. He's blunt and brusque but intriguingly enticing. I'm drawn to the direct and undeviating nature. He's the most authentic person I've ever met. He doesn't camouflage the shadows dancing in his eyes. If anything, he's begging for me to see them. To acknowledge and accept them.

"It's not my story to tell, in all honesty," I start. "But, I've seen monsters, Parker, and not in the way you see yourself. These ones are camouflaged in everyday life as good men. They have solid jobs, and they're attractive, exceptionally so. They're confident, and they're charming. They slay in Armani suits and cars that cost more than some people's homes. They attend Ivy League colleges and drink scotch older than I am. But underneath that, there's nothing. Nothing but the darkness they use to suffocate others. Camryn dated one of those monsters."

His hand tightens on my hip, and my hand moves out to stroke along his chest. "They dated for a long time. If you can call it that. He took *a lot* from her. She was trapped. Almost no one believed her when she tried to tell them what he was really like. She gave up in the end, and it was awful to watch. From there, the thought of trusting myself with someone seemed too big of a risk."

"Fuck, Codi." He doesn't say anything for a long time, his hand resuming its gentle caress of fingertips against my skin.

"Why me?" he finally asks, and if I was more experienced with men, or more specifically, Parker, I could've sworn the question was laced with fear, a heightened uncertainty as to what my answer would be. Why would I give him this part of me? This part I've kept for so long. Afraid of the monsters of the world.

"You were different."

He coughs out an unamused laugh, his free hand coming up to rub his face. "No, I'm not. Codi, you need to start seeing me for who I am. Be cautious."

I shake my head, the palm of my hand dragging across his chest, clenching into a fist in anger. "No. You're not. Trust me. Men like him take things without permission. They hurt you. Purposefully." My voice cracks and I attempt to move from his embrace, but he holds me tight, keeping me close.

"You are not like that. You have your secrets, sure. You're dangerous, and I know that. Maybe you'll hurt me in a way that I'll never recover from, but right now, at this moment, you're far from the monster you claim to be."

His heavy intake of breath echoes in the room for long, drawn-out seconds, the sound thundering in my ears with the thick movement of his inked chest. Finally, his hand snakes out, grasping my chin and tipping it upward. He meets my eyes, a storm swirling in the gray shadows before he drops his chin, his lips caressing my mouth almost frantically.

He pulls from our kiss as fiercely as he starts it. Abruptly. Leaving me wanting. Panting.

"You're sore," he gruffs out, the irritation in his statement clear enough, and I suppress a giggle.

That thaws him, a smile teasing at the corner of his mouth. Seeing how often his genuine smile comes on when we're together is nice. I dislike the forced smirk and calculated grin he uses as a weapon.

"Get some sleep. I'm fucking shattered." He arches away from my body, switching off the dimly lit lamp, before settling back into the same position.

As much as my mind is flicking through thoughts at the speed of light, sleep finds me quickly enough. Lulling my body into a delicious sense of unconscious wrapped around Parker's hard body.

I WAKE BEFORE PARKER, my body stirring into consciousness in the most pleasant way. His hard frame is pressed tightly against the entire line of my back, and his knees bent into mine, his hard cock pushes firmly into my backside.

I wiggle backward, and he twitches against me, his rough groan vibrating against the skin of my neck. He pushes forward, wedging himself into the line of my ass, a deep growl escaping his throat.

I'm no longer sore. Tender, sure, but I don't ache. Not in pain, not like I did last night, anyway. I ache but in an entirely different way. A way that courses over my skin, sending a throb to the apex of my thighs.

"Sugar," he speaks, face still planted into my neck, his voice rough and cracked in sleep. He doesn't say anything more; the question, the plea in his tone, obvious enough.

"*Please,*" I beg, the sound a breathy whimper of need.

I momentarily lose him at my back and listen as he rustles through his belongings discarded by my bed.

I hear the sound of foil wrapping, which I only heard for the first time last night but know I'll never forget.

He's glued himself against my back again before I can take a full breath. His knee pushes up, granting him better access to where he craves to be. Where I yearn for him to be. He slides himself along the length of my center, once, twice, three times, making me wriggle back into him farther, needing more.

"Parker. Please."

He groans. "Fuck, the sound of you begging for it is better than your laugh."

Lining his thick head at my entrance, he pushes in, only to

withdraw again. I chase him backward, my back arching to the point of pain. I feel his smile against my neck, enjoying teasing me.

He does it again, his soft bark of laughter morphing into a pained groan as he withdraws.

"Beg for it, sweet, innocent Codi. Tell your man what you need."

My sex spasms at the sound of his roughly spoken demand.

"You. Inside me."

He *tsks*. "Say it, baby. Say *your cock, Parker*. Let me hear those sweet-as-sin lips turn dirty."

I whimper, and his large palm grasps my hip painfully.

"I want your cock, Parker," I obey, not recognizing the deep, agonized need of my voice. "I want you to fuck me. *Please.*"

The *please* did it. He bites down on my neck at the same time his head penetrates, only this time, he doesn't pull out. He continues forward, stretching me.

I roll my hips slowly against the tenderness his unhurried drive causes inside my body.

"See, fucking is so good, Sugar, because it can be slow," he pauses, burying himself completely. "It can be fast," he echoes the sentiment with a quick retract from my body, rushing forward again. "It can be hard..." He pulls out, stilling for a single breath before slamming himself into me hard enough to make me cry out. Loudly. Desperately. He kisses my neck, sliding back out. "It can be soft..." He slowly pushes inside again. "Whatever way you fuck, it feels so. Fucking. Good."

I moan in agreement, and the arm he has buried under my head reaches down, pinching my nipple.

He fucks me slow and hard, his hips moving with an almost lazy drag but slamming back inside me, causing my body to jerk and my boobs to bounce.

It's exquisite. My bent legs push together in a way that massages my clit, making me whimper his name, to beg for more, to squirm, to cry out, to *come*. Almost effortlessly.

Jesus. It doesn't even feel real. I feel almost delirious, definitely not at one with my body.

Parker grabs my hip, thrusting himself forward, his movements no longer slow. No, fast. Quick powered drives of his hips to propel himself forward, deep within my body.

He groans. He flexes. He growls. He bites me.

God. This man. My body still tingles with the aftershocks of my orgasm, my skin damp with what he does to me.

"Gonna come." He licks my neck, his hips powering forward one last time before his loud, harsh groan empties from his mouth in time with his body's release.

His lips kiss along my neck, over my shoulder, his sharp breaths crawling across my skin.

"Morning, Sugar."

"Good morning."

"Fun fact about me. My favorite way to wake up? Codi Rein wetting my cock."

I giggle in embarrassment and maybe a bit of egotism, feeling accomplished.

"I think it might be my new favorite way to wake up, too."

He grunts his approval, his grip tightening on my body, hugging me close. I'd be lying if I said Parker's want for affection wasn't a little staggering. He holds his body in a way to intimidate, his scowl more common than his smile, and his eyes glower with a darkness I crave to know more about. But when we're together, he's touchy. His body, hands, and lips constantly seek ways to love my body. Whether it's a brief or heated kiss, a slide of his hand against my lower back, or the way he pulls me into his side as we walk. It's constant.

I like it. More than that, I love it.

"Let's shower and go grab a bite to eat. I'm fucking starving." He kisses my cheek, moving away, and I roll with him.

He holds my hand in his, walking a step in front of me toward my bathroom. It's sweet in the same way it's egotistical. Parker Shay is sweet but sinister, and I'm finding he's someone I never knew I was looking for.

"Shower," he instructs, letting go of my hand, and I raise an eyebrow with a defiant smirk.

He winks, and my God, my lady parts spasm in extended after-shocks of what we just shared. Then he kisses the air, a simply blown kiss that's so unmistakably arrogant my legs quiver, and I'm confident I'm about to come. Again. I blink slowly and swallow deeply. His satisfied chuckle rings in my ears as he turns his back, opening my cupboards.

I stand frozen, watching the muscles in his back flex with every simple movement of his body. It's hypnotizing. Closing one cupboard, his eyes meet mine in the mirror, and his sinful smirk teases the right side of his mouth.

"Sugar" He reaches out to the next cabinet, and I watch the line of his tattooed arm. "Shower."

I reluctantly pull my eyes back along his thick arm, landing again on his face. I nod absently. "Yes, shower."

He continues his search as I adjust the temperature of the water.

"Gotta spare toothbrush, babe?"

"Top drawer on the right."

He moves in that direction, pulling a toothbrush from its packet. "You're on the pill," he states, dropping a large dollop of toothpaste on the brush, meeting my eyes in the mirror again. "I don't wanna use condoms."

I watch the way his back flexes as he brushes his teeth. He does it roughly, the movements fast and forceful.

"Codi," he prompts, spitting into the sink and turning to look at me without the barrier of the mirror.

"Okay." I nod, washing my body.

"Okay?" he questions skeptically.

"Yeah, okay."

His head pushes back slightly, shocked by the easy agreement in my tone, and I smile, more than a little pleased with myself.

"Pass my toothbrush."

A dark eyebrow raises, a mix of bothered admiration skating along his features at my demand. "Got any manners you might wanna use?"

I roll my eyes. "*Please.*"

"Fucked you twice, already throwing sass. Cock has changed you."

I laugh. Loudly. My head tips back, and my eyes close.

He's standing directly in front of me when my eyes reopen, staring down at me intently, so much so that my laughter dies immediately in my throat.

Handing me my toothbrush, he leans forward, veering from my lips just before he touches them, moving to my neck to offer it a wet caress of his tongue. "Fucking love the sound of your laugh."

My eyes close softly as I moan, enjoying the sweet attack of his mouth on my skin.

"Turn around."

I do as he says.

"Brush your teeth, Sugar."

Again, I comply without hesitation.

His large hand reaches for my arm dropped at my side,

pushing it up against the ceramic of the tiles and keeping it there.

My legs almost buckle when his other hand skates up my inner thigh, not skipping a beat as his fingers drag across my clit.

"Bet I can make you come before you finish brushing?"

I can't answer. Not with words. I moan instead as two fingers slide deep into my body.

My arm drops, my toothbrush forgotten at my side, and he pauses, "That's not the game, baby."

I stutter through a labored breath, smiling in defeat, quaking with how easily he's learned to play my body. Parker hooks his fingers in a slow drag across my g-spot and my back arches.

"Codi," he warns, and lazily, I lift my arm, toothbrush dragging across my teeth in a half-assed attempt to keep him going. He concedes on a quiet snarl of laughter, his fingers starting their assault again.

"So wet. So hot. So tight. And all *mine.*"

I convulse at the harsh way he speaks, his tongue dragging along my neck, teeth biting into my skin.

He wins. Without effort. I've barely made a sloppy attempt at cleaning my teeth before my body starts shuddering with the beginning of my orgasm. I ride it out, teeth clamping shut on my toothbrush, my hand flying to join my other on the wall.

He twists me as I'm still coming down, moving into the spray of water to wash his body, a smug grin dancing along his face. I'm too drunk on my orgasm to care; eyes hooded, smile satisfied.

Finished, he winks, leaning forward to place a chaste kiss on the side of my mouth and stepping from the shower.

With him gone, I brush my teeth, for real this time, wash and follow his retreat. He already has his boxers and jeans on when I return to my room, his eyes focused on his cell.

I dress in silence, glancing at his half-naked form occasionally, to shake my head at the gloriousness of a Parker Shay shirtless.

It's a given. I'm destined to live in damp panties for the rest of my existence. I should stop wearing them. He's a masterpiece. Crafted, sculpted by an artist, their piece de resistance.

He glances up, a slight, almost coy grin creeping onto his face. His muscles flex, his shoulders lifting to zip his jeans, pulling his belt together to buckle it.

"Codi. *Fuck,*" Camryn's voice travels from the front door, and I startle away from staring at Parker. "Pick your shit up, almost broke my fucking ankle."

Her voice moves closer, with her constant mutterings echoing her footsteps.

My bedroom door flings open, my shoes, discarded in whatever direction they landed in my panicked haze last night, flying through and landing in amongst the mess of clothes covering my apartment.

"Seriously, Codi. This isn't a fucking brothel. Stop leaving your shit everywhere." She enters not a second later, eyes falling on Parker as he pulls his shirt over his tattooed torso. Her bottom lip tips out in appreciation, her head nodding along, eyebrows raised.

"Ryn," I scold, and her eyes flick to me, scanning my body up and down. The playful appreciation has left her, being replaced with careful consideration.

Only thing Camryn Rein takes more seriously than her job? Me. My safety. My heart. My feelings. And at this moment, watching the debate in the denim blue of her eyes, making sure that I'm okay; my heart hurts.

My sister is broken, stuck within the deep darkness of her mind, of her memories. I can't tell if she can't get out or if she doesn't want to. I can't determine if she prefers living in the clouded reality of her mind because that's all she knows or that, really, maybe she's afraid of the pain it will cause to claw her way out.

So I do what I can to reassure her. I smile. I let her know I'm fine, more than, my grin probably giving away more than it should.

She blinks, dulling the fire projected my way, dropping her gaze to my tangled bed sheets, her lips tipping upward. "Glad you didn't cop a knee to the junk this time."

"*Ryn*," I whisper-yell at her retreating back, glowering at Parker's dark chuckle.

Dropping on the end of my bed, I pull my shoes onto my feet, color shading my cheeks. "I can't believe she said that."

His white-sneakered feet move into my line of sight, his hand moving under my chin to tip my face up to his. "She went somewhere pretty dark there for a second. She noticed *we* noticed, then said what she said to lighten the mood."

I feel my facial features soften. "You saw that?"

His thumb brushes along my bottom lip, his eyes lost for a moment before a quick shake of his head brings him back. "Baby, I wouldn't have seen it any clearer if Satan himself was glowing red at the pearly gates. She isn't trying to hide her pain. I think she uses it to deter people." He pauses momentarily, sighing loudly. "See it in Rocco all the time."

I'm more than a little stunned at his openness. He's yet to share anything about his family. I know they don't have any to speak of, but his willingness to share anything further is non-existent.

Not willing to scare him off or bring his inner jerk into default, I nod, letting myself appreciate this moment and his uncharacteristic show of empathy. Especially toward the most important person in my life. Camryn.

"Ready?" He steps back, scanning my appearance from my Tiffany blue colored Converse up my skinny black jeans, white tee, and leather jacket to my messy top knot, haphazardly tied atop my head.

"Like this version."

I walk into his body, kissing his chest. Keeping my arm around his waist, I turn toward my bedroom door, and he follows, head dipping down to drop his lips to my hair.

Camryn's in the kitchen, still dressed in her scrubs, hair much like mine, except there is no purposefulness to the mess in hers. Hers is a result of a sixteen-hour shift, the bags under her eyes testament to that.

She yawns unattractively, not covering the wide expanse of her mouth, as she finishes it with a loud shout.

"Morning," she sings, taking a large gulp of coffee.

"Morning," I echo, and Parker lifts his chin in greeting.

"You guys haven't officially met. Parker, my sister, Camryn. Ryn, Parker Shay. My boyfriend." The words are out before I can swallow them.

Boyfriend. I just actually said that.

I chance a wide-eyed glance to Parker, who is looking down at me, eyebrow raised in surprise.

"As you can tell, my sister has zero experience with men. I'm hoping you find it as endearing as I do." Camryn saves me from the world opening up and swallowing me whole.

Parker turns back to her, moving us forward to extend his hand, which Ryn takes without hesitation.

"Shay, you say?"

He lifts his chin in acknowledgment.

"Kane Shay's son?" she continues, coming around the bench to perch upon the breakfast bar.

His body locks rock solid, and I watch his head move in a

stiff nod. Just once, his stormy eyes pinned to Camryn in cautious consideration.

"I remember the night he died," Camryn declares, oblivious to the concrete form his body has taken, and my eyes flick to his face. "Killed by a shower of bullets, so the news reported anyways."

A gasp escapes my lips before I can stop it, my hand moving to cover the sound a second too late. A quick, shooting tremor slides through Parker's large frame. He swallows thickly, jaw set tight.

"Shit, sorry," Ryn apologizes. "That was really fucking insensitive of me."

Relief seems to loosen his coiled frame at her apology. He pulls me into his body more securely, my front glued to his side. "Don't sweat it." He forces a grin onto his face, settling Camryn's crease of worry currently carved into her forehead. "It was a long time ago now."

I squeeze his waist in apology? Reassurance? I'm not sure, but he winks down at me, silently telling me he appreciates it all the same.

"Guy was a prick. In the end, anyway. No loss on my part."

"I remember it hitting me pretty hard," she offers, unfazed by his heartbreaking statement. "From what I gathered, our fathers were in the same line of *work*." She smiles sardonically, and he coughs out a laugh. There's no humor to the sound, though. A practiced response that screams discomfort that exemplifies the rawness this topic evidently cuts him with.

I want to tell her to stop. To leave it be, but she continues before I can find the words to speak. My focus trained on the storm circling in his gray eyes.

"It scared me," she shares. "Didn't sleep much for a few

years, was always worried the same thing would happen to our dad."

He blanks out at the shared fear, his nostrils flaring in barely restrained fury, the menacing man he promises he is, fighting through, shadowing his handsome face.

The hackles on my neck rise at the barely contained show of aggression, at the hate projecting from his eyes. Camryn sees it too, shifting uncomfortably where she sits, eyes darting to me briefly before settling back on him.

"Anyway," she forces out. "Like I said, insensitive of me to bring it up. I apologize."

They become lost in a tangled dance of anger and uncertainty swirling in their eyes before Parker finally comes back to himself, forcing his false grin onto his face.

"No hard feelings. Nice to meet you. Codi and I are heading out to grab a bite. Let's go, Sugar."

I nod, stepping from his grip to hug Camryn.

"Be careful," she whispers, kissing my cheek, eyes still on Parker.

I'd be lying if I said that uneasiness didn't filter through my veins at that moment. Parker's caginess surrounding his family isn't new, but the monster he so soundly attests to be definitely lets himself be seen when they're mentioned.

I'm not afraid. If I were, I wouldn't walk out the door of my apartment, not with him holding me so tightly against his violently powerful frame. But Ryn's right. Wariness couldn't be considered stupid. I'm right to be cautious of Parker Shay. He has warned me to approach him in that way. That doesn't mean he doesn't set my skin on fire and my heart to electric. Maybe the fear of the unknown is what I'm drawn to. I don't know, and I refuse to let myself read into it. Not right now.

THIRTEEN

PARKER

"You know, you don't have to *steal* from your own mother." Codi's voice hits me as soon as I enter the shop.

"I don't know what you're talking about."

"*Pia*," she accuses, the exasperation in her tone dragging along her name. "I just saw you put it in your bag."

Pia walks into my line of sight first. Her dark hair is split into fighter's braids, her fair skin on show with her body dressed similarly to Codi; tight skirt, flowy blouse. Once upon a time, she would've piqued my interest enough to look at. She's a total brat, though.

She halts her movements, Codi barreling into her and stumbling back. Neither notices my presence, too caught up in Pia and her five-fingered discounts.

"Look,"—the dark-haired thief sighs— "just write it down in your tattletale book and be done with it."

A frustrated growl escapes Codi's lips and an easy grin forms on my face. It's fucking adorable, even her high-heeled foot stamping with the feminine graveled sound.

"It's not a *tattletale* book. It's letting your mom know so she can write the stock off."

Pia rolls her eyes, her head turning and her gaze colliding with mine. "How'd you get in? The door was locked."

I stare at her blankly before turning to Codi. "Ready to go, Sugar?"

She exhales heavily, forcing a smile on her face. "Yep, just let me write something in my tattletale book." She glares at Pia, storming toward the counter.

I watch her, turning back to Pia's dubious face. "You're seriously creepy. That door was locked."

"Let's go." Codi approaches, reaching for my hand.

"I'll leave you to close up, be sure to write down anything else that accidentally falls into your bag."

"Definitely *won't* do that," Pia sings back sarcastically, and Codi pulls the shop door open forcefully, muttering under her breath.

Standing outside, I pull her into my body, inhaling her sweet scent. She deflates against my frame, her arms wrapping tightly around my waist.

"Random fact..." I kiss the top of her head before she tips her neck to bring me into view. "You angry is really fucking cute."

Her indigo eyes narrow. "Random fact," she fumes. "Calling a woman *cute* when she's mad is *not* a good idea."

I smile, and not for the first time, I consider how easily it breaks onto my face in her presence. "See, cute."

She growls, and I laugh silently. "Swearing might help."

She gives me another growl, and I'm a little disappointed I didn't elicit the foot stamp.

"I could use a drink," she declares, attempting to step out of my embrace.

"Forgetting you didn't say hello yet, babe."

She rolls her eyes, and I pull her more forcefully into my body. She gasps, eyes falling hungrily to my lips. Not one to disappoint, I lean down as she reaches up, our lips meeting in eager greeting. No pretense, no playing, a pure unbridled need to taste.

Codi melts against me, the frustration from work easing from her body with every slice of my tongue. Finally pulling back, I drop a kiss on her forehead. "Better?"

She closes her eyes softly, exhaling on a satisfied smile. "Better."

CODI'S laugh rings in my ears, the sound barely heard over the music playing through the speakers in the bar.

She claps, applauding the dickhead who just missed his shot, too focused on Codi standing by the pool table, hip leaning casually against the side to give a shit.

Fucker's been testing my last nerve. I'm shocked he had the balls to come over and challenge her to a game. My eyes showed their warning, not enough to discourage him, though. Codi, being Codi, didn't read his intention, smiling wide and downing the last of her beer as she accepted his request.

Fuckwit. It would feel nice to break his face.

The dickhead pouts purposefully, giving her sad eyes, making her laugh, and I picture stomping his face into the curb. She chants something about him being a sucker, moving to take her shot. He moves strategically, standing behind her to watch her ass as she bends at the hips, taking her shot.

Sinking her final ball, she jumps up, arm extended in the air, a whoop of joy shouting from her juicy lips. She high-fives the guy begging for my fists, and he smiles widely, pleased as a fucking pig in mud to be touching her.

Fuckstain.

She saunters back toward me, her eyes glassy from the beers she's downed since arriving, his eyes watching her ass the entire way. He looks at me as she reaches me, and I flip him off behind her back, sliding my hand over her ass and pulling her closer.

"I won," she announces unnecessarily, a slight slur in her words.

"I saw." My legs open wider on my stool, letting her move between them.

"You look at him like that any longer, and he might start crying," she mocks. "Jealous, baby?"

I grunt out a humorless laugh. "You want his creepy little hands touching you... be my guest," I lie through my teeth, and she laughs loudly, the bells ringing in my ear and stirring my cock to life.

"You're a terrible liar," she whispers at my lips, tongue ducking out to wet her own.

She doesn't hesitate to touch her lips to mine, and she kisses me with the desperation of someone who is a few drinks down and begging to be laid. Not that I'm complaining.

She pulls away, eyes dazed with a potent mixture of booze and lust, skyrocketing my need to be inside her.

"Gonna go to the bathroom, then we'll head off?"

I lift my chin, touching my lips to hers once more before tapping my palm along her ass and telling her to hurry.

Dipshit stops her on her way to the bathroom, and my fist clenches around my glass as I swallow the last of my beer. The kid is seriously searching for a broken fucking jaw. He saw us all-but-fucking only seconds ago. Fucking cunt. Codi laughs at something he says, waving him off and walking away.

Discarding my glass, I move toward him, pool cue held tightly in my hand.

"Touch or speak to my girl in a way that makes me think you're thinking about her naked again, and I'll break this across your face." I lift the cue, and he takes a step back, nodding. "Get me?"

"Yeah, man," he placates. "I get you. Meant no offense. She's smoking hot, is all."

I push the stick against his chest, moving him back two or three steps, and he grabs hold of it as I let go.

"She *is* smoking hot, and she's *mine*. Even think about her while you're jerking your cock, and I'll make sure you're missing teeth."

He holds a hand up in surrender.

"Ready?" Codi smiles up at me, arms wrapping around my waist.

I look at the dickcheese once more before nodding and turning without another glance, pulling her with me.

Our Uber pulls up outside my place, and Codi pulls her lips from mine long enough to crawl out of the car ahead of me. She stumbles slightly, and I watch her readjust her clothing with a wink.

We're both a little drunk. Well, I'm a little drunk. She's a lot. She launches at me again, and I grin through our kiss.

Codi Rein boozed is horny as fuck.

Noted.

I detach our lips again, and she growls her disapproval.

"Baby, you want me to fuck you on the concrete steps of my loft for every fucker to see?"

She laughs, arms stretching out wide. "Happy for every fucker in this city to know you're mine. And I'll touch my man whenever and wherever the fuck I want," she declares loudly, laughing as she finishes.

I echo her laugh with my own, thoroughly enjoying this version of her. "Sugar," I start, and she rearranges her features in mock seriousness. "Big difference with people seeing us making out and watching me fuck you. Nobody will ever hear your sexy little groans and cries pleading for me to fuck you except me. No one."

All teasing falls from her face, replaced with unrivaled lust, making my cock strain in my jeans. I step into her, my arm draped heavily over her shoulders as we walk inside.

We enter the loft in silence, heavy need coiling around us. She follows my lead to my bedroom without question, and I don't even let myself consider how much of a dick I am for enjoying her so much.

I'm doing wrong by Rocco by liking this girl.

I'm doing wrong by Codi by using her until her time is up.

I'm a fucking double-edged sword, fucking two people who don't deserve it and without their knowledge. Right now, though, I don't fucking care.

I kick my door closed as we enter, watching her survey the untidy room; sheets still messed up from where I woke this morning, clothes thrown and discarded across the floor.

"I like it," she states with a smile. "Organized in the same way as mine."

"Take your clothes off."

Her smile freezes on her face, her lips parting with a lustful look. She drops her bag without care, letting it scatter amongst my messy belongings. Her shoes go next; one foot then the other. Pulling her blouse from her skirt, she lifts it over her head, revealing a black triangular cut see-through bra, nipples hard and visible through the material.

"Leave the bra," I scratch out, moving closer.

Her hands reach behind her, moving quickly to unzip her skirt. It falls, a drop of material falling to her feet, and she steps over it, pushing it aside with her bare foot.

Her lace-cut panties are blood red, a complete mismatch to her bra.

She moves to remove the tiny scrap of lace covering her, but I shake my head, telling her no. She backs up as I move closer, her legs hitting my bed before she stops.

"I wanna taste you," she admits through lowered lashes, and reaching her, I lift her chin with my knuckle.

"Tell me how I wanna hear it." My voice is coarse and rough. The thick need I have for her tightens in my throat.

"I wanna use my mouth," she tries, and I brush a thumb along her pillowy lip.

"More. To do what, Codi? You wanna use your mouth to what?"

"To suck your cock," she whispers, and I close my eyes at how fucking hot the hesitant murmur sounded.

"Kneel on the bed." It's said unevenly, the demand harsh in its instruction, but she follows willingly, her body sliding backward onto my tangled sheets.

Moving onto all fours, she crawls toward the edge where I'm standing. I'm trying to determine if I've entered some warped fantasy land. Codi Rein, body barely covered by lingerie, prowls toward me on all fours, begging to take my cock in her mouth.

Halle-fucking-lujah.

Unbuckling my belt, she watches with rapt attention, eyes glued to the bulge straining at my jeans. My shirt comes next, and her greedy eyes skate over my naked torso, bottom lip chewed between her teeth.

"Never done this before," she speaks at my abdomen, hand

coming out to brush along the divot of muscle dropping into my jeans. She uses her fingers to unbutton and push at them, freeing my hips from their confines, my dick stretching the material of my boxers.

"Know that, Sugar."

She glances up at me, nodding, understanding the reassurance I offered her before focusing back on my boxers.

Shuffling forward on her knees, her two index fingers reach up, dropping into my waistband and gliding my boxers over my shaft. She pulls a heavy breath through her nostrils as I spring free, my cock heavy and needy, pointing directly at her.

She takes the invitation, peeking up at me briefly before wrapping her small palm around the bottom of my length and pumping once, then twice.

There's no secret she knows how to stroke a cock. I blew my load in my place of work, surrounded by partygoers from her doing *just* that.

My eyes close on their own accord, relishing in the feel of her stroking me. I shout, the sound landing somewhere between a growl and a groan as her tongue drags along my head, teasing my slit.

She's tentative in her exploration.

Her pouty lips cover my tip, tongue swirling around the head, pulling back and going back again.

"Deeper, baby," I ground out, thrusting my hips forward and pushing deeper into her mouth.

She takes my instruction readily, her tongue coating my shaft on her downward glide. She does that once, twice, taking me deeper still with each downward slide. I hit the back of her throat with an agonized groan, her virgin mouth choking on my dick. The broken sound of her gagging makes me harder still. She draws me from her mouth, her hand skating along me in firm, skilled movements. Dick wet from her mouth, she swallows me back down, satisfied groans slipping from her throat and pulsating against me.

I groan.

She whimpers.

She's inexperienced, sure, but that's not saying she's no good. Fuck no. The opposite, she's into this. Hardcore. Gorging on my dick like it's her very last supper. She takes my cues; she's not just going through the motions. She's enjoying this *almost* as much as I am.

She shuffles closer, pushing my dick to the back of her throat, her free hand moving up to cup my balls, massaging them in time with her mouth.

"Baby. Fuck. That's it. Deep. Just like that."

She drags her mouth back before dropping it down again and swallowing, the walls of her throat closing in on me as her mouth covers me completely.

It's my undoing, and neck tipped back, I groan long and hard as I empty inside of her mouth.

I fall from her lips. She's standing tall on her knees, eyes wide, her hand covering her mouth. She watches me for a loaded second, eyes closing, throat moving in an attempt to swallow, but she stops it.

"Codi—" I start, but she holds up a finger, silently telling me not to speak, and I watch her uncertainty as her throat contracts with the act of swallowing.

A look of utter distaste coats her features, and I suppress my laugh. Dragging a hand over her mouth, her eyes finally open, meeting mine.

She opens her mouth to speak but stops herself, her lips closing tightly. Head nodding, she looks at me confidently. "So, umm... cum is warm and salty," she pauses, tongue dragging along her teeth. "And really fucking gross."

I can't stop the loud bark of laughter that shoots from my mouth, and after the briefest hesitation, she giggles. "Like, seriously, you should've warned me that it would fire at the back of my throat and try to choke me with its unappealing warmth."

My laugh continues, and I move, grabbing her arm and tugging her forward to wrap my arms around her. "Codi Rein, you are one hell of a pleasant surprise."

I like this girl. Really fucking like her. There's no bullshit. Just her. As she is, in all her awkward, innocent, sexy goodness. Fuck, I don't know how I ever stood a chance.

I've got no idea what I've tangled myself into, but I know it's chaotic, twisted, and weaving in a way that might be impossible to ever crawl out of. But right now, I don't want to. I want to enjoy this moment with a woman that, in another life, I think I could have found happiness with.

"No, I'm serious, is not swallowing a deal breaker for you? I'll do it if it is, but if you're not fazed, I appreciate you letting me know."

I look down at her blue eyes, staring up at me widely, and give in to my need to touch my lips to hers. Pushing her backward, her back hits the bed, and I raise an eyebrow. "Think it's worth it if I repay the favor?"

"Swallowing it is."

My laugh breathes across her skin as I pull the tiny bit of lace covering her pussy down her legs. Her laugh joins mine until my tongue meets her clit; her laughter morphing into a moan that arches her back. And in that singular moment, I consider that I need to find a way to cleanse my soul and gain access to her heaven, only to be able to claim her back after I've taken her life.

FOURTEEN

CODI

A thud pulses from one temple to another, and I curse myself for the stupidity of excess consumption. I can't handle beer. It's no secret, no unknown fact, yet, last night, I felt compelled to drink more than my body could handle.

I know why. Parker and I were having *fun*. He and I were drinking, laughing, and playing pool, and the night got the better of me. Not going to lie; that guy who challenged me to a game of pool was a total creeper, but I saw the possessive gleam in Parker's moonlit eyes, and I *loved* it—loved that I stirred that side of him to life. I felt powerful, desired, and *claimed,* and it felt really, really good.

He touched me more. He kissed me more. Gave me his smile. Gifted me his rough laughter. He made me feel cherished, adored, delicate, and *wanted*. He made it known that I was his, and in turn, he was mine. We were an *us.*

All that made me crazed with my need to touch and taste him. I couldn't get enough, clawing all over him like he was my only hope to breathe. He seemed to enjoy it, giving back just as much as I gave. Likely with a little more finesse.

Probably.

Definitely.

I crack my eyes open, glancing at his sleeping form, large bicep thrown over his eyes, the sheet falling precariously low on his chiseled hips. Like most of his body, his arms are heavily inked, and tattoos are artfully placed on his skin. His tricep is, compared to the rest of him, somewhat bare, the word *Lila* inked in cursive script, a white rose, thorned stem and all, underlining the name. It's beautiful and obviously a piece with significant meaning, nothing else to disturb the tanned strip of skin. I wonder who Lila is. Someone special. Someone who means a great deal to him.

My eyes look downward again, over his naked skin, taking in every last toned inch of him. His body is phenomenal. He was likely crafted by an artist with an infinite eye for detail, chiseling every line of his muscle to perfection.

I drop my eyes farther to the part of him hidden from sight. He's hard. That's obvious under the thin material covering him. I consider reaching out to touch him, to drag my palm along the smooth, velvet touch of his skin, but refrain. I need coffee, and I need to pee. It doesn't stop me from lifting the sheet lightly and stealing a look.

His cock lays heavily against his hip. Thick, rigid, and *big*. God, I can't believe that fit down my throat. Okay, maybe not all the way, but deep enough. No wonder I gagged a time or two. I'd be embarrassed if it weren't for how turned on he seemed to be at the sound, hips thrusting forward a little harder every time I choked on him.

But the taste, *ugh*. It wasn't so awful when it would leak from his head as I was doing my thing; small spurts of warm salty sweetness along my tongue, but all at once, in a forceful shot to the back of my throat. God, I had to force myself to swallow it down.

I smile to myself at the recollection of his amused laughter. They're few and far between, but Parker Shay being *playful,* steals large chunks of my heart without warning.

I move from the bed, grabbing the first of Parker's shirts I find discarded on the carpet. It smells like him, and I pull the neckline to my nose to inhale as it falls over my body. I pee, brush my teeth and tiptoe out of Parker's room in search of coffee. The loft is eerily quiet, and I pull my hands farther into the sleeves of Parker's shirt, feeling a little out of place and unwelcome in the space.

I busy myself making coffee, opening cupboards, and working not to make more mess than necessary. The kitchen is meticulously clean, with everything within a specified space. Moving to the fridge, I bend down, searching for cream. Grabbing it, I spin and scream.

Rocco stands on the opposite side of the counter. His hands are braced on the marble, the muscles in his arms protruding from the simple stretch.

"Dude," I breathe out, my heart beating fast in my chest. "Warn a girl that you're standing in the same space, man. You're like a panther. Weirdly quiet for someone so big."

He doesn't speak, his eyes scanning me up, assessing. He starts at my bare feet, moving up my naked legs. I pull on Parker's shirt to cover me more, which earns me an arched brow as his evaluation continues. His eyes cross quickly over my body, finishing on my face, his bottom lip tipping out in quiet appreciation.

The dress down of his eyes wasn't creepy, not in a sexually

charged, unwanted attention kind of way, but still uncomfortable. He was most definitely working to see my bare soul.

"I'm Codi, Parker's, umm... girl...*friend?*" The hesitancy in my voice sounds as lame as the words, and I cringe at the amused smirk that plays along his lips.

"Coffee?" I squeak out, turning back to the machine and pulling an extra mug from the cupboard without waiting for his response.

I feel his stare burning on my back as I rigidly pour coffee, trying to decide whether to continue making one-sided conversation or get swallowed by the awkward silence.

Swallowing deeply, I square my shoulders and turn back. Taking a few steps toward him, I slide his cup over tentatively. "I bet you're a no cream, no sugar type of guy."

He watches me for an additional beat before his eyes drop to the black coffee, his face giving away no emotion as he reaches for it. He takes a heavy sip before his focus returns to me, and it's impossible not to read the skepticism within them. They're like Parker's, almost identical in shape and shade but somehow more threatening, lined heavier with darkness.

"Do you wear contacts?"

I stumble over my words, pulling my mug away from my mouth as I tip it up to take a sip. Coffee spills down my front, and I close my eyes in embarrassment. "Ah. No. No contacts."

He glances at the coffee stain on Parker's shirt before raking his eyes back to my face. "They're purple and familiar," he adds as an afterthought, frowning heavily.

"Really? That's cool. I've never met anyone with eyes like mine. My family all have blue eyes, just not like mine. They're lighter." I'm babbling, running out of breath with my need to fill the quiet, and I curse myself for my awkwardness.

He lifts his coffee to his lips once again, not speaking, and my eyes trace the thick muscles of his arms. His tricep holds the exact tattoo Parker's does; the name *Lila* is scripted along his skin, a single white rose sitting below, its thorned stem under-lining her name.

"You and Parker have the same tattoo. Who is Lila?"

His eyes storm at my words, and his face twists in hate. "Don't fucking say her name," he spits, the crack of his voice more cutting than his words. "Lila isn't your business. Don't ask about her again."

I swallow the lump forming in my throat and nod my head briskly. "Okay."

"Roc." Parker's sleep-clogged voice drifts between us, but neither of us looks in his direction, the fire in Rocco's stare pinning me in place. "Fucking chill, dude. Codi, I see you've finally met Rocco, my older brother. He's a real pleasant, friendly guy."

He approaches, kissing my temple and reaching around me to retrieve the coffee I had made him from the counter. He's dressed only in gray sweats. His torso is naked and still warm from sleep as he wraps his body around mine.

Rocco watches us, brow furrowing at Parker's show of inti-macy before standing and moving from the open space back toward his bedroom. "Clean the kitchen."

"Nice to meet you," I yell to his retreating form, but he ignores me, disappearing from sight.

Tipping my head back, I smile at Parker, who kisses my lips sweetly. "Random fact," he gravels out, his voice quiet. "Lila is our mother's name."

I open my mouth to speak, but he cuts me off. "Don't ask about her again."

Similarly to what I offered Rocco, I nod my head in acknowl-edgment, the movement jerky and uncomfortable. "Okay."

He watches me expectantly, and I shrug. "Random fact, I totally peeked at your naked self this morning before I got up."

His eyes darken with lust, pulling me farther into his body, and I barely contain the small moan that threatens to break from my lips.

"Sugar, I watched you masturbate in your sleep the night I took your virginity. I think I have one up on you." He winks, and my cheeks shade without permission.

He pulls my coffee from my hand, placing it beside his on the counter, hands moving under his shirt to my naked ass. He lifts me without issue, and I wrap my legs around his bare waist.

"Gonna fuck you in the shower, then I'll drop you home."

"What about the kitchen?" I startle as he walks us from the small mess, Rocco's demand stabbing into my conscience.

"He'll get over it. Or not. Couldn't give a fuck."

I'm about to argue, to demand he take me back so I can work my way into Rocco's good graces, but he slides a finger into me from behind, and I gasp in shocked gratification. He's right. Rocco will have to get over it.

"THAT *IS* WEIRD." Camryn glances over at me before focusing back on the road. "So, he just stood there mute the entire time until he bit your head off."

"Yep," I pop my P, and our eyes meet again, Ryn's wide and irritated.

"What a dick."

I shrug. "I don't know what his issue is. It's like I had personally offended him by merely existing."

"He's probably mad at the world for some unjustified reason. Is he hot?"

I hum my confirmation.

"Well, expand on that shit."

"Same height as Parker, but built. Like muscles on muscles, built. Inked-up skin. Blond hair, short trimmed beard, gray eyes, *scary* eyes," I correct. "He's hot, for sure. But really quite, I don't know... frightening? He looks into you, not through you. *Into* you, like he's trying to reach your soul and figure out who you *really* are."

Our conversation moves from Rocco and Parker, Camryn filling the quiet space of the car as we drive with mindless chatter. Pulling up to our childhood home, I grab Camryn's arm as she moves to get out of the car, and she turns back.

"Listen, can you not divulge too much about Parker to Dad? I will tell him I'm seeing someone, but I don't want his henchmen sniffing around, background checking, and stalking my boyfriend."

She nods easily. "Yeah, of course."

We push through the front door, almost colliding with our mother, who stumbles back. The smell of stale alcohol seeps from her skin, and my nostrils flare in distaste.

"Ever heard of knocking?"

Her painted lips twist in disapproval, aging her. It's a shame she's so hateful. The blackness of her soul extinguishes her outer beauty, which like Camryn's, is flawless.

Like my sister's, her brown hair is thick and falls over her shoulders in large waves. Their skin tone is identical, flaunting a natural tan that was unfortunately not bestowed upon me through our gene pool. I didn't inherit many of my physical traits from my mother or father. My blonde hair, creamy skin, and purple eyes are all my own. I don't mind it. Camryn hates her appearance because of this woman.

"Hello, Mother. A pleasure to see you too." Camryn smiles,

the falseness in the gesture aching her cheeks. "I see you've been sucking the souls of helpless human beings again," she gestures to the blood-red lipstick our mother seems to use as a trademark. "Also, this is *our* home. If you don't want us walking in like we're, I don't know, your children, change the locks."

I remove my coat, remaining quiet through their typical hellos.

"Codi," she greets indifferently, ignoring Camryn, infuriating my sister further. But, more than her insults, Camryn loathes her indifference, the ease with which the woman who grew us inside her body can reject her.

"Mom."

She sighs, looking me up and down. "I never understand why you dress this way. Black jeans, white t-shirt. Really, Codi, you have a beautiful figure. You should dress to show it off."

"I'm wearing the exact same outfit. You don't think I should dress to show my fabulous figure?"

Mom rolls her eyes, turning back to Camryn. "More often than not, you're dressed in pajamas. Honestly, Camryn, I've given up on whatever seems broken inside you."

Camryn goes quiet, her face twisting in an unhealthy mixture of hate and pain. It's wrong we even refer to her as our mother. Biologically she may very well be, but there's no love shared, no mother-daughter bond, no bond at all for that matter. The woman is unfeeling and void of emotion except those created to cause pain. Hate. Envy. Spite.

"Have another mimosa, Sarah," I bite out, grabbing Camryn's hand and pulling her through the house in search of our dad.

"Fuck, I hate that bitch."

"She was literally born without a heart. God knows what black storm sits within her chest to make her so awful."

"Ignore her. I'll deal with her later." Our dad's thick voice filters toward us as he comes into view, and we move forward straight into his tall frame, hugging him tightly.

"Beautiful." He kisses Ryn's cheek. "Beautiful." He offers me the same. "You need to come by more. I miss you both too much," he chides, slinging an arm over our shoulders and walking us toward the kitchen.

"Not gonna lie, Dad, your house guest is a bit of a buzzkill."

He laughs, but it's a sad sound. "She knows too much. If I throw her out, she could destroy me." His eyes close in helplessness, and it's so out of place on his perfectly constructed demeanor that Camryn and I share a confused look.

"Not against her disappearing," Camryn teases, and I bark out a snort of laughter.

"Girls," he warns, and Camryn only winks, earning her a kiss to the temple.

"WHAT'S NEW? Tell me what's happening with my girls," Dad speaks, eyes focused on the steak he is cutting.

Ryn takes a sip of wine, twisting the stem of the glass as she places it back on the table. "Working. Same old. Nothing new."

"How miserably predictable of you, daughter."

Sarah sits at the end of the table, leaning back in her chair and nursing her drink. She won't eat. Like always, she'll swallow booze and throw out insults until our father banishes her from the table. It's sad, really. Family dinners, Rein style.

"Codi?" Dad ignores our mother, glancing toward me.

I shrug, chewing my food and swallowing before speaking. "Work's good. Life's good. I started seeing a guy. He's nice."

"Oh, lucky guy, does he know your chastity belt's padlocked shut?"

I cough out a humorless laugh. "Some people are attracted to women who respect themselves enough to not sleep with the first guy that tells them they're beautiful, Mother."

"You're a prude, Codi. Don't sugarcoat it."

My father's fist hits heavily onto the table. "Watch your mouth, Sarah. Or leave us."

She holds up a hand in mock surrender. Retrieving her glass, she swallows half the contents of the glass before reaching for the bottle to fill it up again.

"What's his name?"

I shake my head. "Parker. But that's all you're getting right now. I've only just started seeing him. No need for your minions to be looking into him."

An amused smile tugs at his lips. "Minions. Funny. I don't like being commanded by my daughter, but I'll respect your privacy for now. If or when it gets serious, I'll be checking him out. Mark my word."

Nodding, I refocus my attention on my plate, cutting my steak and the conversation about Parker off as I do so.

"At least you're trying," Sarah slurs. "This one gets spooked by the first man to touch her." She points at Camryn, rolling her eyes. "It's like you've sworn off men permanently. Or maybe they've sworn off you because you're too much work."

Placing her knife and fork calmly on the table, Camryn stands. Her chair drags along the floor painfully as she does so. "Excuse me."

She rushes from the table, and I know better than to follow her. She needs her space right now. It's the only way she tames the nightmares in her mind.

"Go." The menace in my father's tone sends needles up my

spine, but my mother only sighs in boredom. Content that she's offended us all enough, she stands on wobbly feet, moving away to spread misery to anyone else who crosses her path.

"She's so vile. Surely there's a way around having to stay with her."

Dad smiles sadly, reaching for his glass. "I wish, beautiful, but Sarah Rein holds the ability to take something so *unbelievably* important from me," he stresses, and I see the intensity in his eyes, the truth behind his words.

He lets me watch him in silence, a cautious sadness cloaking him. "She has the ability to crush me, in here"—he taps his heart — "in a way, I could never recover from."

His cryptic words cause me to frown. "You *love* her?"

He laughs then, sarcastically, bitterly. "No, Codi."

"Then..." I pause, struggling to understand.

"Sweetheart, I hope with everything within me that you never need to have intimate knowledge of what I just said. Just know that I don't keep her around for her compelling company. I've been forced into a corner I'll forever be happy to be confined to." He squeezes my hand, and my eyebrows knot together.

My dad chuckles softly, lifting my hand to kiss my knuckles. "Nothing to worry your pretty head about, Codi. I'm sorry that you and Camryn are subjected to her hideous nature. If there was any way around keeping her in our lives, that wasn't illegal," —he adds with a grim smile— "know that I would've taken it."

Camryn walks back into the dining room, skin paled, eyes a little dim, but she smiles at Dad and me, and it's genuine. We bring her comfort. We give her peace.

FIFTEEN
ROCCO

Stepping from my room, I reconsider, pausing in my doorway to listen for any sound of them. I'm hit with quiet, and I breathe a sigh of relief. They're nauseating, and her fucking giggle. Fuck. Me. I want to drive nails into my skull. She's so fucking *chirpy* all the goddamn time. Smiling. Waving. She's always doing small insignificant things for me that make me want to like her. She makes me coffee, and always ensures the kitchen is sterile in its cleanliness. She's even memorized how I like the couch cushions because they're always neatly in their place after she's been over. Parker isn't that considerate.

I trudge through our loft with no immediate plans for the day, save maybe working out. Fuck, I need it. Overnight shifts at Ruin are killer, especially in succession. I'm wrecked. My only saving grace is that not being here means I don't have to listen to my younger brother fuck his bitch.

I shiver involuntarily. I don't know what's worse, listening to her moan and beg for more or Parker's rough voice talking dirty. She went from virgin to wildcat in a hot minute. I'm glad that

Parker is getting his fill while he can. Codi Rein is hot. There's no denying that; killer body, perfect tits, pretty little face. He deserves his slice. It just fucking sucks that I have to listen to it.

My eyes narrow as I reach the kitchen, coffee brewed and waiting, my mug sitting neatly beside the pot.

Thoughtful fucking bitch.

I laugh despite myself, shaking my head as I pour my coffee.

Codi. Fucking. Rein.

I MOVE THROUGH DOWNTOWN SEATTLE, refusing to alter my path for anyone that gets in my way. Parker texted me and told me to meet him for lunch. He asked me to meet him at a shop called Blaq, where his sickly, sweet girlfriend works. I almost told him to go fuck himself. But refrained. I like Parker's company, and with the bar and our Rein plan in full swing, we rarely see one another. Unless you count me listening to them fuck, which isn't exactly my ideal bonding time.

I slow my approach when I see them cuddled into one another, smiles big, and focused solely on each other. It gives me pause, and I stop, moving to lean against the cool brick of the wall to watch them.

Parker speaks, making her laugh, and a shit-eating grin forms on his face. He hasn't smiled that freely, that sincerely since Mom passed. He's happy, and I don't know whether to be elated by the fact or pissed right the fuck off.

He leans down to kiss her, her entire body melting into his as they all but fuck on the sidewalk. It's intense. It's intimate—a show of unbridled affection between two people in love.

What. The. Fuck.

I rub my jaw roughly, my anger spiking.

Pissed off.

No two ways about it. My temper boils in my body, coursing thickly through my veins, scorching the small snippets she'd begun to thaw.

Does he not remember? Does he not care? This wasn't the plan. He was supposed to have fun. That's it. He was supposed to enjoy her and pull her in to gain her trust and affection. Nothing more. Then he was supposed to put a bullet right through her brain, watch her bleed, and know, *fucking know,* that he did right by Mom. That he gave Dominic Rein precisely what he deserved. Unequaled agony. Dominic Rein *needs* to live in the reality of hell, his loss and heartache so heavy he can no longer pull himself up. I want him to suffocate in his pain. Choke on it.

I watch Parker break their kiss, touching his lips to her forehead before stepping back. She waves him off, opening the shop door, stopping and turning around one last time to wave again.

I punch the brick wall, startling passersby and breaking the skin on my hand. I turn without another thought, reaching for my cell and texting Parker, telling him something came up and that I'd catch him at home.

SIXTEEN

PARKER

Rocco's been MIA for days now. He does this occasionally, which worries me the same way it pisses me off. Hard. He won't respond to my texts, which isn't unusual, but it fires my anxiety. I need him. I rely on him as heavily as some would a parent. It's been that way forever.

When Mom died, Dad changed. He'd always been a little darker and volatile, but her death killed anything good in his soul. Day by day, his insides grew blacker. He lost his ability for love, and within the blink of an eye, we went from his children, who he cared deeply for, to nothing more than burdens. Reminders of her. A cold reality that she was gone and, along with her, his heart.

When the mood struck or one of us stepped out of line, he parented through fear, fury, and fists. He'd backhand us with blame because, somehow, one way or another, her death was on us. For existing, for making the threat of ending her life more attractive to those who wanted to destroy his business.

Rocco took that on.

Time and time again.

When I fucked up, he stood up and took responsibility. He took hits that were mine more times than I can count. And when there was no way to deny I was involved, he made sure he did something to piss our father off more. He took my heat. And I stood by weakly and watched.

Then Dad died, and the cycle started again with Marcus. Kane's second in command. His best friend. Our uncle. Not that our blood tie meant anything to him. *Family.* He despised the thought. Marcus saw us as a burdened misfortune when he realized we didn't share our father's taste for delinquency and criminality. Still, he stayed. For what? I was never certain. Possibly the connections our name brought him. Likely the money Mira inherited as our guardian.

Mira. His anger rained down on her in violence. Our fuck up, or his, meant she would meet his fists. The only way to keep her safe was through Rocco because, more than hurting others, Marcus thrived on the villain that lived within my brother. The one he craved to nurture into something psychotic. Going head-to-head with a raging Rocco made the guy feel alive.

When we finally managed to escape that hellhole, Rocco worked, doing God knows what, to let me finish school. When we came of age and gained access to our parent's estate, I went to him with the concept of Ruin. He nodded and agreed without question.

He makes sure I eat. He makes sure I sleep. He cleans. He might be fucking psychotic, but he's the only parent I've ever known.

I owe him my life.

But he only wants Codi's, and I promised him that.

I stand, hips pressed against the cool marble of the kitchen counter, considering what the fuck to do about his disappearing act. I might be indebted to him for an eternity, but it doesn't mean he's not pissing me right the fuck off with these vanishing acts.

When he's gone, he's one hundred percent *gone*. I have no way of contacting him. No way of knowing if he's okay. He's also not pulling his weight with the bar. I've been having to do all-nighters more often than not, working to manage stock, suppliers, our financials, and pain in the ass fucking staff while covering the bar when needed.

I'm fucking wrecked. When I do get the chance to sleep, I crash hard and wake the same way. It's a vicious fucking cycle, one Rocco's standing right in the middle of, expecting everything and giving nothing.

I exhale heavily, drinking deeply from my mug, praying it'll fire up my energy levels.

The click of the front door echoes through the loft, and I slam my cup down harder than necessary, spilling coffee over the white marble.

I move from the kitchen purposefully, my body raging with a potent cocktail of emotions I in no way understand.

Roc stops when he sees me, eye black and lip split.

"The fuck, man?" I ground out, not caring about his current state, moving forward to slam my palms into his chest.

He stumbles backward, caught off by my uncharacteristic show of aggression. He knocks my hands away, stepping into my frame. We're nose to nose, anger storming in our eyes, and my temper flares, pissed that he has the fucking nerve to throw attitude my way.

I push him again, but this time he's prepared, his body barely moving an inch.

"Get the fuck outta my face, Parker."

I push him, and he shakes his head, warning me against

touching him again. But fuck him, so I do it again. "Where the fuck have you been, Roc?"

He exhales heavily from his nose. His jaw is wired shut with rage so volcanic his entire body is shaking. "Lay your fucking hands on me again, and I'll make you wish you hadn't."

"Yeah?" I raise my eyebrows, spitting the words in challenge.

"Yeah."

"Fuck you," I seethe, lifting my hands and smashing them against the solid wall of his chest once again.

This time he pushes me back, and I stumble at the strength in his attack. He pauses, giving me the opportunity to back down, his ice-cold eyes warning me to stop.

Correcting my footing, I glare at him. "Gonna tell me where you've been, making me fucking worry you're dead?"

Shaking his head, his scowl comes heavier onto his face. "Gonna tell me you killed the bitch while I've been gone?"

I run at him before I let myself question what I'm doing. I tell myself it's because he's disappeared on me. That he won't tell me where the fuck he goes. But in reality, I know it's because he brought up Codi, called her bitch, and brought up her immi-nent death.

We fall to the ground on impact, fighting for an advantage I will never gain. He's bigger than me. Stronger. He's angrier than I am.

I land a punch or two before he twists, pinning my body heavily against the floor, hand on my neck. "Stop it. Don't make me fucking hurt you."

I struggle in his grasp, my hands and legs moving to dislodge him, but his body mass is too much. I land a few blows into his ribs and kidneys, and eventually, he gives, letting me throw him off my body.

"Fuck is your problem?"

I rub at the tenderness on my neck, glaring at him. "Sick of you vanishing, man. You come back like this"—I gesture to his black and blue face— "more often than not. You're big. You're strong. You're fast. You're letting whoever is hurting you get one up on you. I'm worried about you and running myself into the ground with the bar."

He looks rightfully ashamed, closing his eyes and scratching the back of his neck awkwardly. "Park, you don't need to worry about me. This" —he gestures to his face, shrugging— "is me blowing off steam. Nothing more."

He slides along the ground, moving his back against the closest wall. He stares at me for a few loaded seconds. "You're right. I need to pull more weight with the bar, but that's not what's got you so worked up." He shakes his head, bending his knees and crossing his arms over his chest.

I mirror his position against the front door, focusing on my bare feet.

"Park," he starts, and I close my eyes against the concern in the sound.

"I know," I bite out. "I know," I repeat, quieter.

He waits for a beat before speaking again, his voice carrying the same level of worry. "I told you to enjoy her, not fall for her."

"I'm not falling for her," I argue, but it's meek.

"Don't lie to me. Don't lie to yourself. It's cool if that's what's happened, but you're the one that will be hurt in the end."

I drag my hands roughly against my face, groaning loudly.

"Rein it in."

I twist my neck to bring him into focus, and I hate the way my eyes sting. "She's different, man. I hate... I *hate* that she's a Rein. In another life—"

"This isn't another life, Parker. Her family stole ours. She might be sweet, but you don't have a happily ever after with her. Surely you fucking see that?"

I tip my neck up, feeling the thud of my head against the door through my entire body. It numbs my thoughts, if only briefly, so I do it again.

And again.

And again.

Rocco waits for me to stop, and when I do, I turn my head to look his way. "I don't know what I let myself believe."

"You think you'll sit at family dinners with them, knowing what her father did? Are you going to watch *him* walk her down the aisle knowing Mom's not there to see you get married because he took her from us? Are you going to let him hold your kids, knowing our mom will never get the chance?"

"I get it," I yell, irritated at myself. "I fucking get it, okay?" I close my eyes, slamming the back of my head against the door again.

Rocco gives me the silence I crave, the quiet I need to fight the quicksand of emotion I'm drowning in.

I don't know how long we sit there, the low punctuation of our breathing working to make me feel suffocated and claustrophobic in the vast expanse of our loft.

Finally, when I'm sure I can bring myself to meet Rocco's stare, I look at him, expecting disappointment and animosity to cloud his intense gaze. Instead, I see sadness, maybe regret, and possibly guilt.

"Hate pulling anything good away from you, Parker," he admits miserably. "I see she brings you something you've been missing, but..." he pauses, his head shaking in an unexpected show of emotion. "I can't give you this, little brother. It's not that I don't want to... I *can't*." He thumps a fist over his heart, his words cracking. "I promised her retribution. I've sat at her grave *countless* times and promised it to her repeatedly. I need it. This has gone too far. We need to end this. I need my peace, man," he says through a plea, the desperation in the statement slicing into my heart.

"We need to end this," he repeats, the soft rumble of his tone finishing on a heavy sigh, and I nod.

"Just give me a bit more time with her."

"A week."

Bile rushes up my throat, but I swallow its acidity down. I nod against every protesting muscle in my body. He watches the jerky movement for only a moment before standing.

"Roc," I call before he walks away. I realize how broken and pathetic I look right now; ass planted on the floor, body slumped in defeat, eyes red-rimmed, the cracked dejection in my voice only magnifying my desperation.

He looks back at me, a complete contradiction to my broken self; even battered, bruised, and caught in the nightmares of his mind, he looks collected.

"I can't—" I start, but the words are inaudible, breaking off in my throat before they can fully form.

He walks over, reaching over a hand, and I take it, standing with his assistance. Pulling me into his body, he hugs me fiercely as a tortured sob escapes my lips without permission.

"Never expected you to, dollface—too much of Mom inside you. You've done your part. The rest is up to me. It's on my conscience, Parker." He pushes me back, searching my eyes. "Not yours. This'll be my guilt. Promise me that."

I frown at the stupidity of his statement. He doesn't care for her or love her the way I do. To him, she's no one. This guilt will be all mine. It'll drown me. It will suffocate me until I take my final breath, which'll be more than I deserve. But this is the only thing he's ever asked of me. It's not on him that my weak heart got involved.

"Parker," he pushes, and I nod my lie, agreeing with him to appease the monster stirring within him.

He keeps my eyes, searching for my deceit but believes the storm in my eyes is agreeance and not the hate I feel drowned by. At myself. At him. At Kane. At Dominic.

Stepping back, he cups my jaw, a sinister smile turning his lips. "We've got this, dollface. We'll finally let Mom rest easy. We'll bring her what Dad couldn't."

I watch his retreat with a heaviness in my heart, sickened by the blink of time I have left to love Codi the way she deserves.

One week.

Seven days.

One hundred and sixty-eight hours.

Ten thousand and eighty minutes.

Six hundred, four thousand, eight hundred seconds.

That's it. Then I'll be made to live the entirety of my life without her.

Forty years. Give or take.

Four hundred and eighty months.

Two thousand and eighty weeks.

Fourteen thousand, six hundred days.

All. Without. Her.

I fall against the door, dropping down as my legs give way, and I cry for the first time in eighteen years.

SEVENTEEN
CODI

"I like that you wanted to see me so bad today." I drag a finger along Parker's naked chest, feeling along the line of his pectoral muscle, moving down along the defined ridges of his abdomen and back up.

He grunts out his agreement. His eyes are closed, one arm acting as my pillow, wrapped around my back, hand resting on my bare ass, the other thrown over his head, *Lila's* name once again taunting me with my want to know more.

Parker had texted me around lunch, telling me he needed to see me. I'd bailed from work early, worried something had happened. It turns out he missed me. He turned up at my house in a flurry of hands and lips as soon as I opened the door. We didn't even speak before he'd pinned me against the wall and taken ownership of my body.

It was beyond amazing. He needed to touch me so desperately that he couldn't wait a single second.

Lucky for Camryn, she isn't home. That could've been

awkward. For her, at least. Truthfully, I wouldn't have noticed her presence, not with the wicked things Parker did to my body.

We spent the rest of the afternoon similarly. I think we've now christened most areas of my apartment.

He went down on me in the shower.

I repaid the favor in the living room.

He took me from behind in the kitchen. He's different. His need to touch me has magnified over our few days apart. Not that I'm complaining. I like this Parker.

Now we're in my bed, bodies sweaty and spent. We took our time exploring one another before he let me ride him. Slowly. It was unlike anything I'd ever felt before. I felt him *everywhere*. His hands, his mouth, his cock. His hands worshipped my body as I ground against him, my hips undulating and dragging along his length unhurriedly. I got to see his face as he came, and my God, the look of pure, unrivaled pleasure as he groaned out his release is probably my new favorite memory.

I look at his face, eyes still closed, a small satisfied smirk dusted across his lips, and I can't believe the whirlwind he's brought into my life. We've only known each other for a few short months, but I crave him in a way I never thought possible. He consumes my thoughts and makes my body ache with my need for him to touch me. He makes my heart happy. It beats faster when I see him. It pauses in my chest when he smiles at me. He's stealing it, one large piece at a time, and all I can focus on is when he's going to let me take his.

I glance at the ink on his arm, and before I can give it another thought, my hand reaches out, tracing the script of his mother's name with my finger. His body locks solidly under my touch, but he doesn't push me away. He doesn't reject my touch, so I continue.

I don't speak as I finish the soft brush of my finger, trailing off at the end of the rose. Parker swallows audibly, and I consider maybe I pushed him too far. He's warned me, more than once, not to push him further than he needs to go. I open my mouth to apologize, but he beats me to it, his voice soft and rough in the quiet of my bedroom.

"She died when I was a kid. I was fourteen. She was beautiful and sweet, and everything good in my life."

I rest my chin on his chest, and he meets my eyes with a sad smile.

"We went from a happy family of four to being two lost little boys with Satan himself as a father. Her death changed him. It changed all of us." He shrugs, shifting upward. I move to give him room, waiting as he props himself against my headboard before I shift in beside him, wrapping the sheet around my naked body.

"Not only had we lost our mom, but we were inserted directly into hell. The day we buried her..." He closes his eyes softly, rejecting the memory forcing its way forward. "Was the day my dad died too. What we knew of him anyway. In his place was the devil reincarnate."

"Parker," I breathe, pulling his hand into mine. He takes it easily enough, threading our fingers together, looking at the contrast of our skin.

"How'd she die?"

His hand drops from mine immediately, his thumb and forefinger pressing against his tightly shut eyes. Opening them again, a glint of moisture covers them, and my heart cracks.

"She was murdered. Someone shot her." My hand flies to my mouth, and I can't hold in the tortured sob that escapes my throat. He speaks of her brutal death with complete detachment, and my heart twists with pain.

"They blew her face off. Whoever did it, they shot her in the face." He looks at me, his eyes drilling into my skull, searching for something I'm not certain he's sure of.

I feel sick. My stomach churns with hurt for a fourteen-year-old Parker being subjected to such violence. His mom wasn't just taken from him. She was *stolen*. Her life was taken without considering that she had a family, a husband, and sons that needed her. What kind of monster would do such a thing?

"Did they find them? Who did it?"

His lips curl in disgust, bottom lip pushing out on a quick shake of his head. "We know who did it, but the cops couldn't prove it."

"Oh! Parker." I throw myself at his body, wrapping my arms around his neck and burying my face into his skin. "I'm so mad for you. That's heartbreaking."

He doesn't touch me, his hands staying purposefully at his sides as he breathes through the anger firing through his body.

"We'll get revenge. We'll make them pay," he speaks quietly, the words a loaded threat I don't doubt he'll carry through.

Pulling back, I meet his eyes. "Good. They deserve pain and misery."

His brow furrows in surprise before they turn sad. "They'll feel that in spades, Sugar. Everyone will." His hand reaches out, gliding against my cheek.

"*Hey.*" I reach up, my hand grabbing onto his and squeezing. "Don't feel sad for them."

He closes his eyes with a sullen laugh. "Baby, I don't feel anything for them. I feel sad for *myself*. I'm all but signing my one-way ticket to hopelessness."

I shake my head, disagreeing with him before he's finished speaking. "No. You'll finally have justice for your mom. Only let the peace of that in here." I place a hand over his heart, leaning down to kiss the same spot.

"Could you do it?" he asks, the soft, tortured whisper floating across the space in agonized curiosity.

My brow furrows at the hollowness deepening his eyes. "Do what?"

His tormented gaze skates over my face on a continual loop, working on reading whatever his heart seems to desire. No. What he *needs*. There's a desperation in the panic that swirls in the gray depths holding my attention hostage.

"Take revenge." He finally speaks, his voice scarcely audible. But as quietly as they were spoken, unease spreads up my spine with the threat dripping along the words.

"If someone took Ryn from you. Permanently. If they put a bullet to her skull and took her life. If they left you lost and broken."

My heart squeezes in my chest, the pain leaking into his words forcing me to consider, for a moment, if that were true. I imagine the monster he sees as part of him would most definitely live within me. How could it not? How could the darkest part of you as a person not fight its way to the forefront of who you are? Every dark, damaged, and broken thought would fuel anger, hate, and despair until you no longer recognize the positive parts of who you once were.

I clear my throat against the sudden onset of emotion. "I wouldn't need to. My dad—"

"Take him out of the equation, Codi. It's just you and Ryn."

Silence weighs heavily between us. A kiss of space separates us, soaking us in a question of life and death.

I know what he wants. He wants me to say yes. No, *declare* it. Vehemently. He wants me to admit convincingly that I would seek a bloody and vengeful end to those who would harm my family.

Like him.

I should say yes. Of course. How could anyone question my commitment and my love for my sister? That's what he wants. But could I do it? Play God in that way. Could I take the life of another? Even in the name of revenge?

"I would want to," I admit. "But no, I don't think I would." Shame spreads over my skin as I whisper those last words.

His eyes close. Guilt washes over him so significantly that I can taste it.

"Not because I think it's wrong," I continue, waiting for his eyes to hit me again. When they do, they're skeptical, swimming in the unshed tears readying themselves to drop. "I'd be too weak," I confess. "I'd fold. I'd crawl into a ball of grief and misery, and that's where I'd live my days."

I lean forward, kissing away the tears that have managed to escape, the ones dripping along his unshaven jawline in a slow and steady rush.

"I would hope if that happened, if someone stole one of the most important people in my life, I'd find the strength to inflict pain on them in a way they'd never forget." My head drops, my eyes locked on my hands held nervously in my lap.

A knuckle finds my chin, lifting it to return my eyes to his.

"But my backbone isn't that strong. I'm weak. I'm emotional. I'd fail Ryn because I'd be too damaged and afraid to give her the vengeance she deserves."

His breath has paused in his body. His large body is *entirely* still. It's eerie, the intensity of his feelings shocking him into stone. Yet, I can't decipher where the force of his emotions is aimed.

Finally, after what feels like forever, his body exhales heavily, sagging in relief.

"Because you're good in here." An inked hand presses firmly

against my heart. "Your heart is what's right in this world, Sugar."

I shake my head in disagreement. "No. Love like you have for your mother, even in death, that's what's special. You're fearless, Parker. You're strong and determined, and you'll do what's right. For your mom." The genuine belief in my tone heightens my voice, haunting the space.

"I wish I could keep you forever, Codi."

I sit back again, my eyebrows narrowing in confusion. "Why do you do that? Talk like our relationship has an expiration date?"

He looks uncomfortable with my question, his eyes darting downward, avoiding my scrutiny. "Don't all relationships?"

I think about his question, at the hesitation in the statement. "I like you, Parker—a *lot*. I'm in this relationship, hoping that it's more than long-term. This isn't a fling to me. If it is to you, we should probably end it now," I declare, hurt by his easy dismissal. "I'm not interested in letting my heart become invested if you have no intention of letting yours do the same."

He laughs then, his head tipping back, letting the sound escape into the room. It's sarcastic and unhappily amused. "My heart's invested, Sugar. Trust me. More than it should be."

I frown at why that makes him seem so down. "Good," I state, my hands finding his cheeks and pulling his stare down to mine. "Let's not act like we're doomed before we start."

"Doomed." He laughs sardonically. "Baby, my life was doomed the day someone killed my mom. I knew my life would never be the same. I couldn't imagine how fucking empty it would really be."

"Parker," I soothe, moving to touch my lips to his. "Don't say that. You have me."

He kisses me back, his tongue dancing softly against my lips before pulling back. "I wish you knew what you brought to my life."

"*Bring*, Parker. What I *bring*."

He pauses, his stormy eyes staring into mine. Finally, he nods, and I relax, my breath filling my lungs.

"Do you believe in redemption?"

I pause on his question, considering my answer. "I guess it depends on what you're looking for. Atonement?" I question, but he remains silent. "Who can actually give you that?" I shrug. "Are you looking for forgiveness in yourself? Or from a greater power? God?"

His stoic silence echoes between us.

"I think the belief of one's redemption is up to interpretation. You could do something to hurt someone and have zero guilt. Do you still need redemption? Or is it irrelevant because you're comfortable in your decision and actions?"

"Make sense," he coughs out. "What about if you feel the guilt? If you know you've done wrong."

I stop to consider my words once again. "I guess it depends on what you're looking for. Do you really want atonement? Or do you want to relieve your guilt? There's a massive difference, Parker. Awful people do awful things all the time and never offer consideration to those they hurt. Look at the monster that killed your mom. Does he want redemption? Does he deserve it even though he may not care for it? I think it comes down to forgiveness inside of yourself," I continue. "You can do wrong by someone and apologize a million times over. You can make amends until the day you die, but if that person doesn't *want* to forgive you, does that mean you don't deserve it? Maybe you only ever really come to the point of atonement when you can forgive yourself for your actions."

He watches me intently, bottom lip trapped between his teeth as he gnaws at it. "What about from a greater power?"

"God?" I ask, and he nods. I shrug. "If you believe in God."

"You don't?"

"I've never thought hard on the subject. I find it difficult to place my faith in something I can't see or *know*. I prefer to place it in myself. In the people I love. If I can't find faith in myself, why should I trust something I can't be certain is real? You're responsible for who you are and the actions you take. We should own that. We should strive to be the people we want to be. If you love *yourself*, respect yourself, and trust yourself, the faith in who you are as a person is all you need.",

"What if you lose faith in yourself, though?"

I clear my throat, letting my mind wander. "Then you place your faith in the people that love you, that care for you, to *love* you through your darkest hours."

I let his eyes scan urgently over my face. His hands move to follow his eyes, his callused palms dragging across my skin affectionately. His lips move to do the same, and his breaths come harder as he rushes to see, touch and taste me everywhere. He loves me with his eyes, adores me with his hands, and worships me with his lips. He handles me in a way that shows me he loves me. He hasn't said it, but are words the way you hear someone's love? I always imagined I'd feel it more than any words would convince me, and at this moment, this definite, frantic sliver of time, I *more* than feel it. I feel overwhelmed by it, and I couldn't be happier.

THE NEXT MORNING I walk Parker to the door, my hand in his. I'm disappointed that I have to work today. I'd much rather

spend today as I did yesterday. In bed. Wrapped on and around Parker. My body still tingles with his touch, my nerves buzzing with overused but unfulfilled need.

I've become insatiable. Needing, *craving* his touch.

He smiles down at me as we reach the door, looking at me in a way that makes me wonder if he can read my thoughts.

A blush casts along my cheeks, and his grin comes on wider. "Love when you think of me in that way. You can't hide it. Your body wants me to know," he shares, his inked hand coming to drag along my cheekbone.

"Morning," Camryn grumbles, walking past us without a glance, focusing on the kitchen.

"Ryn," Parker greets, and I smile at his use of her nickname. He has slid into my and Camryn's lives without issue, at complete ease, and I like that—a lot. I wish I felt as comfortable in his space as he is in mine, but considering he lives with Satan's sidekick, I've come to terms with Rocco taking time to adjust to my *sugary* self.

Parker leans down to kiss me, pulling me up and into his body as he does so. Once upon a time, I would've been embarrassed with Camryn standing in the same room while my boyfriend kissed me the way Parker does; openly, intimately, hungrily. But I can't find it in myself to even give her a second thought when he touches me. He's all I see, all I feel.

He pulls back with a gratified smile, pleased that he's worked me up to the point of desperate need. "Random fact, I can't whistle."

"Really?" I laugh. "How odd. I can't wink," I admit sheepishly.

"That's a lie."

I shake my head, pausing to meet his eyes before I attempt

the fruitless endeavor. Both eyes close as I work to close only one, and he laughs loudly.

"Don't try and do that. Ever again."

I hit his arm, but he grabs it, pulling me close once again to inhale the scent of my hair and dropping a kiss on my forehead.

"I'll hear from you."

I nod, gnawing my bottom lip between my teeth as he disappears through the door.

"Do you think you can fall in love too fast?" I turn toward the kitchen.

Camryn pauses, lifting a cookie to her mouth and turning on her stool to face me as I wander over. "Who has the right to tell somebody else if it's too fast?" She shrugs, an irritated look of judgment crossing her features. It's not directed at me. More the thought itself causing distaste in her mind. She places her cookie on the counter, her arms crossing over her chest as she gives me her undivided attention. "I think you need to identify the difference between lust and love correctly," she continues, the contemplative tone in her voice stirring my thoughts as I sit beside her.

"How do you know the difference?" I test, but she smiles with a shake of her head.

"I think it's something relatively personal, Codi. For me," she places her hand on her chest, eyebrows raising in emphasis. "I can hate someone but lust after them. They can railroad my thoughts constantly because I want them to fuck me. The sex can be mind-blowing, but it loses its appeal quickly. That's lust, not love. Not to me."

"I can't imagine Parker's appeal will ever be lost to me."

She considers me for a moment before her head nods in understanding. "Love is different for everyone, I'd imagine. The basis and the basic human need for affection and care would be there for most. But love to me is a decision my heart makes. It makes me crazy with my need to be with someone and not just intimately. It makes me want to share my life, thoughts, and secrets." She swallows deeply. "I want them to creep into my thoughts at any opportunity, and I want to do the same for them. I want them to know when to love me and when to give me space. I want them to understand I'm a crazy, messed up bitch, but love me anyway. I want them to see that my demons aren't what defines me. I want to know that they can see through the darkness in my soul and realize I have something good to give." Her words pause for a breath, her eyes closing in thought before opening again. "Honestly, I want to be borderline obsessed because they should be the most important person in my life and vice versa. I want them to feel everything I feel, but *more*."

What she said was the most authentic and beautiful thing I've ever heard. She's right. At least, I think so. Love should be consuming. Overriding your heart, mind, and soul. "My heart hurts when I'm not with Parker, and it feels this overwhelming sense of relief when I see him again. I feel a little lost when we're apart," I admit, and she smiles.

"Babe. You've been in love with Parker for weeks now. It's shooting out of your purple eyes like glittery rainbows." She grabs her cookie from the bench, taking a large bite, her eyebrows dancing.

"It is not," I defend, embarrassed at the portrait she'd just painted.

She laughs, cookie flying out of my mouth, hitting my face. "Oh," she coughs, covering her mouth. "Sorry."

I wipe my face. "You're disgusting."

"And you're in love. Sickeningly so. Same, same." She shrugs.

I ignore her teasing, wondering if she's right. Have I been

shooting laser beams of love at Parker? And if so, is Parker freaked the hell out or happy about it?

"But I still feel like I barely know him at times. Does that mean I'm falling too fast and stupidly?"

Placing the half-eaten cookie back on the counter, Camryn turns back to me, grabbing my hands. "Fuck timeframes, Codi. If you love him, *love* him. He's allowed to be a little closed off, babe. People are entitled to their secrets. Let him open up to you in his own time."

EIGHTEEN

PARKER

"I've missed you," Mira offers softly as the server moves away.

I grab her hand across the table, squeezing it tight. "Me too. I'm sorry I haven't been around much. I—"

"Parker," she cuts me off, her free hand resting on our conjoined ones. "You don't have to explain that to me. I get it, sweetheart."

I nod, guilt wracking through my body. It's true. I hate that my need to avoid Marcus at any cost cuts off my time with Mira. Maybe that makes me weak. Maybe I should suck it up, but I can't seem to be able to push past it. I hate him with every tiny morsel of my soul. I despise him. He knows it, too. It only makes it harder for Mira when I'm there. She defends me from every insult he throws my way. I know what that costs her. I have told her countless times to let sleeping dogs lie. I don't give a fuck what the guy says or thinks of me. His words mean nothing to me. Less than. But she insists on defending me, on calling him out when he throws his pathetic slurs, thinking I give a shit.

"Anyway." She distracts my dark thoughts, squeezing my hand once more before letting go. "Tell me what's new."

She watches me eagerly, one hundred percent invested in what fills my life. She looks like Mom in these carefree moments, when her spirit is allowed to breathe, no longer suffocated by the devil. Her hair is a little darker than Mom's, but the shape of her face, the color of her eyes, and her complexion are identical to Mom. Rocco seeks Mira out for comfort, to bring mom closer to him. I avoid her for the very same reason. It spikes the most bitter parts of me. Seeing her hurts my heart as much as it calms hers. But I love her, so I let myself feel the pain. Rocco and I are all she has left of her sister.

"Not much, Aunt Mira. Working heaps, the bar is doing well. It's keeping me busy and out of trouble." I smirk, and she rolls her eyes.

"I find that hard to believe, Parker."

The server brings our food, and Mira thanks her with a broad smile and sincere words. Like Mom, she's just so *good*. Deep within her heart, within her soul, she's *good*. This life should've never been theirs. They should've stayed away from Kane Shay and Marcus Dempsey and lived a life not weighed down by loss and violence.

"Eat," she prompts, and I watch her momentarily.

"Mira," I call, and she looks up from her salad, her fork pausing mid-air. "I love you. You know that, right?"

She places her fork back in her bowl, leaning over to cup both hands around my face. "I know that, sweetheart. I love you too. You and your brother are all that matter in my life."

"Parker?"

Mira's hands fall away from my face as I turn to the sound of Codi's voice. She's standing by the table, a small look of uncertainty playing off her beautiful face.

"Sugar," I stand, leaning down to place my lips against hers.

She looks at Mira hesitantly, and I gesture for her to sit. "Codi, baby, this is Mira. Mira, Codi," I introduce them. Mira glances at me expectantly, shaking her head when I give her nothing more.

"Nice to meet you, Codi. Mira Dempsey," she offers her hand across the table. "Parker's Aunt."

Codi takes her hand readily, a large smile pulling at her pink-toned lips. "So lovely to meet you. Codi Rein, Parker's girlfriend."

I watch Mira's reaction closely; the heavy swallow in her throat, the widening of her silver eyes. "Codi Rein," she tests, making sure she heard correctly.

Codi nods, the gesture unsure and anxious as she glances at me for reassurance.

"Lunch break?" I change the subject, ignoring Mira's probing glare.

"Yeah," Codi affirms, looking across the table awkwardly, then back to me. "I won't keep you from your lunch. I just ran in to grab a coffee and a piece of cake and saw you sitting here."

I drop my lips to hers again. More from necessity than anything else; my need, my want to taste her, especially now, almost too much.

She pulls back from our kiss almost shyly, her eyes seeking out Mira again. Coughing, she clears her throat. "I'm so sorry for interrupting your lunch."

"Not at all," Mira smiles genuinely. "You should join us."

"I'd love to, but this one made me pull a sick day yesterday, something I don't often do. The shop was a disaster when I came in this morning," she sighs. "Honestly, I have to get back." She stands. "It was lovely to meet you, Mira."

Mira stands as well, smiling wide. "We'll get Parker to organize a lunch with the three of us to give us a chance to get to know one another."

"I'd like that." Codi grins, the warm affection in her tone stabbing me in the heart as much as the emptiness that will be Mira's promise.

I hold a finger up to Mira, telling her to give me a second, and she nods, taking her seat and turning back to her salad as I follow Codi from the café.

She turns to exit, walking into my frame, and I don't hesitate in drawing her into my body. "You never told me you had an aunt. She's lovely."

"I didn't keep it from your purposefully," I lie. "I don't see her much nowadays. It just slipped my mind."

She watches me skeptically, and to stop her from asking any more questions, I close my mouth over hers, cutting off her train of thought with a deep, wet kiss. She returns it with enthusiasm, her tongue caressing mine in a way that leaves no doubt as to where her mind has traveled. I break the kiss, smiling at the protesting groan she lets out when I do.

"Tonight, baby."

She nods. "Tonight. You working?"

"No, I have the night off. I want you at the loft. I wanna fuck you in my bed tonight."

She bites her bottom lip. "Okay. I'll be over around seven."

I plant a chaste kiss on her tempting lips once more, stepping back before I get lost in her again. I watch her walk away, her head turning back every few feet, smiling and waving each time she sees I'm still there. Fuck, she's a dork. An adorable, addictive dork. Hitting the corner before she turns out of sight, she blows me a kiss, and the grin I no longer need to force around her works its way onto my face.

Mira watches my approach, her silver eyes cutting into my

brain cavity. I sit down without meeting her eyes. Picking up my fork, I shovel food into my mouth to stop my ability to converse.

"I'll wait until you're done, or you can stop forcing excess amounts of food into your mouth to avoid talking about whatever the fuck you and your brother are playing at."

I drop my fork loudly, the sound echoing through the café. I swallow my mouthful, chasing it down with a large sip of water. Finally, wiping my mouth, I meet her intense stare.

She doesn't speak. She doesn't need to; her questions are clear enough.

"None of this concerns you, Mira. It's something Roc and I need to do."

She looks affronted, hurt contorting her features, making her look years younger. "Doesn't concern me? It's *my* sister you're working your revenge plan for."

"*Our* mother. Don't forget that part. *Our* mother. They took her from us, Mira," I spit across the table. "They left us with that monster who used to be our dad. He was no better than Marcus in the end," I accuse.

She blinks down her guilt, once again taking responsibility for the agony our father put us through. But that's not on her. That's on Dominic Rein: him and only him.

"Parker, they never proved Dominic Rein had anything to do with Lila dying. Cops worked their damnedest to pin it on him. They couldn't. Sweetheart, no evidence even suggested him."

I shake my head at her disbelief. "Don't you think the fact that my father seemed to be getting tipped off with details of Dominic's business wasn't motive enough? Or that that intel started giving my father more power. He started claiming more turf, bigger deals. You don't think that is reason enough for Dominic Rein to act out?"

She leans across the table, reaching for my hands, which I

give to her reluctantly. "I'm not saying there isn't a possibility it was Dominic. I'm saying there was no actual *proof*. Be smart before someone gets hurt."

I look down at the table, unable to meet her eyes. "It's done. It's already in motion."

"Parker," she stresses. "Parker, look at me."

I follow her instruction, the strict, demanding tone of her voice leaving no argument. "You love her."

My eyes cut to the side, an overwhelming sense of emotion racking my body, causing water to leak from my eyes.

"You love her," she repeats, and I nod, my eyes glued to the stained yellow wall of the café.

"You go ahead with this. Whatever you guys are planning, it can't be undone. You'll *lose* her."

I swallow deeply, sniffing loudly as I tip my head back. "You think I don't know that?"

She blinks sadly, and I lean across the table, bringing our faces closer together. "You think I don't fucking know that," I repeat angrily.

"Then stop it," she implores, but I refute her plea with a quick shake of my head.

"Your mom and I always vowed we'd keep you and Rocco out of whatever your father and Marcus involved themselves in. She always made me promise that if something happened to her, I'd keep that promise. That I wouldn't let you both fall into the abyss of their darkness."

She sighs in regret, in self-reproach, and I remain silent as she massages her temples. "It cost me a lot," she accuses softly. "My disobedience, my refusal to let you two be swallowed up in their world."

Guilt is an awful feeling, the way it engulfs you, overtaking your mind and physically affecting your body. I've felt shaky about it for weeks now. I've felt weakened by its overpowering strength and felt it threaten to spill over and consume me completely. I don't know how it's stayed contained. But watching Mira, having aged within moments, her delicate features now lined with the worry and the hardship of her life, of *ours*. I know she's endured a lot. More than she deserved. Well and truly. I've let it crash down on top of her, letting it be known that *everything* she has done to protect us has been for nothing. A waste. It was an insignificant collection of years that she would eventually be swallowed up by, no matter how she fought it.

How depressing the realization that the circle of hate my father created has continued without him. Worse, it's expanded. Sickeningly, he'd be proud. He'd be pleased at the rage rooted inside Rocco and me. We were drawn to his evil even before we realized it, though we might never admit it. A moth to a flame. We are nothing but brainwashed little soldiers salivating at the opportunity to wreak havoc, to cause chaos. All for selfish reasoning. We're no better than our father or Dominic. Hurting others, even those we love, to find our place in the world.

We're monsters, Rocco and me. Cold and heartless and definitely people our mother would be ashamed of. The thought agonizes me. *Ashamed. Disappointed.* Would she smile at us as she once did, knowing what we became? Or would she look at us like Mira is now, lost, defeated, embarrassed that we share the same blood?

Maybe it was always meant to be this way. In tragedy, our father's hate will die with us. Rocco and I aren't stupid enough to procreate, so the cycle will finally end. And as much as I hate to admit it, Dominic did right by raising his girls. There's no hate seeping through their veins. They're what's right in this world.

The good.

The kind.

The honest.

The decent.

Their father's evil hasn't spilled inside of them, not like Kane Shay's did to us.

"We're just trying to find our peace."

Her head lifts slowly, sad eyes penetrating mine. "What are you planning?"

I hate the sadness in her tone. The disappointment. It eats away at me, acidic erosion crumbling my cracked conscience. But she holds my stare, demanding an answer.

I sigh. Loudly. "Don't concern yourself with that."

She laughs. Sourly. "Don't be concerned that you and your brother are harboring plans to avenge your mother. Is that a joke, Parker? Do you expect me to sit by and watch the two of you destroy your lives and potentially the life of an innocent girl who looks at you with love in her eyes?"

"I'm not asking you, Mira. I'm *telling* you. I have enough weighing on my conscience. Your added guilt isn't needed."

"Then *stop* whatever you're planning. Clear your conscience," she pleads, her hands grabbing onto mine and squeezing tight.

"Not an option."

"There is *always* an option. Always. I get that you feel cornered, that you think you owe it to your mom. Trust me, Parker. *Trust me.* I knew her better than anyone else. I know that whatever you and Rocco have created in your mind as a necessity would only break her heart."

She would have been better to stab my heart with a perforated blade, rip into my lifeline and steal my life from my body. It would've been less painful. Her words are true. I was happy enough to keep my ignorance within the chaos of my mind. But having Mira vocalize the deepest depths of my self-loathing destroys me. No matter which way I turn, I hurt the ones I love. She's wrong. I don't *feel* cornered. I am. I'm surrounded at every angle by my warring emotions. I'm caught in a trap with no possibility of escaping. I'm imprisoned by my loyalty and torn open by my heart.

I can't win. But I guess I always knew that. I just never knew how brutal the fallout would be or how affected by the collateral damage I would become.

NINETEEN

CODI

I knock.

I wait. *Again.*

I check my watch.

Seven-thirty.

I move my ear against the solidness of his front door, listening for something, anything. But *nothing.*

I rummage through my bag, searching for my cell. No missed calls. No texts. Nothing, except me, waiting in the darkened hall of Parker's building.

I recall our conversation in my head. He told me tonight. I told him seven. He agreed with a quick, hard kiss on my lips before I walked away.

I call his cell. *Again.* But unsurprisingly, nothing. Voicemail. Not even a single ring.

I huff my annoyance, turning on my foot and moving away from his door in quick, hurried footsteps. I'm irritated. I'm hurt. I'm confused.

Is it so much to ask for a simple phone call? A single text

telling me something had come up? That he had to cancel instead of leaving me to stand at his unanswered door like a fool.

I don't even let myself worry that something has happened to him. That something is wrong. The time I've spent with Parker has taught me that he forces distance when things get too much. His mood has a direct link to our connection. If he gives too much or reveals something about himself that he didn't want to, and he turns ultimate prick.

His aunt. It has to do with me meeting her. His lie about her slipping his mind was so ridiculous I almost laughed. He's made a point of making it known that, with the exception of Rocco, he has *no* family. I could pretend she was a pseudo-aunt with no relation or a long-time family friend, but their eyes gave that away. Eerily similar in color. Genetically, they're related. I have no doubt. So, he lied with his nonchalance, and now he's bailed on our plans without the courtesy of informing me.

I throw my bag into my car and drop into my seat, slamming my door in frustration. I hate this. The games. The unknown. I despise feeling insecure or unsure. More than that, I loathe that a *man* has the power to make me feel that way.

I drive home, cursing Parker. I'm ready to tell him I love him, and he pulls crap like this. He's cut me. He's made me second-guess myself because I could've sworn he felt the same way. But if you cared for someone, truly, in the way I do him, could you disregard someone's feelings so easily?

Camryn glances up from the couch as I walk into our apartment.

"Thought you were seeing Parker tonight?" She pauses her movie, turning back to me.

I shrug, dropping my bag without care and shuffling to the couch to fall beside her. "He stood me up. I knocked at his door for twenty minutes without an answer, and his cell was turned off."

Her eyebrows pull together, the dark hairs almost touching in her confusion. "Is he okay?"

I hug a cushion, rolling onto my back and placing my feet in her lap. "He's fine. He's in freak-out mode, I'm sure of it."

Throwing the remote on our coffee table, she angles her body with her arm draped across the back of our couch. "Care to elaborate?"

I shove the cushion onto my face, groaning into the soft material. I stuff it behind my head, my hands moving into my hair, pulling at the strands in frustration.

"I was going to tell him I loved him tonight," I confess. "And I was pretty confident he feels it back. But I ran into him today. He was having lunch with his *aunt*."

"Okay," she drags out, her head shaking in her unspoken *and...*

"First, he told me he had no family. He told me that numerous times."

She shrugs, caught in her indecision as to whether she'd dwell on something so trivial.

"Second," I continue. "She was incredibly friendly until I told her my name. She couldn't hide her shock. It's like she somehow knew me. It was weird, and Parker changed the subject immediately."

"Babe, our dad is *our dad*. People know him. Maybe she recognizes the name Rein."

"Mm," I grunt out. "Anyway, we made plans, and then he was a no-show. Too coincidental. He shuts down whenever I get remotely close to knowing more about him. Or turns into an ultimate jerk. I deserve more than being cast aside without a word."

She nods her agreement, squeezing my ankle. "True. You should knee him in the junk again."

I laugh, pulling the cushion from behind my head to throw it at her face.

"Okay, okay." She holds up her hands in surrender. "A head-butt to the nose will suffice," she laughs, and I groan aloud.

"Codi, talk to him. Tell him it's not cool or a deal breaker for you. Make him understand. If you're not happy with something, let him know. You deserve the best from him, not this shit."

I nod, sighing heavily. "What are you watching?" I glance at the TV.

"Reruns of Sons."

"Mmm... Charlie. Nice."

Reaching forward, she grabs the remote, turning her episode back on, and I let my mind go numb, trying not to think about Parker and when he'll decide to reach out again.

"CODI." My leg shakes, and I groan, attempting to kick off whoever has hold of my leg.

"Codi," Ryn yells, shaking me harder, and I startle awake.

"What the hell, Camryn?" I rub my eyes, dragging my body up into a sitting position.

"You have a guest," she declares with wide eyes.

My eyes find Parker immediately, standing a step or two away from the couch, body swaying with the obvious effects of alcohol. I frown at him.

I've seen a whole range of different versions of Parker over the last few months, but not this guy.

His hands are stuffed in his pockets. His eyes are glassed

over and hooded in an effort to keep them open. A small smile plays on his lips when our eyes meet.

"Sugar," he stumbles, attempting to remove his hand from his pocket to wave hello, leaning against the arm of the couch to stabilize himself.

"You okay?" Camryn steps into my view, and I nod, standing and squeezing her arm in reassurance as I move past her.

"Yeah. I'll see you in the morning."

Parker leans in to kiss me when I'm close enough, but I pull back, glowering at him. He staggers sideways, and I shake my head in irritation.

"Go to my room, shower, and start sobering up. I'll bring you coffee."

His head pushes back on his shoulders, eyebrows raised in shock. It's a little hard to tell in his inebriated state.

"Prefer you join me in the shower," he slurs out.

"Pfft, good luck with that."

Rolling his eyes, he saunters off, a slight stumble in his walk, and I pause to watch him, caught between a strong feeling of irritation and concern.

It can't be coincidental that he stood me up to write himself off the day I met his aunt. He's panicking. I don't know why. But whatever the reason, I'm not down with it. I won't be treated so poorly. I won't be fed riddles without knowing how to solve them. I made that clear from the beginning.

I place his coffee mug gently on the bedside table, walking back to my bedroom door to close it quietly. Back pressed against the wood, my head turns toward the bathroom, listening to the strong sound of the shower echoing into my room.

I could go in there and check on him. But he'll be naked. He'll be wet. And he'll most likely attempt to touch me. And he'll be wet. And he'll be naked. And I most likely won't be able to say no.

Pushing from the door, I move around my room, tidying, working to occupy my hands as I wait.

And wait.

And wait.

When the shower finally shuts off, I can see every available space on my carpet, not one item discarded along the ground. I've found a total of eight things I was positive were lost. I've changed my sheets. Re-fluffed my pillows at least four times and remade Parker's coffee because the first cup went cold.

He shuffles from the bathroom, wrapping a towel around his defined waist. He's wet and practically naked, and I congratulate myself for not following him into the shower initially because, *goodness.* His tanned skin taunts me, the majority covered in colorful tattoos that ripple and stretch as he moves through my room. Wet droplets run down his broad chest, dropping along the divots of his abdominal muscles before being absorbed into the charcoal towel I may never wash again.

"Clothes stink like booze and cigarettes," he coughs to clear his throat uncomfortably, and I nod vigorously.

"I'll, umm... throw them in the wash if you like."

He nods, stretching an arm up to hand them over. I move to take them from him, but he pulls at the same time I do, and I stumble into his body.

His wet and naked body.

I breathe heavily through my nose, closing my eyes against my want to lean forward, ever-so-slightly, to press my lips to his bare chest.

"You didn't say hello." His words are still slurred, if only somewhat, but his voice sounds deeper, rougher, being tainted by booze.

"Parker," I warn, pulling at the clothes gripped tightly in his hand.

"Sugar," he replies, the threat in his tone mirroring mine.

Sighing, I lift my head. "You'll get your hello when I've put these in the wash, and you have the decency to apologize for standing me up."

He doesn't attempt to keep me in place again, his hand freeing its grip on his clothes as I pull them again. I swallow deeply as I dart from my room, needing space from his mixed signals and the war between my temptation and my mind.

Feeling calmer from the forced distance between us, I load Parker's clothes in the machine, struggling to comprehend why people fall into relationships. It's exhausting.

The miscommunication.

The secrets.

The push and pull of power.

God. I want to love someone and be loved in return. Why does it have to be so complicated?

He's in bed when I walk back into my room, sheet tucked around his waist, inked chest on show, coffee mug held tightly in his hand. He glances up at me over the rim of his cup as I enter.

"Like what you've done with the place." He skates his eyes around my tidy room, a forced smirk on his lips. "You redecorate?"

"It was an organized mess. I knew where everything was." I arch an eyebrow defensively. "You should try it."

He shakes his head. "Nah. Like you said, I know where everything is."

I remain glued against my door, eyes stuck on the beautiful man tucked into my bed. He's the ultimate contradiction. His body, strong and muscular, dwarfs the size of my bed. His firm mouth is set hard, the muscle in his jawline ticking in time with the grind of his teeth. Everything about him screams risk—everything except his eyes.

His eyes are drowning in sadness. They're ashen with shame. They're swallowed by regret.

Finishing his coffee, his body stretches to place the mug on the bedside table, pulling his skin tightly along the rigid line of his side, showcasing the easy divots of his ribs. Righting himself, his eyes fall to his hands, massaging heavily at his knuckles, the unconscious movement an uncharacteristic show of uncertainty.

"I think you were gonna tell me you loved me tonight." His eyes don't lift from his hands, and while there is confidence in his simple statement, grief is paired with his words. I move closer to the bed, stopping when my knees hit the end. His head lifts, the glassy effects of booze having left his eyes, only to be replaced with anguish, with misery.

"I wanted to tell it to you back, Codi. Fuck did I want to." His voice cracks, and he clears his throat in embarrassment, his neck tipping back, eyes trained on the ceiling.

I wait quietly, patiently. I don't even attempt to decipher his mood. I am not attempting to predict where this conversation is going.

Finally, after a fully loaded minute of silence, he drops his head, eyes clashing with mine, and I can't stop myself from speaking from working to reassure him. Crawling onto the bed and over his body, I straddle his waist, my hands resting on his cheeks, my eyes searching his. "Parker, it's okay not to feel it back. I'm okay with you taking more time to sort through your feelings."

He nuzzles into my palm, eyes shutting in his need to feel me *more*. "Sometimes I feel time isn't our friend, baby. I... *shit*, it's not that I don't feel it back. I just... *fuck*." His hands find my waist, pulling me into him more solidly, his nose dragging across my collarbone, inhaling my scent. "*Baby,*" he groans desperately, his hands flexing on my hips almost painfully.

"You're not ready," I state.

His breath stutters at my words, his head shaking against the cotton of my shirt, body wracking with silent cries.

"*Parker.*" I push him back, bending to catch his eyes, but he shuns me, dropping his face to avoid me. I lift his chin, my brow knotted with concern. "Parker," I repeat, and the harsh shadow of his eyes meets mine as tears leak down his cheeks.

"I'm not ready. Nowhere near fucking close, baby."

He's talking about something entirely different. He communicates that well enough through the storm in his eyes, through the cryptic words he uses, but before I can question him further, before I can push him to elaborate, he kisses me.

It's fierce.

It's desperate.

It's every emotion he can't let himself vocalize tied up in the fraught need of his lips. I taste his tears on my lips; their sweet saltiness is quickly lost, swallowed by the wet caress of our tongues.

His hands grab my work blouse, ripping it open, the buttons flying in every direction as he tears it from my body. His hand flicks expertly at the clasp on my bra, his lips never leaving mine as he divests me of the white-laced material.

He flips me onto my back in a quick, effortless move, our kiss breaking as he yanks at the material of my skirt. I arch uncomfortably, pulling at the back zipper, and within seconds, I'm naked, my panties ripped from my body in a similar fashion to my shirt.

Only then does he pause—when I'm completely naked, sprawled openly on my bed, my chest heaving with labored breathing.

"Fuck, you're beautiful, Codi. So. Fucking. Beautiful. I made you happy, right? Even for this short time. I've made you happy?"

My hands reach for him, and he comes without hesitation, bracing his body above mine, his eyes moving frantically to read mine.

"*Baby,*" I soothe, but he shakes his head.

"Tell me, Codi. *Please.* Tell me I made you happy. That I've made you feel loved."

I nod my head as frantically as his eyes search mine. "Yes," I agree. "You make me happy."

"Will you tell me, even though you know I won't, *can't,* say it back?"

I close my eyes softly, my hands moving up the hard plane of his chest, resting over his heart. My eyelids open, and his moonlit gaze bores into mine, and while I have zero clue of what is happening right now, I want nothing more than to see some of the insecurity fade from his eyes.

"I love you, Parker."

His eyes close in a relieved mixture of pain and fulfillment, and my heart eases from the constricting knot in my chest. Because in that broken moment, his happiness outweighs the demons in his mind. For that split second, I let myself believe I could be enough to take away the monster in his heart.

Leaning down, his mouth opens over mine, and this time his kiss is a soft, loving *feeling.* He explores my lips, my tongue in a whispered caress of his own, and I moan intimately at how good it feels.

Stretching my thighs open, he lines up at my entrance, sliding in without preamble.

I gasp.

He groans.

And our kiss breaks.

"Open your eyes," he demands in a whisper, and I comply, letting our eyes anchor as he moves slowly in and out of my body.

Parker's fucked me slow, and he's fucked me hard. He's played my body expertly every time we've touched. But he's never made love to me. Not in the way he's doing now. Something's changed. Everything about the way he's touching me feels different. It feels more intimate. More meaningful. Just *more*.

Our lips sit a breath apart the entire time, our quick inhales and exhales of air tickling my lips with the dare to connect them. That would mean losing his eyes, and there's no chance of that happening. His tongue darts out occasionally, just to tease my bottom lip, and my breath catches.

I clench around him, my body preparing itself to explode around him. My legs wrap firmly around his waist, and I pull him onto me more forcefully.

"Tell me. When you come. *Tell me,*" he growls, and I do exactly as he asks. I tell him I love him with a heady moan, working to keep his eyes through the whole thing, letting him see the sincerity of the moment, the truth in my words.

He comes a moment later, his vocal cords giving me nothing but a rough groan as he empties inside me. I see it, though. In his eyes. I see the love staring down at me, and I let that fire my hope that whatever's plaguing his mind, I can destroy it.

TWENTY

CODI

We lie as close as any two people could in a single moment. Our naked limbs intertwine, the hard line of his stomach and the soft of mine pressed together in a kiss of skin. My breasts are pushed heavily against his chest, his heart beating fast and capably in his body, so loud I can feel it thumping against my skin, causing mine to do the same. His right arm pillows my head, his head twisted into my hair, tipping my neck back securely, giving him full access to my face. My left arm offers him the same cushioning for his head, my nails dragging up and down the naked skin of his back; over and over again. Up and down. Continuously. Our free hands lay entwined between us, his thumb running endless circles along my wrist.

We're quiet, save our breathing, content in watching one another in the muted light of my bedroom.

The monsters in his mind are plaguing him, dancing in the forefront of his mind so eagerly I can see their torture. It shines from the gray pools, hurting my heart.

I wish he'd talk to me. Confide in me and tell me what's drowning him so heavily in hate.

He warned me *he* was a monster. That he was dark. From the very beginning. Still, even now, I don't see it. Not the way he does, anyway. I see dark and twisted thoughts circling his mind. I see the need he feels to be consumed by them. But what I cling to, what's most important, is that I see his want to drown them, to suffocate them from the oxygen they use to breathe until they're no more. He wants to divest himself of their presence within him.

He's punishing himself for something. Suffering through demons, he doesn't understand. He's conflicted, and I don't know how to help him. I feel powerless.

"Random fact," he croaks out, pausing to clear his throat. "I didn't cry at my mom's funeral. I wasn't allowed. My father warned us not to embarrass him with *theatrics.*"

My heart cracks at the fourteen-year-old boy I can see in his eyes. Stripped away is his power, his secrets, his dominance. Pushed aside is the thirty-two-year-old *presence* of a formidable man. In his place is the lost, scared little boy, wrapped around me, his big gray eyes dropping tears that run onto my arm.

"How fucked up is that?"

Lifting our joined hands, he runs them along his socket, angrily removing his tears as he drags a rough breath through his nose. The question is rhetorical. He's not searching for reassurance. It's said as a statement, a cold declaration of fact.

Falling into silence again, his eyes stay pinned to mine, content in seeing me cry, in letting me see him broken.

"Tell me yours." His delivery is harsh, brusque, and demanding, but I hear, I *feel* the desperation in the request.

I swallow down my sadness and helplessness. "My mom is a horrible human being. It's like she was born without the ability to love. She's a drunk. A mean one too. I can't recall the last time I saw her sober."

I sigh in defeat as I talk about my mom, about the nastiness she showers upon everyone.

"She hates us all," I continue, shifting closer, pushing our bodies more forcefully together, finding reassurance in his solid frame. "She makes certain we're all aware of it. Especially Camryn. She treats her the worst. I don't understand how a parent can treat their children so poorly, so hatefully."

"She's the stupidest fucking bitch ever to exist. She doesn't see you for the beauty your heart holds. If she doesn't cherish that, she doesn't deserve the breath in her body."

I laugh lightly, bringing our hands up to kiss his knuckles. "I was always afraid that the evil that seemed so deeply rooted within her soul was hereditary. Was I destined to be so nasty, empty, and unfeeling?"

"Not possible," his jaw tightens, his expression hardening again. "You're so good inside, baby. So good," he repeats softly, lowering his gaze.

"My dad," I start, and any anger that had softened only moments ago spikes, and his hand, still wrapped around mine, clenches involuntarily. My brows pull together, uncertain at his unprovoked show of aggression. "My dad," I repeat cautiously, my eyes narrowed on his reaction. He schools his expression, his face now uncomfortably blank. "He's why I'm good. The hate in her doesn't exist in him. He showed me love. He's kind and generous. My dad has good in his heart. He gave that to me," I declare vehemently, forcing him to believe my words.

But his blank stare continues, his entire face void of even a single emotion. His heart betrays him, though, thudding wildly in his chest.

"Wh—"

"Lets fuck," he cuts me off, the words laced with... *rage?*

"Parker," I test, but he ignores me, his face buried into my neck, his teeth sinking heavily into my skin.

I gasp in surprise. Unprepared but ultimately turned on.

"I'd really like you to meet him," I attempt to bring our conversation back, more than a little confused by his severe mood swing and wanting to decipher his intense change.

He laughs at my request, the sound sarcastic and hateful. "No."

He moves quickly, flipping my body easily. My stomach to the mattress, he bites my shoulder. *Hard.* I cry out in pain as my body arches into his assault. Wanting more.

"No?" I question, letting his calloused hands drag roughly over my sensitive skin.

"No," he cuts out, grabbing my hips and pulling them toward his groin.

My hands move upward on their own accord, bringing me onto all fours, but he growls. "Tits on the bed, arms out, ass up."

I gulp down a shaky breath, nodding.

He's angry. Vibrating with his quiet fury. I'm so confused, but a lot turned on. His teeth sink into the cheek of my ass, and I cry out.

In pleasure. In pain. In shock.

My neck tips back as his name hisses from my lips, his hand grabbing my hair and yanking hard. His lips tickle my ear, and I shudder.

"Stay the fuck down, Codi. Understand? Nod."

I attempt to do as he says, but his hand is wrapped so tightly in my hair that he's bruising my skull.

He laughs, his tongue dragging along my neck before using his grip to push my face down again.

"Fuck," he spits. "You're a fucking wet dream, Sugar. You

should see yourself; back swayed painfully, ass in the air," he growls, dragging his palm down my spine. "I can see your ass and your pussy displayed just for me," he continues his rough-spoken words, his fingers sliding through the seam of my ass, pausing over my tight entrance. I gasp, unsure of the feeling of him touching me *there*. His hand continues down, his fingers sliding against my wet heat, and I whimper as he slides them into me.

"So wet." The words are rough, lost in a growl, and almost inaudible. "Love when I play with your sweet little body, don't you, Sugar?"

He pumps his fingers in and out of me twice before removing them. I whimper at the loss, wanting to scream for him to keep going. I push back, chasing what he just took from me, and his dark chuckle echoes into the room.

He *tsks* me, sliding his dampened fingers up the line of my ass and massaging the tight pucker. I push forward, away from him in surprise, but immediately move back again, wanting to feel the foreign feeling again.

"Like that, baby? You like me playing with your untouched ass?"

I moan. Or beg. Whatever the sound, it's desperate and needy, igniting Parker's fire further. My mouth opens with a silent gasp as the thickness of his thumb slides into me.

"*Fuck*. Codi. God. Baby."

His disjointed words tumble from his mouth, the finesse in his movements lost as he rushes to line the head of his cock at my entrance. He pushes forward while simultaneously thrusting his thumb inside me, filling me completely.

"God. I wanna fill you up." His free hand grips my jaw, turning my face to slide his fingers past my lips and into my mouth.

"Suck," he snarls.

He's a blistering contradiction, a mess of conflicting emotions. His anger is palpable. I can taste it, dripping over my body in passion. His pounding thrusts, the rough grasp of his hands, the savage sounds he makes. But caught up in his fury is a beautiful desperation to *love* me. Every brutal touch of his body against mine is severe in its caress but bound in devotion.

In all the ways we've been intimate over the past months, I've never felt anything like this. He's hijacked my entire body, and I never want to regain control. Not when being owned feels *so* incredible.

I obey his thundering growl, my lips massaging his fingers as I suck hard.

A thick roar rolls up his throat, releasing from his strained neck on a cracked moan.

His movements falter, the finesse I'm used to from his touch pushed aside by his spiraling need.

"*Fuck.* I wanna keep you forever."

I want that too. I want to feel cherished in the same way I feel owned. I want him to claim me. Completely.

My heart.

My soul.

My body.

"Parker," I whimper around his fingers, and he drags them from my mouth, wet with my saliva, roughly down my jaw, down the underside of my body. He pinches a nipple, and I cry out. He does it again, and I buck against his violent thrusts, forcing his hand and cock deeper into my body.

Then I'm falling. I've lost all sense of reality. I'm no longer real. I'm floating. My entire body pulses with the most intense orgasm of my life.

I scream out his name. My voice a level of desperate I should be embarrassed by, but I'm not. I beg him for more. For him to keep going. To go harder.

My knees buckle, and he follows me down as I collapse onto my bed. I cry out at the loss of his thumb, but his hand clamps onto my shoulder, his body slamming against mine just before he stills, my name roaring from his lips as he empties inside me.

We lay like that, his sweat-slicked chest plastered against the dampness of my back. He's heavy, and my breathing is labored from not only exertion but also the weight of his body. But I wouldn't want it any other way. With this closeness, almost feeling suffocated by him, I'm relaxed, at peace, and *complete*.

Whether he vocalized the words or not, Parker Shay declared his love for me. If he'd shouted it, it still wouldn't have been as loud. He made sure I felt every tortured inch of it. In a way, this was better than three small words that could have been said without truth. Using his body to demonstrate there's no lie there. It's not possible. I felt his truth. I felt it filter from his body into mine, the sincerity in the silent declaration undeniable.

His lips meet the nape of my neck, a soft caress of his mouth against my skin.

Rolling off my back, he lands against my mattress, his head turning to meet my eyes. The red-rimmed tell of his eyes solidifies my thoughts. This was as emotional and meaningful for Parker as it was for me.

"I hurt you?"

I shake my head softly, my cheek still plastered against the softness of my pillow. "No."

"I... I was tryin'..."

My hand lifts to touch his cheek, resting there as my thumb drags along the socket of his eye. "I know, Parker. I felt everything you were telling me."

His eyes close in relief, a thick breath pulled through his

nose. He lies like that long enough for me to think he's fallen asleep. The heavy thud of his heart and the shallow intakes of air between us were the only sound in the otherwise quiet room.

"I can't meet your dad, Codi," he speaks, startling me as his eyes flicker open. A morose look of acceptance sits painfully in his eyes, and I watch him silently, trying in vain to read anything in the vagueness of his statement.

"Why?"

He shakes his head and copies the action with an irritated sigh.

"One day soon, you'll figure it out. I hate the fact that day will ever come. But it will." He blinks, his gray eyes opening again, searching the depths of mine. "I hope you remember this the moment you figure it all out." He lifts his palm to my chest, resting it gently over my heart. "If you remember this, I hope you'll find a little understanding as to why and maybe hate me a little less."

My forehead lines in irritation. "Stop it. You're always talking in these confusing riddles, alluding to our expiration date approaching. I just told you I loved you, and whether you want to vocalize it or not, you told me back."

He swallows heavily, his lips turning down in the beginning of a frown.

"If this is your way of trying to end whatever this is to you," I gesture between us, "be upfront. I don't understand your riddles, and quite frankly, I don't want to."

He pulls me closer, lining our bodies until they're touching, from the forceful thud in my chest to the tips of our toes. "Not what I was getting at, Sugar. Trust me when I say the last thing I want in this world is for us to end."

My body relaxes at the intensity of his words. "Good," I smile, leaning forward to touch my lips to his.

Maybe I should read into the haunted look in his eyes more and try to decipher why he seems utterly broken in the happiest moment of my life. But if I'm honest with myself, I'm petrified at what appears to be plaguing him. For the first time in my life, I've found something, *someone*, that I want to hold onto with everything pulsing through my body. This also means that I've opened myself up to real heartbreak for the first time in my life. And that scares me—more than anything. Worse, I feel as though he's teasing me with my heartbreak. He's dangling it in front of me, ready to crush my heart but loving me as fiercely as he can before he does it. I just don't know if I should be grateful or terrified.

TWENTY-ONE
PARKER

The sun begins creeping into her room from the split in her curtains, and I'm panicked and irrationally angry that Mother Nature seems to betray me by letting the sun rise. I need it to stay down, just for a few more hours.

I haven't slept, and my eyes feel weary. But I find myself praying for *more* time. Just to watch her sleep. I want to stay lost in the unappealing allure of Codi asleep. I smile despite the turmoil swirling inside my gut. I thought that first night that it may have been an uncommon picture; her mouth open, breathing thick, and eyes almost *open* as she slept. But I was wrong. It's just how she sleeps. Crazy to imagine these irrelevant details are the parts I'll miss the most. Bile runs up my throat, and I swallow the need to vomit because that would pull me away from where I want to be right now. Staring at an unconscious Codi, wondering how the fuck I'm supposed to survive in life without her. Worse, knowing she no longer breathes on this earth.

I thought burying my mom was the most painful moment of

my life. I've replayed it in my mind over and over again. For eighteen fucking years. I've let the agony of losing her brutalize my conscience until all I thought I would ever feel again was hate.

Then I met *her*.

I met Codi.

And I fell in love.

Now the pain I felt burying my mom is a distant memory I can't seem to recall because *pain* doesn't come close to describing the feeling that's been flooding my system for weeks, *months* now.

I want to cry. I want to scream. I want to *run*. I want to take Codi and run as far away from this fucking cesspool of a life I've created and never look back. I want to disappear. But he won't give up. He can't. I know that, and I can't even hate him for it.

I don't deserve Rocco's loyalty because I no longer want to return it. I want to betray him in a way he would never forgive me for. I want to take away his chance at peace. For my own selfish reasoning, I want to stomp on any possibility he had to seek the revenge he so desperately craves.

I don't deserve Codi's love because everything we've based our love on has grown from an almighty lie. The greatest betrayal, Codi gave me her heart, and I took it. I claimed that beating son-of-a-bitch knowing, fucking *knowing*, that I'd crush it in my hands and watch the pain in her eyes as I did it. I'd also steal the life in the same eyes.

My phone vibrates where it remains, discarded on the table beside Codi's bed. Reaching over, I grab it, glancing at Codi to make sure it didn't wake her, but she groans rolls over, and pulls the comforter further up her body, almost covering her face.

Rocco's name lights my screen, and I wait for it to end. He's been calling me non-stop for days. All calls were unanswered, and all texts were ignored.

My time is up.

My time is up.

Fuck, I don't even know how to comprehend that. I refuse to listen to his voicemails. They'd be reaching a level of desperate anger I give zero fucks about right now. I'm dealing with my own desperation, sorrow, regret, and fucking heartbreak.

My phone vibrates again, and I shake my head, switching it off to cut Rocco out of my head. Dropping it to the ground, I roll back, taking in Codi's sleeping form. I reach out, sliding my hand over her messy nest of hair.

She stirs, rolling onto her back, stretching and groaning before settling again. I pull the blanket away from her body, my eyes devouring every inch of her glorious skin. I want her. *Bad.* Just one more time. I'd kill to fuck her, slowly, and stare into the purple depths of her eyes, so she knew how much I fucking love her.

Instead, I kiss her lips softly, pull her blanket back up and dress as fast as possible.

I run home, approaching the loft through the back entrance to avoid coming face-to-face with Rocco. His car sits quietly beside mine in the empty undercover parking lot. It's early, the building still asleep, and my feet sound ten times louder, padding along the glossed cement as I jog toward my car. I slide in, switching the ignition on before my door closes. I reverse on a screech of my wheels, flying from the lot at excessive speed.

Reaching Ruin, I'm fucking grateful for the locked door, relief flooding my system knowing that no one's inside. Legging it up the stairs toward my office, I grab the first bag I see, dropping to my knees in front of the safe, keying in the code. I should feel ashamed. I should feel disgusted with myself. Keying in my mother's date of birth, my *dead* mother's, my *murdered* mother's. I should feel sick with regret about stealing money from Rocco.

But as I throw wad of cash after wad of cash into the backpack, I only wish I could move faster.

My cell vibrates in my pocket, and I slam the safe door, yanking it from my jeans. Codi's name lights my screen, and I tuck the phone between my shoulder and ear, answering as I zip the backpack.

"Sugar."

"Hey, baby," she greets sleepily. "Where'd you go?"

Jogging back down the stairs, I key in the alarm code, slamming the club door closed behind me. "On my way back, I just had to pick some shit up. Ryn home?"

"Uh. I guess. I haven't checked."

"Wake her, baby. Both of you get dressed. I just gotta put gas in my car, and then I'll be there. Be ready."

"Wh—" she starts, but I hang up, throwing the backpack onto my passenger seat and pulling from Ruin without a backward glance.

I'm back at Codi's within half an hour. I've rejected five calls from Rocco and ignored at least a dozen texts.

Fuck.

I barge through their apartment door without preamble, my eyes working to seek them out.

"Why the fuck are you both still in your pajamas?" I growl, stalking toward them.

Camryn frowns, taking a sip of coffee and looking at Codi as she shakes her head.

"Parker," Codi starts toward me, and I move closer, grabbing her arm to drag her toward her room.

"You need to dress. *Now.*" Looking back over my shoulder, I glance toward Camryn. "You too. Pack a bag. You're going away."

Codi yanks on her arm, and I tighten my grip.

"Ow. You're hurting me. Stop it," she cries, working to pull away from me again.

"Stop fucking fighting me. I fucking told you to be ready. Why aren't you ready?" I'm yelling. I sound like a fucking psychopath, but in my panic, I couldn't give a fuck.

Camryn pushes at my shoulder. "Let her go, you fucking jerk."

Dropping Codi's arm, I look between the sisters, sweat covering my entire body.

"*Please,*" I beg, but neither one of them move.

Stepping into Codi's space, I cup her cheeks. "Baby. Please listen to me. You need to go away." My voice is soft and coaxing as I stroke my thumbs along her creamy skin, my eyes penetrating hers with my desperation. "*Please,* Codi. I don't have time to explain. I need you and Camryn to *leave.* There's enough money in my car for you guys to survive comfortably until I can work this out. You'll take my car."

Codi's hands grab onto mine, squeezing my wrists. "Parker, you're scaring me. What's going on? *Talk* to me."

I'm shaking my head before she's even finished speaking, my hands dropping away as I step back. My heart is heavy in my chest, the thick, prominent pounding echoed by the incessant vibration of my phone in my back pocket.

I pull at my hair, pacing in circles.

"FUCK," I yell.

My cell starts again, and I pull it from my jeans. "FUCK. OFF." I throw it against the wall, watching it shatter into a million pieces.

Turning back to the girls, they're huddled together, a shared look of wariness cast across their features. "I'm trying to protect you. How can you not fucking see that?"

"Parker," Codi whispers, and I roar, hurling a vase across the room as the tortured sound cuts through the quiet.

"I. CAN'T. FUCKING. TELL. YOU. WHY."

Camryn steps in front of her sister, a glazed look of indifference sliding over her face. "You need to leave. Now."

I laugh, my head twisting to the side at the sardonic sound. "Fuck this."

Marching toward Codi, I grab her arm, dragging her toward the door. "You can go like that. You're to drive for as long as possible before you're too tired to go further. There's enough money to buy clothes when you get wherever you're going."

She fights me the entire way, pulling at my arm, working on releasing hers. But I'm stronger. I'm more determined. I have to be. It's her life I'm protecting.

"Don't use your credit cards or your cell. Nothing that could let someone track you. Understand?" I keep talking, ignoring the scratch of her fingers trying to pry me from her arm.

"DO. YOU. UNDERSTAND?" I repeat, turning to meet her eyes.

She glares at me, and I'm so focused on the fury in her eyes that I don't see her free hand coming up to slap my cheek with extreme force. I close my eyes against the sting, turning back to face her. "Let. Me. Go."

I watch her silently, stepping into her body and moving her backward. Her petite frame hits the wall with a thud, and I stare into her eyes, working to convey my thoughts and feelings enough for her to understand.

"Codi. Baby. *Sugar*," Her eyes soften at the endearment, and I cup her cheeks, moving my lips against hers. "I'm trying to keep you safe, *baby*. Let me keep you safe."

"You're scaring me," her lips move with her whispered

words, brushing the soft cushion against mine, the faint taste of salt from her tears teasing my taste buds.

"I'm sorry," I push my lips forward, kissing her softly. "God, Codi, I'm so fucking sorry for everything. For being born into the family I was, and that our fate was already planned out before we ever had a chance. I'm so *fucking* sorry for pulling you into this shit storm. For putting you in danger. If I knew," I start, pulling a hand from the dampness of her cheek to rest it over the wild thumping of her heart. "If I knew how good you were in here." I press my palm against her fast-beating heart. "I would've made fucking certain none of this touched you. I would've fucking *killed* myself to guarantee that."

I drop my face, joining our foreheads, running my nose along the smooth line of hers, and kissing her almost hysterically. My lips caress hers heavily, our shared tears dropping into the wetness of our kiss, making me frantic.

I pull back as severely as our kiss started, breathing laboriously, the pain in my chest magnifying with every agonizing inhale of air.

"Please."

Her indigo eyes stare into mine, the color glistening under the thick tears falling from them. Her breaths hit me sharply, the quick, stuttered sound echoing the loud rasp of mine.

"I can't," she whispers, her teeth biting into her bottom lip to stop it from trembling.

"FUCK," I roar, my fist meeting the wall beside her face and crushing through the plaster. Pulling it from the hole I'd created, debris falls along her shoulder, and I grab my hair in frustration, moving away.

Codi doesn't move. Her body is stuck against the wall, arms glued by her side, the eruption of my anger sitting not an inch away from her beautifully sad face.

She's afraid. This should add to my guilt. To the disgust I feel for myself. It doesn't. If anything, it fires my hope that maybe she'll understand the weight of my plea and leave.

"What the fuck do you have to stay here for?" I scream, continuing my desperate attempt to get her to listen. "We can't be together, fucking trust me when I tell you that. Your mom is a sociopath, and your dad's a fucking criminal."

Fire spikes in her eyes, and I know I've hit a nerve. Just the wrong one. She's no longer afraid or cautious of me or my words. No, now she's angry, her eyes narrowing.

"Get out," she grits, finally stepping away from the wall, her fists clenching.

"Tell me what's keeping you here," I challenge, every word I speak, seething with frustration.

"Camryn, call the police." She glances at her sister and then back to me. "Get. Out."

I hear the tell-tale sound of a dial tone, and I know Camryn's eagerly given in her sister's demand. Why would she not? This probably reminds her of every bad decision she made in her past. The ex Codi so artfully avoided giving me full details about. Without doubt or hesitation, she would protect her sister, whatever the cost.

Fuck.

This was not how this was supposed to go down. Shit, they should've been gone by now, having put as much distance between themselves and Rocco as possible.

I take a tentative step toward Codi, my voice soft. "Codi—"

"GET THE FUCK OUT OF MY HOUSE," she shouts, the shrill sound of her voice cracking her vocal cords. It's also the first time I've ever heard Codi swear. Outside us fucking, and even then, it's only been when I've demanded it from her, wanting to listen to the sweet, soft desperation of her voice turn dirty.

I hear Camryn's quick-fired words in the background.

Ex-boyfriend. Aggressive. Violent. Threatening. In danger.

It hurts hearing the demise of our relationship vocalized. I'm not an idiot; our relationship was well and truly over, but hearing the words slices into my already broken heart in a way I'm not ready for.

I'm fucked. If I stay here, I'm beyond fucked, so I move to the door. Sick with the feeling that I've failed everyone.

My mom. For trying to steal away her vengeance with my selfish desires.

My father. For being *so* fucking weak and not being strong enough to follow through with the one thing in life he wanted and *needed* more than anything.

Rocco. For working to pull the one chance at peace he has away from him.

Codi. For loving her and taking her love in return.

Myself. For losing everything important to me with my stupidity.

Every accomplishment I've set out for has been an implosion of disaster.

I'm a fucking mess.

My heart sent me on a path for peace, and in the end, it turned out to be my downfall. The part of me that was supposed to hold something true, something real, fucked me over so badly it has taken the life it anatomically gives me away.

Pulling open her front door, I glance back, my soul aching with the heartbreak sliced along Codi's face.

"Go to your dad for me, Sugar. Tell him my name and who my dad was. Tell him you're in danger. If I can't keep you safe, he can."

With that, I step through the doorway, letting her door slam heavily behind me.

I drive slowly back to the loft, trying to figure out how I tell my brother that he can't kill Codi. I can't ask him. I can't beg him. He's already told me it's the one thing he won't give me. It doesn't leave me with any other option. I'll tell him that if he *needs* her dead, he'll have to kill me first. I'll shadow her for the rest of her life if necessary, ready to move into the line of any bullet he aims her way. And if by some miracle, he manages to get around me, I'll kill him. With my bare fucking hands. I'll choke his last breath of life from his body and stare into his eyes as I do it. I'll make sure that the last thing he ever sees is my betrayal.

He's sitting on the couch when I walk into our loft—staring at nothing. Still as a statue. Rocco's way to center himself. He doesn't look up or acknowledge my presence, and I know he's pissed. Shit, I knew that days ago when I started ignoring his calls. But now, I can feel it vibrating off his frame.

I sit on the coffee table in front of him, and it groans under my weight. Bracing my elbows along my knees, I massage the palm of my hand, eyes focused on Rocco's profile, the tick of his jaw, the heavy pulse in his neck.

Finally, he turns, meeting my stare, and in amongst the fire, the anger in his eyes, I see the hurt, the pain my disloyalty has caused. "I've been trying to call you."

I nod.

"For days."

"Yeah," I cough out.

"Phone's off now."

"Not off, just smashed into about a million pieces."

He snorts out a disinterested laugh but asks, "What happened?"

Dragging a palm along my face, I sigh loudly. "Guilt at ignoring your texts and calls got a little much."

He pushes forward, his body's stance mirroring mine. Our faces sit close enough that I can feel the warm push of air from his lungs dance across my face.

"I threw it against a wall at Codi's when I was trying to convince her to leave town. To run."

My confession is quiet, said without remorse—an honest statement of fact.

Nothing more. No emotion crippling or spiking my words. Maybe he'll read that in my eyes.

The anger.

The guilt.

The hate.

The sadness.

The acceptance.

"I can't let you follow through with this, Roc. I'm sorry. I'm so *fucking* sorry," I breathe, forcing myself to keep his eyes and not look away from his wounded scowl.

"I can't let you kill her. It's not an option." I shake my head, swallowing the feeling of betrayal threatening to spill from my mouth.

The hatred in his eyes darkens, drilling holes into my head as he sits there silently. He doesn't utter a single fucking word, just stares me down, demanding I take my words back.

Finally, he stands, and my neck tips back to keep his face in view. The look of disgust that transforms his features is eerie as all hell, and I brace myself for impact. For a swift, fast fist to my jaw. But it never comes. He moves out of the living area, pacing aimlessly as he works to quell the uncontrollable anger radiating from him.

He stops, turns toward me, fists clenched, but stops. He

cracks his neck side to side, breathing forcefully through his nose.

"You think you have a say in this, *brother?*" He spits his last word, making sure I don't misinterpret the repulsion in the term. He's making this about family, about loyalty. Something I can no longer let myself be controlled by.

I stand, moving only a few feet away from him. "Yeah," I nod. "I do. I love her, Rocco. I fucking *love* her. I can't live in a world where she doesn't exist. I won't do it."

"We had a plan. A. Rock. Fucking. Solid. Plan. You don't get to back out now. Not when we're this close. No fucking way."

"You even look in Codi's direction, you'll see me. I'll be there. Rain. Hail. Fucking shine. Night. Day. Whatever the fuck. I'll be right there."

He laughs, his thick shoulders bouncing with the sarcastic sound. "*You're* going to keep her safe. From *me?*"

"I won't need to. You only need to know that to kill Codi Rein, you'll be forced to go through me. Know that the moment you pull that trigger, I'll move into its direct line. I'll take the bullet you meant for her and let it kill me."

His nostrils flare, and the self-assured smile that graced his lips only moments before drops away, replaced with a thin line of disbelief, pain, and heartfelt betrayal.

He shakes his head, forcing out a shaky breath, his throat working overtime. "You promised me this. After everything I've fucking done for you. *You promised me this.*"

I nod, my jaw wired shut as I'm thrown back eighteen years, eyes locked with Rocco as our mother was lowered into the ground. He's looking at me, boring into my eyes with the desperation in his, begging me for solace, for support. Only this time, I can't give it to him.

"I know," I rasp, giving him nothing more. But, really, what is there to give? A half-assed apology for taking his chance at freedom. It would mean shit. Nothing. Because as sorry as I am for taking something from him, it pales in comparison to what I'm taking for myself.

"And if I kill her anyway?"

I had hoped he wouldn't go here. I'd hoped he would've stormed out of the loft, ranting like a fucking psychopath, and saved me from this. From this last stab to his blackened heart. The final and most likely the most painful part of my betrayal.

"I'll kill you. You won't just be dead to me in the figurative sense. I'll hunt you down, and when I find you, I'll steal every last ounce of life from your body."

A single tear runs down his face, along the left line of his jaw. Just one. But it's more than I've ever seen from him, and I know I've irrevocably killed any bond we shared.

My love for Codi Rein has forced away the one single person in my life who fought for me harder than I fought for myself. The worse part is, I can't even regret it because it's the right fucking thing to do.

Rocco turns, walking toward the door. He pauses, hand to handle, not looking back as the rough cut of his voice hits me. "You're asking me to choose between my love for you and Mom. You're asking me to choose between the person who gave me life and the person who just threatened to take it without hesitation. It makes it harder knowing your love isn't with me. It means I gotta choose between the person who showed me what love was and the person who no longer cares enough to give me theirs."

With that, he's gone, our front door closing with a loud bang that sends a shiver up my spine. The problem is, right now, I'm no better off in knowing how safe Codi is. Sure, Rocco knows I won't be a part of this plan for revenge we set out for months ago, but that doesn't mean he won't continue on his path. He admitted that much. And what hope do I have he'll concede to my threat when he knows my loyalty is no longer with him? My heart has succeeded in derailing my allegiance. There's now no question Rocco was always right to doubt me because, in the end, my loyalty to family never stood a chance. Not against Codi. Not against the things she forced my heart to feel.

I've sealed my fate to a life of solitude. Of loneliness. I've irretrievably damaged my relationship with Rocco, and I'm destined to live without the woman I've given my heart to.

TWENTY-TWO

CODI

I stare out the window blankly as Camryn drives. I feel her stare, the quick, worried glances hitting my profile every few seconds. I should reassure her with a smile or carefully chosen words. But I can't bring myself even to pretend.

What I want more than anything is to tell Camryn to turn the car around. To stop. I don't want or need to see our dad. I want her to drive me to Parker's, and I want him to explain. I need him to divulge the monsters in his mind. I want a reason, a *solid reason* as to why our relationship was doomed from the beginning. I gave my heart to him, and whether he wanted to admit it to me or not, he gave me his back.

How do two people who love one another lose out so badly? I want answers. I want a justified reason as to why I have to feel as heartbroken as I do right now.

"Are you okay?" Camryn's voice finally hits me, the skittish glances no longer satisfying her need for reassurance.

"No." I drop my head against the window, closing my eyes.

"Babe," she prompts, and I turn my head, opening my eyes to

bring her into focus. "You'll have answers. Dad knows Parker's family. He made that clear before he left this morning. We'll make Dad tell us."

She turns back to the road, weaving through traffic, and I watch her. "What if I don't want to know? His dad was a criminal, and so is ours. Do I really want to know?"

She shrugs, not looking back at me. "You can't go on like this for the rest of your life, having zero understanding as to why the person you loved and who *clearly* loved you right back couldn't make it work."

She's quiet for a moment before she speaks again, this time glancing at me as she pulls into our parent's driveway. "Maybe there'll be a resolution. Someway to take back what you and Parker had."

"He doesn't seem to think so."

"He's a boy, Codi. They're stubborn. He'll fight reason because he's decided something else in his head. You'll need to make him see. *If* that's what you want after we speak to Dad."

I take a deep breath, nodding. "Thanks for coming with me. I feel weird, you know? He told me I was in danger, and he one hundred percent *believed* that, so I should feel afraid. I'm more confused, though," I shrug.

"Babe. Fuck. Parker was pretty hectic just now. Something big is going on. I need to make sure you're safe. That's our priority here, okay?"

She waits for my nod of approval, which I offer her with a sad smile. She reaches for my arm at the same time I reach for my door handle, and I pause, turning toward her.

"You're allowed to be confused. You're allowed to feel shaken by this. Shit, I feel this way, and I'm not in love with the guy."

Throwing my door open, I wait for her to move around the

car before walking to the front door. It's early, so we enter without knocking. Our demon mother will no doubt still be sleeping off a hangover, so at least we'll be saved from her insults.

"Do you want coffee?" Camryn asks, and I nod, following her lead into the kitchen.

Coffee in hand, we move toward my dad's office, and my heart moves into my throat, choking me. I don't *feel* as though I'm in danger. But Parker assured me I was. That I needed to be protected. I wished he had explained the who and the why. What have I ever done to make someone want to cause me harm? Exist? That's about it.

"Hi, Daddy," Ryn greets softly, her knuckle tapping quietly on his office door.

"Girls." He glances at his watch, then back to us. "It's early. Did you come for breakfast?"

He's dressed for his day, even this early in the day. A navy button-up shirt rolled up at the sleeves is tucked into his dark dress pants, black polished shoes dressing his feet. He's impeccable, not a single hair out of place—a complete contrast to the chaotic mess of Ryn and me. I'm surprised we took time to change out of our pajamas. We each threw a pair of jeans and a shirt on, stuffing our feet into our shoes before racing out the door minutes after Parker had left. Not a single word was spoken as the thick echo of our front door sounded through our apartment. Parker's absence in the space was stifling, and we couldn't get out of there fast enough.

Moving to Camryn, then to me, our dad kisses our cheeks, embracing us. I hold on for a second longer than expected, squeezing his colossal frame against mine. His clean, masculine scent soothes my nerves, and I step back from his embrace a little calmer.

"I need to talk to you, Daddy."

His face morphs into one of careful consideration, nodding solemnly as he gestures to the couch in his office. He waits for us both to sit, me next to Camryn, before he sits along the arm of the chair across from us, his hands moving to adjust the legs of his pants before meeting our eyes. Dropping my coffee onto the small table in front of me, a sick feeling crawls under my skin.

"The guy I've been seeing, Parker," I start, and he nods, the kindness in his face dropping away immediately at the grave sound of my voice. Seeing this side of him, being given a glimpse into the man Parker so easily labeled a criminal, is scary. His lips move into a thin line, his nostrils flaring, the steel shade of his eyes swirling in paternal disquiet.

"He hurt you, baby?"

"No," I placate, meeting his eyes to let him see the truth in my words. "He says he knows you, that you'd know him. He told me to come to you, to tell you his name and his father's, and to tell you I'm in danger."

Our dad glances at Camryn and then back to me, leaning forward, the concern etched along his handsome face only moments ago replaced by a thick fury.

"He was talking in riddles about you being able to keep me safe. He tried to get Ryn and me to leave town. To run away. When we refused, he told us to come to you."

"*Name*," he cuts out the quickly spoken demand, and I swallow heavily.

"Shay. Parker Shay. His father was—"

"Kane Shay," he speaks over me, and I nod.

He stands quickly, his arm coming up to rub the back of his neck. "*Fuck.*"

A quick intake of air pulls my attention. Our mother stands at the threshold of the door, eavesdropping. Her face is contorted in a way I've never seen, fear etched along every feature.

"Leave," my dad grits out, and she hurries away without throwing a single insult.

"If Parker Shay says you're in danger. He'd be right." He closes the door, moving back toward the couch Camryn and I are sharing.

"But..." I take a breath to speak, but he holds up a single hand, silencing me.

"He would know because he and his brother are the only two people on this planet who want to cause you harm."

"No." I shake my head. "*No.*"

"If there is a threat on you, Codi. It's from him. *Directly,*" he combats the panicked sound of my voice with quiet sternness.

I stand, pacing around his office. "That doesn't make any sense." I turn back, looking between him and Camryn. "He loves me. He's trying to protect me. He wouldn't want to hurt me."

"It's a lie."

"Dad, it's not," Camryn finally speaks, shifting forward in her seat. "I've seen the guy. I've met him multiple times. I saw his desperation this morning to get Codi out of harm's way. He loves her."

He massages his temples, sighing loudly. "Sit down, Codi."

I do as he asks without argument, crossing my arms over my chest and hugging my arms—a shield. Against the words my father is about to give me.

"Did Parker tell you that his mother died when he was young?"

I nod, working to keep my brain from recalling the gruesome details of the way he lost his mother.

My father takes a breath to speak, stops, rubs his jaw, and sits along the arm of the chair again. "His family thinks our family killed her. You don't need specifics, but we were *competitors* in certain markets. He was gaining traction, he—"

"Oh my God," I cry, my hand covering my mouth, the stuttered breath shaking across my open palm. "You did it. You murdered his mom."

"No."

"Not you, but one of your minions. Oh my God," I sob, folding down onto myself.

It all makes sense. Why he hates my family, and why he refused to meet my dad. Why he fights so heavily against the monsters in his mind. Holy crap. I can't even blame him for seeking revenge, but it makes no sense that I've been dragged into it all. His hate is aimed at my dad, not me.

"I assure you, Codi." My dad touches my arm, and I flinch at this touch, not having noticed him moving. "Our family had *nothing* to do with Lila Shay's death." He kneels in front of me, imploring me to believe him. "I know Kane thought differently, but I had *no* reason to take that woman's life."

"You just said." I stand again, moving away from him. "You just admitted that his business was crushing yours, that—"

"*CODI*," he yells, calming his voice before speaking again. "Look at me. In the eyes," he demands, and I do as he says, needing to find truth in his declaration. "I. Did Not. Kill. Lila. Shay. *Trust me*. I had *nothing*, absolutely, fucking nothing to do with the murder of Parker's mother."

My eyes search his desperately, tears tracking down my cheeks, wetting my shirt. "*Why* blame you then?"

He shrugs. "I was the obvious answer. As clichéd as it is, rival crime families kill one another off to gain turf. Sounds so fucking juvenile. The police investigated me, my business, and my associates, for months. *Months*, Codi. There was no evidence to pin her murder on me because I had absolutely nothing to do with it."

I look at Camryn, my face pleading with her to tell me what

to believe. Her eyes are fixated on our father, and I wait for her to turn to me. When she does, I know that she believes him without her speaking a single word.

"I don't know what to believe," I whisper. "It still doesn't make any sense. Parker loves me. He would never hurt me. I'm confused."

"His brother?" Dad questions, and an uneasy feeling crawls painfully up my spine.

"Rocco's intense. I definitely got the vibe that he didn't like me. I didn't ever sense he was having murderous thoughts, though."

"From the information I've gathered over the years, Rocco Shay is unhinged. Dangerous. He fights for fun. He'll let his opponents get the upper hand, to begin with, I assume, because he enjoys the pain." A distasteful grimace crosses his face. "Then he beats them within an inch of their life, smiling the entire time. Kane also had a few *very* dangerous men working alongside him, his second in particular, Marcus Dempsey."

He moves toward his desk, his stride purposeful. "You've met Rocco?" he glances up, waiting for my nod, before hitting the keys along his laptop. "Did you meet Marcus? Anyone else in the family?"

I shake my head, but he doesn't look up at me, too focused on his screen. "No. Except for his Aunt. Umm... Mira's her name."

He pauses his attack on the keyboard, his eyes meeting mine under the dark line of his lashes. "Mira is married to Marcus. I can't imagine she was involved in this plan, whatever the fuck it is. She was Lila's sister."

Flicking his laptop around, I glance at the mugshot lighting his screen.

"This is Marcus Dempsey. Have you seen him before?"

I move closer, pulling the computer closer and shaking my

head. I stare into deep blue eyes, so dark their color is almost indistinguishable, yet I see no soul. No feeling. Just *nothing*. His strong, angular cut jaw is dusted with a light shade of facial hair, his blond hair just close to his head, a dark beauty spot kissing an inch above his top lip.

He's scary. He's attractive. He's *empty*.

"You're going to go upstairs to your old room. You will not leave this house until I have this sorted. Do you understand me?"

I stare into Marcus' dead eyes, not listening to a word my dad spills. His smooth voice tickles my ears, but I can't move past the soulless man staring into my eyes, like evil itself is being gifted a ticket to my inner psyche.

Slamming the screen shut, I push the laptop away, considering he was charged with Rocco and Parker's care after their dad died. They lived with the devil. I'm sure of it.

I stand abruptly, looking at dad and Camryn without meeting their eyes. "I need... I'm.."

"Codi, did you hear me?"

I nod. "Hmm. Yeah. Stay here. Don't leave."

"Baby," he speaks again, standing to move toward me. "I won't let anyone harm a single hair on your beautiful head. Do you understand me?"

I nod into his embrace, letting him offer me the reassurance he's craving. "You are safest here. I can protect you here. This'll all be over before you know it."

Over before you know it.

I hate to even think about what that means. Who gets hurt in the process? Marcus? Mira? Rocco? *Parker?*

Bile rushes up my throat. I push back from my dad, running toward the small bathroom in his office, emptying the contents of my stomach.

Camryn rubs my back, whispering words of reassurance in my ear. I hate myself for wanting to tell her to go. To leave me.

"I'm fine." I brush her off, standing and moving to the basin. I splash my face with water, palming my eyes sockets. I rinse the taste of vomit from my mouth. My father is on the phone, and his voice echoes through the room, too soft to hear his words but still causing anxiety to prickle at my skin.

I push past Camryn and my dad. "I'm going to my room."

I close the door behind me, listening as dads quietly soften, "give her some space," filters through the wood.

I stand there, plastered against his office door, regulating my breathing for a minute or two. My eyes flick around the space, trying to find calm, but I can't focus on it. Pulling my cell from my jeans, I dial Parker's number before I remember it's currently sitting in about a million pieces in my lounge room.

I look to the front door, my feet moving before I can stop them. Mom's car keys tease me from their discarded position on the entry table, and I glance back to my dad's office door before picking them up as quietly as possible. Holding them in my hand, I pause, waiting to be caught, for my dad to barge from his office and yell at me to stay put. Instead, I'm met with silence, the sound stifling in such a large space.

I open the door quietly, closing it back over before running to my mother's Audi. I'm pulling out of the driveway before I've let myself second guess what I'm doing.

My father would tell me I'm being careless and putting myself in danger.

Camryn would tell me I'm being impulsive. That I need to give myself time to think, to consider everything I've just been told.

My mother would tell me I'm stupid. That if I get hurt, it'd be my own fault.

Maybe she's the only one with any sense. I know I'm being careless and impulsive. I know this could be the stupidest decision I've ever made. I'm already hurt. What's a little more pain if it offers me closure?

Parker Shay was the first thing in my life I've ever wanted. I need to know if it was all a lie. I need to know if his love was, *is* real. And even if it was all a game. A carefully crafted plan for revenge, I need to make sure he's safe. Because whether he feels it back or not, I love him.

TWENTY-THREE

PARKER

I pace the polished concrete floors of our loft, pausing at every insignificant sound. My breathing is sharp. I can't fill my lungs. I feel like a junkie waiting for his next score, scratching at my skin and tearing at my hair. I'm a fucking mess. My mind, my emotions, they're a fucking train wreck.

I don't know who I'm trying to protect anymore. Who deserves it more?

Codi. Rocco. Mom

Mom. Rocco. Codi.

Me.

Fuck.

Rocco hasn't come home, and I have no fucking idea where he is or what he's doing. God, he could be at Codi's place right now. That gives me pause, and I shake the thought from my head. No. I saw the fear and the worry stamped along Camryn's face. She would've made her sister do as I said. I have to trust that Camryn saw enough sense to seek out Dominic.

Dominic Rein.

I want to kill that motherfucker. If he hadn't taken something important from Rocco and me, this story might have ended differently. Maybe Codi and I could've found love in an honest way, not a road paved with deceit and lies. It's his fault. All his fucking fault. He's taken everything from me and continues to do so.

The click of my front door sounds, and I turn, watching it open, my feet stopping their continuous pacing. Mira's soft smile hits me, and my heart seems to start the beat it forgot to manage only seconds prior.

I pull my first full breath of air.

I drop to my knees.

And I cry.

My head falls into my hands, and I beg her to help me. To fix it. To save Rocco. To protect Codi. To tell mom to forgive me.

Mira rushes to my side, her ass hitting the hard floor as she pulls me into her arms, my head falling to her lap as she holds me. I've been here before, broken and *fragile*.

Eighteen years ago, Mira held me just like this. Offering my comfort when I found out my mom had died.

She soothes me for what feels like hours. Crying on and off, Mira rubs my back. She sings to me. She talks to me. She tries to reassure me that we'll survive.

The only difference now is I'm twice her size, not the other way around. I'm not a boy. I'm a grown-ass man. Falling apart in a way that I never thought I'd experience again. I assured myself I'd never let anyone get close enough to cause this type of pain again. Heartbreak is worse the second time around. You'd think it'd be more manageable. You've felt it before, so the suffocating emptiness, the excruciating helplessness doesn't catch you unaware. You *expect* to feel it. You don't account for having your heart ripped to pieces when it was only starting to heal. Having the raw scars pulled apart, inch by inch. Making you feel the pain you once upon a time thought would kill you happen all over again. Worse, the cruelty of the realization that the person who had started to heal those shattered pieces of your heart is why it's been decimated again.

Then imagine all of that was your fault.

The pain of your heart being ripped apart is *nothing* compared to knowing that the *reason* your hopeless heart felt anything good could be taken away from you. Finally smashing the damaged part of your heart into a million irredeemable pieces.

I feel like my lungs are collapsing. I feel as though everything inside of me is being severed in two, torn to pieces.

This time I don't believe Mira's words of hope. Her reassurance sounds like fairy tales. All lies to my ears, and this makes me cry harder. But I don't stop her. I let her try because she is all I have left. She's the only person in my pathetic existence that still loves me.

I don't know how long we sit there. Long enough for my tears to run dry. For my rough sobs to morph into staggered breaths.

"Thank you for coming," I finally speak my first coherent sentence, and her hand pauses briefly on its glide along my back.

"Always. Whenever you need, Parker. You know that."

I sit up. Knees bent, I rub the wetness from my eyes. My eyes feel raw, my copious tears having cut like sandpaper. I drop my head, steadying my breathing before I can look at Mira.

"Our plan was to kill her. To take her life. To steal away the good from Dominic like he did to us."

Her eyes close tightly, tears dropping along her cheeks. I can see so much of my mom in her. The beauty in her sadness. It gives me pause because split seconds like this magnify the way I miss her, and for a confused moment, I consider I should've gone along with Rocco's plan.

"I fell in love with her," I laugh, the sound full of misery and heartache. "*Fuck*. It was so easy to do. The instant I met her, and she smiled at me." I recall her genuine grin, her dancing flirtation. "I was gone. Fuck, Mira. I never stood a chance."

I crack my knuckles, looking away, considering the months that unraveled from that first encounter.

"I pretended for a while. I let myself believe I was enjoying her, that it was nothing more than me playing with her before..." I shrug, not wanting to repeat the words. *Kill her. Take her life.*

"I don't know who I was pretending for—Rocco or me. Lying to Roc gave me more time with her, sure. But I think admitting the truth fired my self-hate. I failed her, Aunt Mira." I drop my head, my shame filtering through my words. "Mom. I failed her. The last thing I could give her was vengeance, and I couldn't do that."

I feel her in front of me, and I lift my head to stare into stormy gray eyes, just like my mother's. "You did *no* such thing. Vengeance is not what Lila would've wanted, Parker. God, it's the *last* thing she would want."

"It's what she deserves," I argue.

"I don't disagree. But not this way."

She grabs hold of my hands, squeezing tight. "The last thing you could do for your mother, the *one* thing she would want for you, *more* than anything, is your happiness. She only ever wanted you and Rocco to be happy and loved."

"Dominic Rein killed any chance of that when he shot her in the face." Rocco's voice startles us both, and I move quickly to stand.

Mira steps in front of me, working to protect me from the blistering anger radiating from Rocco. This woman, fuck. She's tiny. Petite and fragile, she's never questioned putting herself in harm's way for Rocco or me. It's earned her a fair share of beatings. I have no doubt, even though she would never tell us outright. But I've seen the bruises. I've watched her nurse broken bones brought down on her by that psychopath our dad trusted with his life.

Rocco notices the movement, the seemingly insignificant step that placed her in front of me, his face twisting in hurt. She's betrayed him and made him feel the way her husband does. *Unhinged.*

"You don't need to protect him from me," he spits.

"Not what I was doing." She moves toward him, unconcerned by his bristling anger. "You're both messed up by whatever ill-directed plan you've created in your heads in search of peace. I'm protecting you from one another."

He pulls her into his body, hugging her to his side, his eyes never leaving mine as he kisses the top of her head.

"Nothing ill-directed about it, Mira. Their family stole something from us. We planned to do the same to them. An eye for an eye."

Planned. That's the word he used—past tense.

Stepping from Mira's embrace, he moves closer to me. "You're dead to me. You're the one person who was supposed to have my back. Like I've had yours. You were supposed to be on my side. MY SIDE," he yells, his finger crashing into his chest repeatedly. "I needed this. *I. Needed. This.* I thought you had a fucking heart, Park. I thought you had good inside you. How fucking twisted is it that I'm the only one that *family* means something to, that is guided by loyalty."

"Never questioned that, Roc. Always saw that in you."

He barks out a laugh. "You can keep your bitch. I won't

touch her. I'll do that for you. But that's it. We're done. You couldn't love me enough to offer me peace, so fuck you."

Panic rises, flooding my body, and I step forward. "Roc. *Please*. You and Mira are all I've got. I'm sorry," I whisper. "I'm so fucking sorry. For being weak. For failing you."

"Save your fucking tears." He gestures to the water coating my cheeks, the ones I didn't notice falling. "Save your fucking apologies. They don't mean shit."

His words are spiked with hurt, disappointment, with regret. His eyes glisten with the tears he rejected from me. Every word he speaks feels like a stab in my gut.

I've lost everything.

Everything.

Every pivotal moment we've shared in life as brothers flashes in my mind, and I close my eyes against the sting of their memory. Of the betrayal I've served to him because I fell in love.

I hate myself.

I despise myself.

He's right. I searched, fuck did I search, but in the end, I couldn't find it in myself to give him the one thing in life he's been looking for. I couldn't love him enough to let him try to find his peace.

He's right to cut me off. I'm the most selfish motherfucker on this sorry planet.

Locked in our stare, I long to reach out, to pull him into my body. To hug him and let him reassure me that it will all be okay. That we'll survive. We've survived worse. Haven't we?

"Parker." Codi's voice hits me, and I stumble back, searching for her.

Standing by the door, her eyes skirting between Rocco and me, apprehension coloring her messy appearance.

Her shirt is on inside out, one jean leg folded up, the other pulled down. Her hair is tied haphazardly on her head, and thick clumps have fallen from her untidy bun. Her creamy skin is blotchy and red, and her usually brightly shining eyes are dull and hollow in her face. She's been crying, *is* crying.

Why the fuck is she here?

I tried to save her. She said no. I told her to let her dad save her, and now she's *here*. I've betrayed my brother and family, and she's ignored everything.

I stalk toward her, rage and fury tickling under my skin. "You fucked it," I yell in her face, caging her in with both hands punching at the wall by her head. "You fucked everything," I spit, my eyes shaking with the fury drowning me. "She deserved vengeance. Our revenge was for *her*. For *us*. She was stolen from us. Her life was *stolen*." My breath stutters, tears forming in my eyes as fast as they fall along my cheeks. "You were supposed to be our retribution. You were our way to retaliation, a way to make it *right*. If only slightly." I shrug my large shoulders before leaning in close, breathing in the scent of her hair.

So sweet. So familiar.

Forcing my hand away from the wall, I hover it over the creamy column of her neck, my entire arm trembling with the indecision of the movement.

Right here and now, I could make it right. She wouldn't stand a chance. My palm would close over her throat, and I'd steal her last breaths.

My mother would be avenged.

My brother would have peace.

I'd be left with nothing.

And Codi would be dead.

Dead.

Clenching my hand into a fist, I pull it away, slamming it into the wall repeatedly.

"You fucked it," I repeat. "You fucked everything." My scream cuts off with a pained shout. "You took my heart, and you made it yours. *You made me love you.*"

Codi stands statue still through my tirade. Her frame is shaking, and tears leak from her eyes. But she refuses to back down. She holds my stare, letting every emotion clawing from her body rip her apart.

The disgust I feel for myself leaks heavily into my declaration. I am placing the blame for giving over my heart on her like I didn't force this upon her. Like I didn't hijack her peaceful life with a lie and take ownership of her heart.

"Worse, you forced me to understand *him,*" I accuse, betrayal dancing in my eyes and slicing through my tone. "I hated my father. I despised the angry, evil man he became. But I get it now." I nod, my gaze tracking over her face, the love I feel for her driving its way forward, pushing aside my hate, if only momentarily. "If someone took you away from me, if someone *stole* you from me, brutally, like your family took my mom, my soul would be lost too."

In an uncharacteristically intimate show of affection from someone barely holding their humanity in place, my large hands cup her cheeks, pushing up into her hair as my face moves forward, my nose skating along her jaw. "I'd go black," I whisper. "I'd happily walk into the bleak, empty depths of hell and make sure everyone I came into contact with felt my hate."

I stay buried in her skin, my face moving to touch my lips along her neck and against the hurried beat of her pulse, erratic in its alarmed state.

The monster she's spent the last few months convincing me didn't exist is very much alive. Vibrating with indecision and volcanic anger.

Pulling back, I move my hands to my head, my palms skating

along the shorn sides, elbows coming in to close my tortured face away. My jaw is set tight, a heavy tick pulsating in the rigid line. The line of my neck is strained, thick cords of muscle prominent with the tension in my body. When I let myself see her, my eyes would show her the swirling mass of contradiction inside me. I'm lost with the unconscionable love I feel for her. But that love is shadowed with hate and clouded with the vengeance I so desperately desire.

Our feelings are a disaster. Twisted and pulled in every direction by fear and need. By intimacy and hate. By loyalty and devotion.

Our affections are a mess.

Our love was tangled. Knotted and impossible. Neither of us has a single clue as to how we unwind it. On how to make it right.

Looking into her eyes, she understands the heaviness inside of me. She's trying to understand the pain I've lived with for almost twenty years. Maybe, in reality, the agony and the heartache of my life were always there for her to see, painted clearly on my features. Perhaps it's begging to be seen. I never thought so until now, but staring into her clouded purple eyes, I know she sees it all.

"Your plan for revenge was based on a lie, Parker," she whispers. "All this hate, it's aimed in the wrong direction."

Pain slices through her accusation.

I scowl down at her, pushing away from the wall, irritated that she'd come in here, after *all* I've lost, and defend *him*.

She glances at Rocco, the color in her face fading with what she reads on his face. But as scared, as intimidated as she is, she steels her spine, standing upright and meeting his glare head-on.

"Lying bitch," he spits. "You don't know shit."

"*Rocco*," Mira interjects, but he silences her with a sidelong glance.

"I spoke to my dad," Codi continues, her focus now on Rocco, working to convince *him*, disregarding me. "Your dad believed it was our family, but it *wasn't*. He promised."

Rocco's laughter slides across the loft with hate. "Oh. We should believe your dad. He's a real fucking standup guy."

"Would I be here if I thought it were true," Codi bites out, anger flaring in her eyes. "Would I put myself in harm's way if I knew deep in my heart my father took the life of your mother?"

He shrugs. "You're stupid enough to fall for my brother when he was playing you. It seems your stupid knows no bounds."

Pain cuts across her face. A part of me wants to reach out, to reassure her. To tell her it wasn't a lie. Not in the end. Convince her my love was, *is* real. But a larger part of me is pissed she's here. I've lost *everything* because I was stupid enough to fall in love with her, and she couldn't love me enough to keep herself safe.

My heart is thumping heavily in my chest. So loud I can hear it. I'd guarantee I could see it on my naked skin if I took the time to look.

"He told me the police investigated him for *months*, Parker. There wasn't a single shred of evidence."

"Dominic Rein is a career criminal. He knows how to cover his tracks. That means shit all."

She closes her eyes against Rocco's argument, taking a deep breath before opening them again.

"I believe him. He has no reason to lie to me about this. He didn't do what you think he did. He didn't kill your mom," she finishes weakly.

Fuck. I want to believe her. How easy our life would've been if that were true. But it's not. No one else has a motive. No one else had the means.

"I've lost everything because of you. *Fucking* everything. My family." I point at Rocco. "My heart," I spit in disgust. "*Peace.* I've got nothing left. *Nothing.* And you come here after I've thrown *everything* away to save you. Worse, you put yourself in danger to defend *him.* To defend the man that stole the greatest part of me."

Our eyes lock, and so much passes between us.

Loss.

Regret.

Hurt.

Betrayal.

Love.

Hate.

"Who do you think you are?" She seethes, moving forward to push at my heaving chest. "How fucking dare you. *You* did this. YOU," she screams. "What the hell did I have to do with this? Nothing. I was living my life peacefully, and you *forced* your way in. I pushed you back. More than once, but you kept coming back."

Every emotion exchanged has been lost to her pain, to the hurt I've caused her. It twists her face, wets her eyes, shit, her body is trembling with it so hard I'm surprised she hasn't lost her ability to stand.

"You made sure I didn't stand a chance. You took the purest part of me." She stabs at her heart. "The part I guarded so heavily, and you claimed it. You *stole* it."

Her chin trembles unwillingly, and she bites down on her bottom lip to stop me from seeing it. Her lip pales against the trauma of her bite, and I want to reach out and free it.

"I can't breathe anymore." Her hand wraps tightly around

the column of her neck, her breath stuttering as she lets go. "Because I don't know how to exist without you. How *fucking* stupid is that?" She whispers bitterly.

She thinks it's stupid, but all I can find in myself is relief. I'm not alone in how I feel or how I feel consumed by her. I can't stomach having to survive this torturous journey of life without her.

Gone are Rocco and Mira. All that remains in the hollow space of the loft is me, watching as my heart bleeds out in front of me. I can taste her heartbreak. It's so potent, so rich. But that's always been Codi. *Real.* Genuine. No façade. No pretense. She's always offered me what I could never give her back. *Honesty.* The deepest parts of who she is.

"Your brother's right. I'm as stupid as they come. You played me, and I danced right into your little game. Eyes closed. Heart open."

Her words are quiet. They are hauntingly broken. Her pain holds me hostage, slicing through me and remaining, forcing me to reconcile how much I've hurt her.

"Screw you," she sobs, her face twisting in irritation as the cry slices from her throat jaggedly. She drags in an uneven breath, her arm moving angrily to wipe away her tears. "Screw you," she echoes, more forcefully this time. "For standing here and throwing blame and hate my way. How *dare* you tell me that I've taken *anything* from you. I gave you everything in here." She touches her heart again. "I gave you everything," she repeats softly. "And all you've given me in return is a broken hymen and a shattered heart. The only things I'm left with now are pain, regret, and blame."

The truth of her words hangs heavily between us. The fury in her blazing eyes dares me to disagree. They challenge me to argue against the fact that I'm the biggest fucking asshole to ever walk this planet. The men I so fiercely despise; my father, Marcus, Dominic; their indiscretions, their flaws, the evil that lives inside them, is nothing, fucking *nothing* compared to the rotting soul I host within my body.

I can't dispute her words. Not one spoken syllable. She gave me *all* of her. Every inch of her body. Every fragment of her soul. Every morsel of her mind. And every last shred of the love inside her oversized heart.

Everything.

"I'm sorry your mom died," she spits, the fury inside her eyes having claimed her, coursing through her veins with unrelenting control. "I'm sorry she was taken from you. I'm sorry you've let your pain manifest into hate. I'm sorry the both of you are so rotten inside you can't see any light when it shines down on you. I'm sorry that all your mother would feel is disappointment that the two people she spent her short life loving turned so hateful."

Her words hit hard. They steal the breath from my lungs and cause my feet to stumble backward with the force behind them.

Because they're true.

I know that.

Rocco knows that.

Codi knows that.

"FUCK YOU," Rocco rages, stepping toward her, and before I've registered what he's doing, his gun is held tightly in his grasp, barrel pointed straight at Codi's face as he stalks toward her.

I push her back without a single thought, Rocco's gun hitting me right over my heart. My nostrils flare, and I shake my head.

He refuses to meet my eyes, looking over my shoulder at Codi. "I promised him I wouldn't kill you," he bites out, his arm shaking with his Glock tucked against my chest.

"Rocco," Mira cries, her small frame trying to force her way between us. She yanks at his arm, desperately working to move the gun from my heart. "Stop. *Please.*"

"Maybe I should kill *him* and his bitch. Rid me of his disloyalty and get the revenge I fucking deserve," he threatens, emotion clogging his throat.

"Can't let you do that."

Rocco startles at the rich voice that filters across the loft and our eyes seek out the source.

He's bigger than I imagined, easily standing eye to eye with Rocco and me. His build is similar to mine, not as bulky as Rocco, but not small, still muscular, even for a man in his mid to late fifties. His brown hair is neat, his face clean-shaven, and his skin is free of ink. His hands are held palms out, mid-way up his body, his feet slowly walking into the loft, eyes darting to his daughter, then back to Rocco.

Dominic Rein. The cause of the nightmare that is my life just walked into our loft, a stance of surrender in his cautious approach.

TWENTY-FOUR

CODI

"All you Rein's seem to have a death wish," Rocco snarls, moving his aim to my dad, who ceases his approach immediately.

"*Fuck.*" Camryn walks through the door, stumbling over her feet when she sees the gun. My heart seizes in my chest. I'm petrified. Camryn is now open slather, prey to an unhinged and manic Rocco.

Rocco startles at her appearance, his gun moving to her and back to her dad almost immediately.

"I told you to stay in the car, Camryn."

"Codi's in here." She glances at me, swallowing thickly. She pauses only briefly, concluding that our dad is Rocco's bigger threat. She ignores his bristling frame, moving fast toward Parker and me.

Rocco lets her walk right past him, unconcerned with her arrival. She reaches me in seconds, grasping my hand, eyes wide and panicked.

"I should just fucking kill you." Rocco steps closer to our

dad, his finger tickling the trigger safety of the black semi clutched his hand.

"You could." My dad agrees. "But it won't give you what you want. The revenge you so desperately seek. The vengeance Lila deserves."

"*Don't* FUCKING SAY HER NAME," Rocco screams, his heartache evident in the way his voice cracks.

A pitiful squeak breaks from my lips at the fury unfurling from Rocco, and Camryn pulls me into her body. She shares my fear, her body shaking as it wraps around mine. Rocco is waving a gun in our father's face, his temper unhinged, spiraling with every chaotic second. The slightest movement or wrong word could push him over the ledge he's balancing along—the fall resulting in a bullet in my father's brain.

The thought makes me sick. My eyes close at the rush of bile racing up my throat, threatening to spill on Parker's polished concrete floors.

Dad holds his hands up again, apologizing silently for speaking their mother's name.

"It didn't take her life. I—"

"STOP," Rocco yells, eyes closing to find some semblance of control as it spirals from his grasp. "Stop. Fucking. Talking."

Quiet descends in the loft, the labored breaths of Rocco's panic filling the space.

"Nah," Rocco speaks again, calmer this time. "Killing you would be too easy." He drops his gun, stepping backward, looking toward Camryn, Parker, and me. "No. I want you to live in the pain I have. I want you to feel the hell of life when your heart is missing."

My heart aches for the words he speaks. They're so flat, so broken, so empty. He's lost. He's working to find placement for the anger that lives deep inside of him, that's rotting his soul.

Eyes on my dad, he lifts his gun again, pointing it toward where Camryn and I are huddled together. "Parker, move."

Parker's arm reaches behind, pulling Ryn and me tightly against his back. "I can't let you do that, Roc."

"I SAID FUCKING MOVE," he roars, the words cracking over the volcanic eruption of his voice.

Mira's soft voice hums in the space. I can't make out her words, the quick-fired mumble of her tone impossible to decipher. Chancing a look up, she's moved into Rocco's space, her small hands cupping his cheeks as she tries to catch his eyes.

"I think you need to lower that gun."

I twist my head toward the unfamiliar voice, a growl of warning rolling through Parker's body and vibrating along mine.

He looks similar to his mugshot, taller than I imagined. Smaller than my dad but not short by any standard. I'd recognize him on sight. The only thing his photo didn't do justice to was his eyes. More so, the look within them. The emptiness in the deep blue of his iris. Windows to nothing but death and hollowness. Windows to *nothing*.

When I met Parker, I saw darkness where he claimed a monster lived. When I met Rocco, I theorized that if Parker was the monster he so confidently claimed he was, his brother might have been the devil himself. Now their menace is nothing. It's not fear-provoking. It's not threatening. Not compared to him.

I've never been frightened of a human being. I've been intimidated, sure, but not *frightened*. I've never had every nerve ending within my body zap with warning, with anxious uncertainty from laying eyes on one person.

I've never seen anything like the vacancy of any human emotion, as evident in Marcus Dempsey.

His gun hangs loosely by his side, a sick smile twisting at the corner of his mouth as he blinks slowly, casually taking in the scene surrounding him.

"You fucking liar," Parker shouts, stepping toward Rocco. "You promised me," he accuses, pain lacerating his words as his fists clench by his side. "You had no fucking intention of keeping your promise if you called *him*."

"I didn't tell him shit," Rocco argues, his shock at Marcus' presence clear enough in the deep furrow of his brow.

Marcus bounces on his feet, his teeth grinding as his eyes flick around the room. He's jittery, but not from the chaos unfolding in the loft. No, he's relaxed by that. His body moves to lean against the front door he only moments ago stepped through. A fine sheen of sweat lines his forehead, eyes depressed into his skull. The veins in his neck show heavily against the pale tone of his skin.

"Dominic." He nods, light eyebrows rising in insult. It's a front, though, the faux confidence in the sound. He's on guard. Cautious as he assesses my father's position and the threat he offers.

A look of hatred I've never seen crosses my father's face and casts severely across the space.

"What have you taken, Marcus?" Mira's hesitant voice scratches against the harrowing silence.

His nostrils flare in irritation. "Your need to protect Lila's spawn is embarrassing, Mira. So defective you couldn't have children of your own, you've latched onto your *dead* sister's offspring like a vulture." His last words whisper into nothing. "Maybe you're happy she died. Maybe Dominic didn't kill Lila. Maybe *you did*."

Rocco moves to step around his aunt, murder in his eyes, but Mira is faster, side-stepping at the exact time Rocco does, keeping him protected from the threat of her husband.

"No," he laughs. "No. You're right. You're too weak to take such charge of your life."

The softness in Mira's face dissipates, replacing itself with hate. A smile teases at the side of her lips, and I'm momentarily stunned by the malice in the gesture. Gone is the seemingly fragile beauty. In her place, a villain that could, without question, stand toe to toe with the devil.

"Marcus, this is why you've never been able to replace Kane, why his associates never even contemplated doing business with you. You're imbecilic."

He stands to full height at her insult, unleashed fury making his already jittery behavior shake more prominently.

"Of course, I could have children," she continues. "I just never wanted to subject a child to a life with you as their father. The world is a far better place without you having procreated."

He laughs then. The rich, rough sound thundering in my ears. Wiping away his nonexistent tears, his eyes move to Camryn and me, settling as his laughter dies. His stare is knowing, one of calculated power that makes the tiny hairs along the back of my neck stand on end.

Parker pulls me farther into his back, shielding me from Marcus' view. Marcus' focus remains on where he could see me moments ago, his gaze shifting to Parker's midsection, where his tattooed arm is no longer visible, instead twisted back, holding me against him.

Finally, this scrutiny deliberates up to Parker's body, settling on my eyes, currently peeking over his shoulder. "Codi. It's nice to meet you in person finally," he soothes, a familiar smile on his lips.

I swallow thickly against the way he says my name, so significant it causes discomfort and uncertainty to creep up my spine.

"Don't fucking talk to her," Rocco spits, stepping closer to the superficially impenetrable armor that is Parker.

"I told you, Rocco. You need to lower that gun. I can't let you carry through with your *plan*. I wanna destroy this piece of shit Dominic more than anyone." His eyes slice to my dad, bitterness and contempt forcing his hand to tighten on the gun held in his palm. "But not with her."

Rocco's bottom lip pushes out in challenge, his shoulders squaring the barrel of his gun aimed toward me, Parker standing between us like my own personal shield.

"What makes you think I would give a shit what you think?"

Marcus shrugs, taking a step forward, forcing Rocco and Mira to move closer to Parker and me.

"You know how often Kane reamed me in front of my subordinates because of information I acquired through my concrete source? It took me some time to realize the piece of shit was feeding me false information."

My gaze moves to my dad as he steps forward. "I will kill you where you fucking stand," he seethes, his eyes shading with panic.

"Uh-ah," Marcus *tsks*, lifting his gun toward Camryn, his eyes glued to my dad.

He's scared of my father. That's obvious. He might be holding the gun, but even the protection of a weapon hasn't removed the fear from his eyes as he watches my father uncertainly.

He waits a moment, making sure my father doesn't move. The threat to Camryn's life significant enough to keep his feet glued to the floor.

"Who was your source?"

It's the first time I've heard Parker speak, the rough sound vibrating through his entire body against mine.

Marcus smiles. Genuinely. It's sick and twisted but full of pleased triumph. He has something. Something solid. Something he deems wounding enough to inflict maximum damage.

His tongue darts out to wet his lips, his teeth following to chew the same spot. He eyes everyone in the room for the briefest of seconds, his eyes falling on me for a few moments longer than everybody else. It's unnerving. It's unsettling, and I step closer to Parker's back to protect myself from the calculated look dilating his pupils.

Finally, his eyes move back to my father and stay.

"The first time I met Sarah, she didn't know who I was," he starts, and the look of defeat that crosses my father's face mixes with regret.

"I told you," he grits, but Marcus shushes him, finger to his lips, a look of reprimand on his amused face. The move is condescending and only menacing by the way in which the gun in his hand remains pointed in Camryn's direction.

"As I was saying, the first time I met your mother." He turns to Camryn and me. "She had no idea who I was. She was just happy to escape the confines of your father's rules. She was drowning her sorrows in some seedy bar on the outskirts of town. No protection, no bodyguards, even considering who she was married to. Seems you never actually cared, isn't that right, Dominic?"

My father doesn't answer, and his eyes remain focused on the gun in Marcus' hand. "I'll kill you," he whispers.

Marcus laughs. "Oh. I don't doubt it. I imagine there'll be a few casualties as my story unfolds."

"I made Sarah feel good. She was so... *stupid*. God, she gave away secrets before I'd even bought her a drink. *Big* ones too." His eyes light up as he speaks, enjoying his stage, us the unwilling audience.

"Getting her to open her legs wasn't much harder." He smirks, and I feel an overwhelming need to be sick. It's sad how easily I could believe she would betray my dad's confidence in business BY divulging secrets that caused him damage. I'm disgusted that she'd let this psychopath touch her. *Intimately.*

"Kane was so *impressed* with me." He moves his gaze over Rocco and Parker. "My *source* had given us greater ground. We'd hit Dominic where it hurt. I was feared. I was respected. Sure, I could never tell him where my information came from, especially because I was sleeping with the enemy. Shit, he wouldn't hesitate to put a bullet between my eyeballs if he knew. Fucking ungrateful piece of shit he was. He didn't give a shit about loyalty."

"Says the guy who was fucking his adversary's wife."

Rocco's voice is hard. Unfeeling, a bored indifference radiating from his large body. He doesn't give a shit about Marcus' story any more than the rest of us. He might also be wielding a gun, but unlike Marcus, he's not stupid. There are people he cares for in this room. He wouldn't risk using it without Mira and Parker out of harm's way.

Marcus ignores his comment, moving on with his story. "Sarah found out who I was eventually and threatened me. Laughable. She knew she was as fucked as I was if our relationship got out. If Dominic here," he gestures to my dad, "wouldn't kill her, Kane sure would have. She disappeared for a little while. I gave her time because I knew she'd come back. She always did... *does.* In the end, she fucking frothed at betraying Dominic in any way she could. Sharing details on business transactions. Fucking me like her life depended on it. Life was good."

He pauses, letting us all soak in my mother's deceit.

Sighing, he turns to my father. "But you knew. In the end.

Or at least suspected. You cut her out. Let her hear half-truths. You made me look like a fucking fool," he spits.

My father doesn't deny it. He only stares at him with hate and fury in his eyes.

"Your piece of shit father started humiliating me in front of my subordinates," he says to Rocco and Parker. "He'd backhand me like I was a useless little bitch." He glares at Mira, disgust in his words.

"Seems fitting." Rocco smiles.

Marcus refuses to respond, his neck cracking in irritation.

"Sarah and I became desperate. We started using. Drinking. We got sloppy." He looks at me, and my breath catches at his meaning, trying to understand what he's saying.

"Then your idiotic, fucking cunt of a mother saw me. *Lila,*" he spits. "Thinking she was more important than she was. She was a nosy fucking bitch who knew too much. So I acted. She would've gone straight to Kane. He would've killed me, Sarah, and Codi. Not only was I sleeping with the enemy, but I'd also knocked her up. *She gave me no fucking choice.*"

My breath comes out in a stutter. My hands shake in front of me.

I'd also knocked her up.

He would've killed me, Sarah, and Codi.

"No," I splutter in disbelief, side-stepping from the protection of Parker's body. My eyes seek out my father's, and in that single moment, I know it's true. He looks *into* me with love, but pain and regret sit at the forefront.

He's not my dad. Not biologically. No, I'm the product of an evil and twisted man. *His* blood runs through my veins. The good I thought I'd been passed down from my father doesn't exist because it was never mine. My hands find my mouth, and I cry silently into them.

My whole world is a lie.

Everything I thought I knew was a lie.

"It was *you*." The soft, broken whisper is unlike anything I've heard from Rocco. "You did it. You took a gun, pointed it in her face, and blew it off. You killed her. YOU FUCKING KILLED HER." His voice cracks open with the scream ripped from his throat.

Everything moves in slow motion. Ask me when it was all over, and most likely, I wouldn't recall a single detail, but here in the moment, I see it all like a replay. Every movement happens sluggishly.

I *hear* it all.

I *feel* it all.

I *smell* it all.

I. See. It. All.

Parker steps back, not purposefully, more as though the force of Rocco's words have propelled him backward. He grunts in pain. The sound moving through everyone with force unlike any other. We can feel his heartbreak. That single tortured sound gives us access to the moment the final slivers of his heart shattered to pieces. If I concentrated hard enough, I'd smell the salt of his tears working their way down his face. His movement isn't graceful. He stumbles as though he's been hit forcefully, unsuspectingly.

A roar breaks from Rocco's throat, disturbed and haunting. A sound I won't ever forget. It ricochets from my fingertips down to the tips of my toes. The loss and anguish in the sound are so poignant I can relate to the devil living within Rocco's body. Unleashed now that he knows his entire life, everything he's been working toward for the last eighteen years has been a lie. His hate and rage are so loud it fills the room. His feet move forward, the same time, his arm stretches up, gun aimed at Marcus' heart.

Marcus is faster, though, and before a split second passes, he pulls his trigger first.

I imagine Lila and Mira had a relationship like Camryn and me. One of an unbreakable bond. One that would ensure you do everything you can to protect one another. No matter the cost. You'd lay down your life. You'd give your very last breath. There isn't a single doubt in my mind that when Lila died, Mira took on the maternal role for Rocco and Parker. One of nurture. One of protection.

She's faster than I predicted, and more than anything else from today, I think I'll remember the tear. The single droplet falling along her cheek as her body moved to shield Rocco's. The heartbreak that her husband, the man she promised her life to, had killed her sister. But her final moments weren't in revenge. They weren't in hate or vengeance. They were that of a mother. A strong, fearless woman who laid down her life to protect her children. She took her final breath right before Marcus' bullet pierced her skull, knowing she gave it to protect her sister's baby. She did what she promised. She gave Lila her word, and she kept it.

The sound was terrifying. I don't know if it was the release of the bullet, the eerie sound as it flew through the air, the moment it connected, or the strangled choke she made as it happened. But it was sickening.

Worse, though, was the blood. The smell, the metallic spike that hit that air at the same time her blood coated my face and body. I can still feel it, wet and warm, freezing me in place.

Everything seemed to kick start back into full speed from that moment. My father's gun was out before anyone registered it, and Marcus' life ended similarly to Mira's. It was quick and bloody, but no one spared him a glance when his body slumped to the floor.

I watch helplessly as Rocco cradles Mira's lifeless form, his eyes shut tight, his big body rocking, stuttered sobs breaking from his lips.

"Someone fucking help me," he stammers. "Get it off her face." His hands wipe hopelessly against her skin, trying to move the blood from her face. Parker drops next to him, hands limp at his side, his jaw shaking and tears falling like Rocco's, heavy and consistent.

I didn't see Camryn move, but she crouches beside Mira's body, a small bowl and a washcloth alongside her. She washes away the blood with care, cleaning her face.

"You're a fucking nurse. Do something," Rocco demands, his large bloody palm coming up to caress his Aunt's face.

"She's gone, Rocco. It was instant. There's nothing anyone could've done." The emotion is thick in Camryn's throat, and I swallow the sob threatening to break from my throat.

My dad's voice echoes softly in the background. His tone is somber and matter-of-fact, but I can't focus on what he's saying. All I can see is Mira lying lifeless in Rocco's arm, the pool of blood coating his legs and arms as he cradles her along his lap.

He looks like a child. A scared and grief-stricken little boy. He continues to rock her, apologizing over and over again. His soft-spoken *sorry* echoed along the emptiness in the space.

Parker holds her limp hand in his, his free hand covering his mouth, blinking against his tears every few seconds to let them drop.

Camryn sits beside them, watching and not speaking or moving.

And I stand here. Unable to move. Unable to speak. Barely breathing.

I just saw two people die.

Two.

One of which happened to be my biological father.

Parker gently brings Mira's hand to his lips, kissing her softly. "*I'm so sorry, Mira.* Fuck am I sorry. I love you." He touches her face, his thumb skating along her eye socket. "Tell mom I love her when you see her. Tell her I'm sorry, too, for everything."

He places her hand along her abdomen, resting his over hers as his eyes meet Rocco's. A fresh wave of tears hit them both as their eyes anchor. A sob breaks from Rocco's throat, and he nods. Parker follows the movement, his jaw wired shut, his bottom lip trembling as he swallows the cries he desperately wants to let go.

Finally, he stands, moving toward me. His eyes skate over me, over the blood decorating my skin, over the tears tracking down my face. He picks me up without speaking, cradling my body against his, and that does it. Burying my face into his neck, I cry. Thick, fat, ugly tears. Loud, uncontrolled, messy sobs.

For Mira.

For Parker.

For Rocco.

For Lila.

For my dad.

For myself.

How messed up this tangled web had become. The foundations our lives were built on were twisted and hateful, deceitful, and deceptive.

Because of my mother.

Because of my *father*.

Because of Rocco.

Because of Parker.

TWENTY-FIVE

PARKER

I can't seem to control my sobs. Or hers. Any comfort from the soft drag of my palm up and down her back as I carry her is lost against the tortured breaths escaping my throat and the tears dampening her hair. My body shakes in perfect rhythm with hers. My sobs are rough, and Codi's are gentle and broken.

I shut my bedroom door, attempting to close off the horror of our day and shutting it away as I break the threshold of my bathroom. Placing her on her feet, I brush away the matted hair from her forehead; it's clotted with blood, staining the white-blonde color a vibrant red. Mira's life is now painted along our bodies in a reminder of what I just lost.

She lets me undress her without dispute, her eyes empty, staring at the spatters of red covering my shirt.

I drop to my knees, tapping her ankle, and she lifts silently, letting me divest her feet of her shoes and socks. Even the souls of her chucks look as though she's stepped on a red ink pad.

Codi, now free of her ruined clothing, I stand and strip mine from my body. She stands quietly as I adjust the shower water and follows wordlessly as I guide her into the spray.

This is probably a bad idea. Showering when cops will be descending on the loft in minutes. I heard Dominic on the phone, his quiet declaration of two shootings requiring emergency services. But I watched Codi look over her hands and arms, seeing Mira's blood covering her skin. She was seconds away from losing it, her eyes darting between Marcus, dead on the floor, and Mira, fate the same, cradled in Rocco's lap as he sobbed and begged for her to come back.

Fuck. Maybe I didn't pull her away for her. Maybe it was for me. Because I know I was barely holding on.

Standing under the rain of water now, her head drops slowly as she watches the water turn red as it washes the blood from her body, and like me, her body shakes violently. "Help me get it off," she cries frantically.

I pull her tightly against me instead. She struggles, her small frame twisting and pushing against mine, trying to move me away. Then her body goes limp, and I hold her up. Her legs have lost the ability to stand, and her hands move to grab instead of push. She pulls me closer, her loud, incoherent cries breaking against my naked chest.

I let her cry, mourning the multitude of blows she's just been delivered, and I mourn my own.

My aunt.

Mira.

The single beacon of light in my life over the last eighteen years.

The woman who helped raise me and who showed me love. The woman who showed me kindness and disregarded every need in her own life, including her safety, to protect Rocco and me.

Gone.

Forever.

Dead.

Dead.

Shit. I don't even want to begin to imagine what her death means for my life going forward. What it means for Rocco. Jesus, she's what kept him sane and alive.

I'm barely aware of the thick, tortured sound breaking from my throat, so lost in my grief and anguish, I can't find a way to rein it in and find any semblance of control.

Codi offers me what I gave her, support. She lets me cry into the crook of her neck, her hands pulling me in close.

I don't know who kissed who first. I can't recall which one of our tortured souls took that desperate step in needing *more.*

Reassurance. Support. Comfort. *Distraction.*

I want to think it was her. That Codi was the one to push us over the vicious storm of grief swirling between us, searching for *my* comfort. Letting me help her detach from the world we no longer wanted to be a part of. But I can't be sure. Because as quickly as the first taste of her kiss came, she fought against her want for distraction that sex could give her as heavily as I fought for it. She went from kissing me hysterically, her legs crawling up my body to wrap herself around me as tightly as she could, to pushing me away. Her small fists hit my chest in time with her weak sobs.

I push forward, and her back hits the wet tiled wall brutally. I ignore her fists and kiss her again.

She kisses me back. Clawing at my shoulders to pull me closer. The desperation in the way touch forces our intimacy into a frantic mess.

I'll pull away, and she'll yank me back.

She'll push at my chest, her cries coming on harder, and I'll kiss her deeper.

Before I knew what was happening, she'd reached between us, my cock held tightly in her hand, and she guided me to the heat of where I wanted to be more than I wanted my next breath.

I don't hesitate, pushing forward into the suffocating choke of her pussy.

She sobs, and I cry.

We fuck hard.

We fuck angrily.

We make love while drowned in hate.

We let our hearts connect as we drift further and further apart. The heaviness of what we've experienced has cast us astray, moving each of us into an abyss from which we can never be sure we'll find our way out.

The hate pouring between us morphed into the lust that always seemed to cloud us. It is raw. It is real. It is soul-shattering and *sad*.

Our tongues war. Our teeth clash. Our tears collide. Our bodies come in an explosion of misery and heartache, orgasms so powerful our legs buckle, and we slide down to the cold floor, our minds empty and hollow.

As much as I hoped she'd never regret this final broken moment between us. One so intimate and raw it'll haunt me for the rest of my sorry days. I knew my hope was futile. Her body already shakes with the shame and remorse of what we just shared.

Eventually, she pulls away, and we stand on unsteady legs. I help her scrub the clusters of dried blood from her creamy skin. She lets me wash her hair. Her neck is tipped back into the shower spray, and I watch the deep red dye of blood rinse from her hair and disappear down the drain.

She waits for me to wash, watching in an empty daze as the last of Mira rinses from my body before she shuts the shower off.

We dry ourselves in silence, an awkward heaviness falling between us as Codi refuses to meet my eyes.

"Sugar—" I start, but she cuts me off, wrapping her towel tightly around her body, eyes darting anywhere but to me.

"Do you have some clothes I could borrow?"

I wait for a beat. *Fuck.* I need her to look at me. I need her to talk to me and let me explain. I need to tell her I love her. To say the words. To vocalize how I feel. But she won't give me the opportunity, so I nod silently, moving back into my bedroom to find her a pair of sweats and a sweater to change into.

She rolls the waistband of my sweats over three or four times to keep them secure on her hips and to ensure they fit her. I dress, and she refuses my eyes the entire time.

"*Sugar.*" I try again, but this time Rocco's thunderous roar breaks me off, and without a moment of hesitation, I run toward the sound.

Dominic attempts to hold him back as he tries to move back into Mira's space.

"Mr. Shay, I will not hesitate to arrest you if you impede forensics from doing their job." A short, round older man tries to reason with Rocco.

"What's there to fucking know? That stupid cunt shot her." He throws a hand out toward Marcus' body. Numbered cards are placed near his body and his gun as a man takes shot after shot of his lifeless body with a large camera.

"*Sir,*" he begins again, but I move into his space.

"Roc. Let them do their job. The quicker they do that, the quicker they're out of here." I push at his chest, forcing him to move away from the detective.

"Touch her in a way I don't like, and I'll fuck you up," he threatens, and I close my eyes in irritation.

"*Roc,* fucking chill before they arrest your ass."

"I'm not going to lay a single finger on her. I want to start taking statements, though. I need to ask you all a few questions. I'll start with you, Mr. Shay." He indicates to Rocco. Rocco stares at the detective blankly before his eyes flick to Dominic Rein and back again. He dips his chin as he moves toward the living area to sit down.

Dominic is standing by Codi and Camryn, his voice soft, undecipherable in the hum of activity in the loft. Codi's eyes reach mine, locking for a long and vacant moment before scanning the desolation in the room; Rocco, Mira, and finally, Marcus. Her father speaks the entire time, his lips moving fast with the words he's working on getting across.

Camryn nods the entire time, taking in everything her father says. He has to prompt Codi, his hand coming up to cup her jaw to bring her focus back to him. She flinches at his touch, and I watch the fleeting flash of pain hit his eyes before he drops his hand. Finally, she nods, the emptiness in her eyes still present.

The detective moves away from Rocco, moving to Camryn, and Codi steps away.

"Parker." I shift my attention to Dominic. "I'm sorry for your loss. I didn't know Mira personally, but I know she was the last family you had."

I nod, refusing to speak. What am I supposed to say? Thank you. For what, an empty veil of apology that wasn't necessary? Dominic Rein had nothing to do with the lifeless body of Mira's slumped across my floor. No. That blame is on me. On Rocco. On the piece of shit Dominic lodged a bullet inside of.

He doesn't expect me to say anything, stepping into my space, his arm moving around my shoulder in a show of support for any unknowing bystanders. His eyes tell a different story, though. One of direction, of complete focus. Of calm.

"Dempsey came here in search of Mira, understood?"

I stare at him blankly, but he ignores my look of confusion. "They argued, like always, only this time she came here, *afraid*. We were all here, meeting you, Codi's new boyfriend when she turned up."

I swallow uncertainly. "Nod to let me know you're keeping up."

I follow his instruction, and he breathes a sigh of relief. His eyes glance toward the detective, still with Camryn, then back to me.

"He came in, saw me, lost it, shot her, turned the gun on me, and I retaliated in self-defense. Nothing more. Nothing less. Understood?"

I barely have a moment to respond before he looks beyond me, smiling grimly. "Detective. I'll imagine you want to speak to me next." Then, without waiting for a response, he steps from the false embrace he'd forced me into. "Parker, as I said, anything you need, son, come to me."

He walks away, moving the detective back toward the living area, and I stand there, stunned.

It's clear as fucking day these cops are on Rein's payroll. Evident in the lax way they're approaching the crime scene. Hell, Codi and I were in the shower when they arrived, and no one batted an eyelid. Not to mention the way every one of them didn't *notice* when Dominic pulled each of us away to school us on what *actually* happened. It didn't happen if they didn't see, right? As far as they can tell, our stories all line up because that's precisely what happened. Crooked cops. Fucking convenient as all hell.

What I don't understand is why Dominic Rein is protecting

Rocco and me. He could've thrown us to the wolves and made us pay for our misguided revenge plan. One that included taking the life of his youngest daughter, but instead, he's using cops he has in his pocket to protect us.

And I have no fucking idea why.

Codi is standing close by, and I watch her focus on the man taking shots of Marcus.

"Relation?" he asks, startling Codi from her stupor.

"Sorry?"

"Family member of yours?" he repeats, indicating toward Marcus.

She shakes her head vehemently. "No."

"Sorry," he mumbles. "My mistake. Just thought, you know, your eye color is the same, almost purple."

She turns without letting him finish, her eyes connecting with mine and shifting away again.

The detective approaches, and she pulls her arms into the too-big arms of my sweatshirt, listening as he speaks. She answers his questions in a clipped response. Single words. Quick movements of her head, confirming and denying. Her answers would be the ones her dad placed along her lips, following his instruction without quandary. Why wouldn't she? Her dad just committed murder. Sure, it was to a piece of shit like Marcus Dempsey, but still, she goes off plan, and her dad pays the price.

They'll take Dominic into custody. Something I can't imagine he'd be an amateur with. He would've known that with the story he'd placed into our mouths. They'll have to. Shit, he confessed to killing Marcus. Through self-defense, something all our reports would've corroborated, but the timeline of events will still need to be proven. Jesus, he could be charged with homicide, for fucks sake. He'll likely be acquitted because of the circumstances and the dirty cops pocketing their monthly paychecks for such moments, but what a gamble to take. For what, scum like Rocco and me?

The detective approaches me last, and I follow Dominic's instructed lead. I follow the timeline of events he created to the letter. I feign shock, denying memory of points I'm unsure how to answer.

Dominic leaves with the detective a short time later, and Codi and Camryn watch on in subdued horror. Mira and Marcus' bodies are taken at the same time, Rocco's horror and anguish a little more unrestrained.

That leaves the four of us. Standing in the loft, death, and betrayal dancing around us like an almighty storm.

"You okay?" Camryn finally speaks, her softly spoken question aimed at Codi.

"Okay?" Codi spits, her arms crossing over her chest in defense. "What wouldn't I be okay about? The fact that I discovered the man I'd fallen in love with had only pursued me with the intent of revenge, of taking my life? Or maybe what doesn't sit right is that our mom is a lying, deceptive bitch who lied and cheated our whole lives. That's not news, though, is it?" she shrugs.

"I didn't mean—" Camryn whispers, but Codi ignores her, her voice rising with every second.

"No. It was probably that our dad, the man I've loved my entire life, who taught me everything in life, isn't actually *my* dad. No. My father actually happened to be one of the evilest human beings ever to exist. I'm spawned from two of the blackest souls I've ever known. *Yay me.*"

"Codi—" Camryn tries again, but she's too gone to notice.

"Add *all that* to the fact that I just saw two people shot dead, one of which was my fucking *dad,* and ask me again if I'm okay,

Camryn. *Please* do because all that's on my mind right now is reassuring *you*."

Her eyes are focused on the pools of blood. Parts now dried against the floor of the loft. I can see her shaking from here, her whole body vibrating in shock, but before I can move in to comfort her, Camryn beats me to it.

"You're right. Let's get out of here," she whispers, and I wanna scream *no*. I want to pull Codi back into my room, into the shower. I want to share that perfectly broken moment when all we had to lean on was one another. When she clung to me and cried, let me be her rock, her support.

But I don't. I stare at their retreating forms trying to find a reason to ask her to stay. But she said it herself. Our relationship was based on a plan for revenge. Sure, it morphed into something completely different, something one hundred percent real, but that doesn't matter right now. All that matters is that once upon a time, she was nothing more to me than a body I would dispose of, one I would strip the life from and discard like yesterday's trash.

She pauses at the threshold of my door, and hope sparks in my chest. It's stupid that I'd even consider she'd ever forgive me one day. That we could move forward like none of this ever happened or start over, fresh and unscathed by my failings. The hope dies as immediately as it sparked, even when her head turns back, bringing me into focus, and our eyes anchor for a long torturous moment.

It's incredible what can be conveyed in a single look. It's frightening that the eyes hold so much power that verbal communication is unnecessary. I guess what they say is right, our eyes are the window to our soul. Right now, Codi's soul has been extinguished. The dullness in her gaze holds none of the glow of life I'm so used to seeing in her. It's gone and replaced with heartbreak and sorrow. She no longer knows where she belongs in the world. She looks lost and scared.

Her whole life, from the very beginning, has been a lie. Me included. She was content in the simplicity of her life, and now that's been taken away.

She blinks, and tears fall down her cheeks. She looks at me again, and I see it, her goodbye, crystal fucking clear in the purple eyes I've come to adore. It shines out at me in hate just before she turns and walks out of my life.

"How could we have been so fucking wrong?" Rocco's voice startles me. I almost forgot he was here, so caught up in watching Codi walk from my life, I'd forgotten the hell I was now left in. "How?" he repeats the word, stuttering along his broken breath.

I turn, walking toward the living area and dropping down beside him.

He turns toward me, the redness rimming his eyes, bordered by the wetness of his lashes. "How did Kane not fucking see what was right in front of him? He was supposed to fucking protect her, and his best friend killed her. His piece of shit brother-in-law was responsible for this agony all along."

Our mother was never safe. Not with Marcus around. Kane forced *loyalty* down our throats. He preached it time and time again. Yet, right under his nose, his trust was being violated regularly. By the one person he placed his confidence in, probably more so than anyone else.

I want to think I'd know if Rocco was lying to me forcefully. Maybe my father didn't want to see it, or perhaps the power of his position inflated his ego so heavily that he couldn't consider, for a second, that anyone would betray him. His stupidity wrote his downfall. Unfortunately, our mother became collateral in his idiocy.

"I killed her," Rocco admits softly, and I turn to him, confusion lining my forehead. "Mira," he clarifies. "I was so caught up in my misguided need for revenge that I killed her. I may as well have pulled the trigger myself."

"Roc—"

"Fuck. Even the bullet was meant for me." A fresh wave of tears hit him, and he angrily brushes them away. "He was going to fucking kill me, Parker. Without a single hesitation. His own fucking nephew. I didn't even see her move. I saw the gun, saw him pull the trigger, and then she was there. Before I could even comprehend she'd moved, the bullet..." He closes his eyes tightly, his hands pulling at his hair, a thick sob ripping from his mouth.

"She. Fucking. Died. For. *Me*. Why the fuck would she do that?"

Using the back of my hand, I wipe away my tears. "She loved you, Roc. She loved us. She made a promise to Mom to protect us. She did right by Mom," I finish softly, knowing the love that ran through Mira's veins. She wasn't our mom, not technically, but she was close enough and the only one we'd known for the past eighteen years.

"I need to get her blood off our floor. It doesn't belong there. She shouldn't be remembered as a pool of blood on the ground," he declares out of nowhere, standing quickly and moving away.

"Roc—"

"Help me. We need to get rid of any reminders of *him* as well. I want everything from this day to go. Far the fuck away."

We spend the next few hours scrubbing the floors, watching the diluted red liquid pour down the sink. The last of Marcus and Mira's lives washed away down the drain.

"At least he's dead," I speak at my feet when we're done, standing in our kitchen, lost in emptiness in uncertainty. "I just wish I'd been the one to pull the trigger, not Dominic."

TWENTY-SIX

CODI

"At least you're dressed," Ryn comments, moving into the room, a long-sleeved black blouse tucked neatly into her black pants.

I glance down at my attire, similar to hers, but ignore her comment, refusing to speak.

"I want you to try and talk to him today, Codi. You can't go on like this. It's not healthy."

I raise an eyebrow in challenge. "Pot, meet kettle."

Her head shakes from side to side, anger, and disapproval twisting her lips.

I offer her the same, my head turning away to avoid the judgmental glare in her eyes. "My trust and my love were violated. Same pretext."

Her bottom lip tips out in disgust, her head once again shaking hotly in disagreement. "Parker is nothing like him. He's a good person. You know that, Codi."

"Why are you defending him?" I bite out, betrayed by her want for me to look past everything that happened without question.

She saw what happened. She knows what he did. He inserted me into his foolish sea of hatred, and now I'm drowning in it too. I can't catch my breath. I can't find the strength to swim out of my anger and hatred.

Because. Of. Him.

"Babe, I'm not defending anyone. I'm not justifying his actions. I'm not telling you what he did was okay. I'm also not telling you that he's the most disgusting human being on the planet, completely lacking any soul."

She moves in front of the TV, thwarting my view of Jax Teller in the shower, and I scowl over at her. She huffs, rolling her eyes and leaning forward to retrieve the remote. The screen goes black, and she throws the remote out of reach, turning back to me.

"I was watching that," I grumble, crossing my arms over my chest.

"Look, Codi. I get it. I *get* why Parker did it. I'd die for a chance at vengeance. I'd do anything to kill the monsters in my mind. To finally find peace and not be woken by my nightmares."

I look at the sincerity, the truth on her face. The scowl stamped along my face eases because, more than anything, I would want that for her too.

"I would take it in a heartbeat. I think about how good it would feel to kill *him,* to rid his body of breath, of life. To take from him what he so effectively has taken from me. So, I *get* it."

"Ryn," I start, but she shakes her head, moving closer, sitting on the coffee table, and leaning forward.

"He was a kid, Codi. A little kid whose mom was *murdered.* Brutally. And when she died, the good in his life died with her. He's known nothing but hate and the want for blood since that moment. You can't hate him for that."

"I don't," I admit softly. "I don't hate him for wanting revenge. God, when he told me, I told him never to feel sorry for the people that brought that onto him. I told him to find his revenge. But he *used* me."

Ryn sighs loudly, her shoulder dancing in an almost shrug, her head moving with indifference. "He thought our dad did that to him. It was a logical thought. No one would have assumed Sarah and Marcus had woven such a fucking cesspool of deceit."

"Don't bring *him* up."

"Codi, babe, you'll need to deal with this sooner or later. Dad's hurting. You've cut him out."

"Dad?" I spit. "Oh. My dad's not hurting. He's dead."

"You know what I mean."

I look away in shame.

"Back to Parker. He and his brother wanted revenge, and they deserved that. They deserved peace. Sure, their hate was misguided, but that was because they were fed a lie for the entirety of their lives. You can't resent Parker for that. They paid the ultimate price. They lost the only family they had left," she adds accusingly at the end.

She waits for me to speak, but I have nothing to say. Everything she said rang true. *Everything.* But that doesn't mean all is forgiven. How could it be? Everything we built our relationship on was deceit. I don't know what was real and what wasn't. I can tell myself that every tiny snippet of vulnerability he showed me was true, but I don't know that any more than I think he does. Surely, he's confused about where his lie started, and his truth began. Of when his lie morphed, with or without his knowledge or permission, into something forbidden. He knew our relationship could never go any further. That's why he talked in riddles and spoke of our expiration date.

I was planning for our future while he was planning my

funeral. I saw marriage and kids, and he saw my death as his peace. I fell in love while he was still lost in hate.

Is it even possible to fall in love when you're so drowned by hatred? They say the line between love and hate is a thin one. That I understand. You can love someone powerfully but become so burned by their betrayal that the intensity of your feelings morphs into something unpleasant. Gone is the sense of completeness, happiness, and contentment. In its place, the festering echo of emptiness, pain, misery, and regret begins to eat away at you.

But can it really be said for the opposite? Is there really a thin line between *hate* and love?

How can an immense feeling of animosity turn into something of fondness? How can you start aiming to inflict pain and impose the worst possible kind of hurt on someone but find love? The two feelings don't go hand in hand, not this way. It's impossible to build a foundation of love, a deep feeling of infatuation and affection, on feelings of hostility and loathing.

I *hate* Marcus Dempsey with everything inside of my body, and I know deep in my heart I would never have found it in my heart to *love* him even if he was my dad, biologically speaking.

So how could Parker have ever truly loved me when his innermost thoughts, his deepest feelings for me, began in bitterness? I guess, in truth, he never actually told me he *loved* me. Sure, his actions showed he cared deeply for me. But maybe that was guilt. Perhaps I misread it all along.

Tears sting my eyes, and I will them not to fall. I'm so tired. I feel stupid. Melodramatic. I can't control the swell of emotions coursing through my veins. It's frightening how the thoughts in your mind can elicit such powerful *physical* reactions in your body. People regularly claim they're ruled by their hearts. But I disagree. The mind is *so* dominating, so consuming. In reality, that overwhelming need in your heart, that burning desire you can't ignore, is powered by the driving thoughts in your head. In your unforgiving and relentless mind.

If I could remove Parker from my mind, I'm confident that the suffocating pain I can't seem to escape from would dissipate. It would go, and I'd be given a reprieve from the chronic agony my mind is insisting I live through. Day after day. Hour after hour. Minute after minute.

My grief hits me wherever and whenever the hell it wants. I can feel stronger, more collected, plodding on, persevering, and *boom,* I'm crippled with anguish. Fresh tears will hit me out of nowhere, and every moment spent with Parker replays like a movie, torturing me with what I've lost, and it's only been a week. Is this the torture I'll be subjected to for the rest of my life?

I wrestle with every negative emotion possible.

I'm drowned in grief, struggling to find my breath through the genuine agony of my heartache, the stuttered sobs that force their way into my throat, and the endless supply of tears that sap me to the point of dehydration.

My anger spikes when my grief has consumed me for hours and days. I feel hate. So much that my skin burns with animosity and rage. At Sarah. At Marcus. Dominic. Kane. Rocco. Parker. *At myself.*

Then the despair hits—the loneliness. I'm moving through the monotony of life, no longer wanting to survive. Not without him. Without the man that cursed us to live without one another by inserting me into an ill-directed plan of revenge.

I go to bed every night missing every last thing about him. I fall asleep with tears in my eyes and self-hatred blackening my fragile heart. What kind of idiot longs for someone who caused them so much pain?

It seems I do. Achingly so.

Am I convincing myself he was *more* to find forgiveness for myself? For wanting him, knowing I shouldn't?

My dreams are filled with him.

The smile he rarely lets free; the sweet, damaged sweetness to the gesture.

The way he'd touch me like he couldn't help himself; the need was too great. His addiction to me is just as dependent as mine on him.

The strength of his body.

The demons in his eyes.

Even unconsciously, he consumes me.

That's why I crave the single moment when I wake. The quiet breath between unconsciousness and awareness when I feel *nothing*. When my mind is pushed into a state of rest, and it's yet to catch me up.

I feel free.

Unburdened.

My heart isn't broken.

My mind isn't consumed with Parker, and I can take a single breath before it hits me again. Like a freight train. Forcefully. Fatally. Unforgiving.

I wonder how long I can survive this murderous routine without wanting to die. My torture begins every morning, and I count down to that moment again, if only to be able to fill my lungs with air and not pain.

The overwhelming need to cry is the worst. I can't fight it. No matter how hard I try, and hell if I don't try my hardest to keep them at bay. But I'm hopeless against their power.

So I hide. In my bathroom, doors closed, water running, trying to shut myself away. If Camryn knows, she doesn't let on. I'm grateful she offers me my broken moments in solitary.

I consider that I'm grieving him as though he's dead. He's

lost to me. Likely forever. But it always gives me pause because in those moments, hidden away to let my grief paint my face with the saltiness of my tears. I allow myself to consider his pain after losing his mom.

Could I survive this for almost twenty years without it irrevocably changing something deep in my soul?

I know I couldn't, and I forgive him that bit more in those retrospective moments. Until one day, I began to reflect on whether I ever really blamed him.

"You ready?" Camryn pulls me from my thoughts, and I nod solemnly, standing to readjust my clothing.

"I've never been to a funeral," I state unnecessarily, and she nods, handing me my purse as we leave our apartment.

The drive is quiet, a thick emotion drifting between us in the car.

"I can't get the blood out of my mind," Camryn finally speaks. "I don't understand it. There was no exit wound. Obviously, I understand the science behind it. The heart continues to pump blood even without brain activity. It's the nerve cells," she explains as she drives. "I just... It was a tiny wound. A single bullet, but the blood, on her face, on Rocco's hands as he tried to get it off, only to make it worse." She exhales heavily. "I just can't get it out of my head."

"She died in slow motion for me," I admit. "I don't remember the blood, apart from what was on me. But I remember seeing her face, this one single tear falling along her cheek as she stepped in front of Rocco." My hand covers my face, and I work to control my breathing, not wanting to become lost in my emotions. "I remember thinking that I would've done the same. If it was you. If it were your child, I wouldn't hesitate. All I can try and force peace from is the fact that Mira died doing something she'd never in her life regret. That has to stand for something, right?"

HIS BLACK SUIT hugs his body perfectly. A thin black tie, roughly loosened, hangs around his neck. The delicateness of the petals from the rose tattooed along his neck peek from the crisp white dress shirt underneath his dark jacket.

Like the one inked into his neck and the one inked along his tricep, a single white rose is held loosely in his hands. He hasn't noticed me. He hasn't noticed much of anything. His eyes remain downcast, like Rocco's, staring blankly at Mira's coffin. She hovers above the earth, readying to be lowered as her family says their final goodbyes.

There aren't many people here. Rocco and Parker, a few other unfamiliar faces. No one of importance to the two brothers, neither having acknowledged their presence.

My dad, Camryn, and I keep back for respect more than anything. I'm not sure if our family would be welcome. It's better this way, with us standing away. Still paying our respects but trying our best to do it respectfully.

An older man officiating the service speaks in a quiet drone of words. I'm not listening to what he's saying. It's not personal, not to Mira. It's a customary collection of words that are undoubtedly recited at every service. Instead, I kept my focus on Parker. On the single white rose held in his hand. The one that seems to signify loss for him. Maybe that's why he's inked it into his skin more than once—a reminder of all he's lost in life.

My heart aches for him. In every sense.

It hurts for the pain he must be feeling.

But it longs for him too. I miss him, and I hate myself for

that. It feels wrong admitting that at someone's funeral. Mira should be the only thing on my mind. I know I didn't *know* her, but that's why we're here, supporting the people grieving her. But all I can think about is how my heart beat faster when I saw him again. How I'd give anything to meet his eyes, just once. How I miss the sound of his voice. The feel of his hands. The touch of his lips. His smile. His smell.

All the things I shouldn't let myself admit. Because I hate him. He pushed me over that thin line of love and hate. With excessive force. He sent me sailing to the other side, lost in the negativity of my emotions, and I don't know how to claw my way back.

Rocco steps forward, dropping his rose, identical to Parker's, along Mira's coffin. He whispers his words of farewell too quietly for the rest of us to hear. But I respect that. His goodbye is between him and Mira. No one else. It's theirs. No one else should be privy to those final words.

Finally, he steps back, and Parker moves forward. He brings his rose to his face, eyes closing as he inhales the soft warmth of the scent. I watch as he touches his lips to the top petals, pausing briefly before dropping it next to Rocco's. His goodbye is said silently as well, his lips moving without sound.

Stepping back in line with his brother, his face finally lifts, and our eyes connect. I was ready for the pain, for shock, for anger even. I wasn't prepared for the vacancy in the swirling gray storm in his eyes. The emptiness. The nothingness. He barely even reacts before focusing back on Mira's coffin.

The coffin begins to lower, and watching her descend into the earth is awful. I choose to focus on Parker and Rocco instead of Mira, and I'm grateful they have one another.

Their hands connect, holding on tight. So forcefully that even through their suit jackets, I can see the muscles in their arms shake with intensity. The angular cut of their jawlines are wired shut, and I know it's to stop the sound of heartbreak from escaping their lips. Their heads turn, bringing one another into focus, and their eyes stay that way, anchored as Mira disappears, now nothing more than a wooden box ready to be buried in the dirt.

His eyes meet mine for a split second again, but he turns, walking away without a backward glance.

"Are you gonna follow him?" Ryn asks softly, watching their retreat.

"And say what? I'm sorry for your loss, you know, the one the man who spawned me forced upon you when he killed your aunt."

I turn and move in the opposite direction Parker and Rocco left in, dad and Camryn fast on my heels.

"You know, negative, mean Codi, I don't like her much. Seriously, I get your life is a lot fucked up right now, but we're here." She gestures between herself and Dad as she rushes to keep up with my power walk. "We're *trying* to be here for you, and you're shutting us out. Let us help you."

My feet stop, and I sigh, turning toward them both. I see the pain in my father's eyes, the want to fix what seems to have broken between us now the truth has forced its way in and pushed us apart. I look away fast, unable to meet the hurt in his face without feeling shame for the way I'm acting.

"I'm allowed to feel lost right now," I whisper defensively. "I'm allowed to have a selfish minute and try to work out the mess in my mind. I *need* that. Let me have it," I argue, the fight in my words lost, the demand sounding more like a plea.

"Camryn," Dad warns her off, and I sigh in relief.

"Codi," he starts, and I swallow the nerves in my throat, meeting his eyes. Eyes that are so different from mine, so similar to Camryn's. *"We're* your family. You're allowed to be mixed up by everything that's happened, but when you're ready, you come to us. We'll be waiting, and we'll move on together. As a unit. The three of us. As we've always done."

The hope in his voice magnifies my shame. Dominic Rein is formidable, respected, and assertive. Yet here, he's just a simple man, a dad, trying to do the right thing. Even when everything inside him is screaming for him to take charge, to *make* me see. But he knows me. Almost as well as Ryn does. And he knows I need this.

TWENTY-SEVEN

ROCCO

Standing on the outside looking in, I take in the opulence of Codi's apartment building. Of course, it's overtly showy. She is a Rein, after all, and her father does nothing by halves.

Once upon a time, standing out here like a fool would have pissed me off and fueled the fire of my temper, having to *wait* for a Rein no less. In reality, my entire life has been me on the outside of the Rein empire, staring in. Waiting, watching. It was all in vain. Not that I had any way of knowing that. Still, a pointless endeavor that caused me nothing but a more profound pain.

Attempting to get into the building would've been futile, so I've been forced to loiter, hoping like fuck Codi will eventually appear.

"Rocco." Camryn Rein pushes through the glass, stopping only a few feet from where I stand. "What are you doing here?"

Her face forces memories I'm struggling to suppress to flash into my mind's forefront. *Blood.* Lots of it. Coating her hands. Her forehead creased in concentration as she worked to clean the oozing red liquid from Mira's face.

She did it, though, without hesitation, without knowing fuck all about us. Aside from the small, insignificant fact that Parker and I had plans to off her sister, of course.

I clear my throat, standing to full height as I bury my hands into the pockets of my jeans. Her eyes skate over me in bored indifference. Her gaze moves over my body, across my chest, and to my face without a single emotion.

I offer her the same dress down. Her body is hidden under ill-fitting light blue scrubs that cover her from chest to toes. She wears a hoodie on top, combating the cooler weather and further hindering my ability to see what her body looks like.

Her brown hair is tied haphazardly on top of her head, no care has been taken to make it neat, and her face is free of makeup. The freckles across the bridge of her nose are a shade darker than her complexion, and her eyes a denim blue.

"I'm looking for Codi." I step forward, and she shuffles backward, an eyebrow rising in an unmistakable warning to back the fuck off.

"Forgive me if I'm not overly forthcoming on my sister's whereabouts, you know, considering you had plans to take her life."

I work to quash the amused grin threatening to spill onto my lips. "I deserve that. I'm not here for me, though. I want to talk to her about Parker."

Her teeth worry at her bottom lip, indecision plaguing her. "What about Parker?"

"About the fact that he's in love with your sister, and they belong together, and I'd appreciate it if they sorted that shit, like fucking yesterday, so I can stop watching him wallow."

A small bark of laughter shoots from her lips, transforming her face. She's hot. She just doesn't want anyone to know it, so she hides under her baggy clothes and resting bitch face.

"Thank fuck. Codi refuses to leave the apartment most days. Something's gotta give," she sighs heavily, checking her watch as she moves a few more steps away from me. "She went out to grab... *groceries* maybe half an hour ago. She'll be back any minute."

I nod my thanks, and she twists on her heel, walking down the sidewalk without a backward glance. She pauses about ten steps down, taking a breath before spinning. "He hurts her again, and I'll hunt him down and kill him."

I feel an eyebrow rise on my face, and this time I don't attempt to hide my smirk. "We should hang out sometime."

"HA," she yells, louder than necessary. "In your dreams, Romeo. I like a little less psycho with my sex."

"I didn't say anything about fucking, dreamer."

Her confidence wavers, but she schools it quickly enough, exaggerating an eye roll. "Try not to kill anyone while you're waiting for Codi. Let's not do this again."

My quiet laughter follows her retreat, and I watch her until she disappears from sight.

I despised the Rein girls for most of my life. I hated what I thought they stood for, what I thought their family cost me. Situation the way it stands, they should loathe me, likely fear me and the fucked up thoughts that cloud my mind. Yet Camryn Rein didn't look at me with contempt or alarm. They're good people, they were raised right, and Parker and I don't deserve the good in their hearts. That doesn't mean I won't fight to convince Codi otherwise.

Parker's hurting. It's not just losing Mira that's spiraling him into a self-destructive depression. He fell in love, and he believes he lost it. My brother is nursing a broken fucking heart, and it's the one thing I have no experience in helping him heal.

He's thrown himself into work. I can't get him to leave that fucking club. He's there all hours of the night and most of the day. He locks himself away in his office, doing fuck knows what. He comes home to shower, catches an hour of sleep if he feels so inclined, then he's back out the door.

I'm not allowed to mention his woman. He loses his fucking head, and I'm done with him having his man period.

Moping. Sulking. He refuses even to try and make it right between him and Codi. He won't talk to me about it. He closes it off as not up for discussion.

"You've got a lot of nerve coming to my house."

My head tips up, watching Codi shift nervously in front of me, her words fierce, body language painting a different story.

I glance at the pint of ice cream clutched tightly in her hands.

Groceries.

Fucking women.

The plastic spoon in her hand tells me she started drowning her sorrows in sugar as soon as she left the shop.

Reaching forward, I grab the ice cream, holding out my hand for the spoon. She frowns but hands it over, moving to sit beside me.

"Is this my last supper? Sharing a meal before you stab me with my spoon?"

I bark out a laugh. "What is this?"

"Cookie dough with chocolate fudge sauce."

Nice. I take a large mouthful, watching her as I swallow it down.

"Nah," I speak again when my mouth is empty, shoveling another heap onto the spoon. "That threat died when your dad killed... your dad."

She rolls her eyes, snatching the spoon from my hand and stealing my mouthful. "Hilarious. Regular comedian you are," she speaks around the fullness of her mouth, her words slurring together as a drop of ice cream flies from her mouth. She throws her hand over her mouth, having the decency to look embarrassed.

She hands me back the spoon, and we sit silently, passing the ice cream back and forth.

"I'm sorry he killed your aunt," she finally whispers, and my breath falters.

Fuck. She feels guilty. Who is this girl?

"Codi, Mira's death is on Marcus. Maybe on me as well. But no one else."

"I can't believe he was my dad," she admits, and the pain in the words makes it obvious enough I'm the first person she's trusted with that statement.

It's odd that she would confide that in me, but maybe she sees the messed-up maze of my brain and is looking for someone to help solve her own.

"He wasn't," I retort. "Trust me, Codi. Marcus Dempsey cared for no one but himself. He was an evil motherfucker. He knew you were his your whole life and never attempted to reach out. Laying that out there was his way of inflicting maximum pain before he died. Don't let him win."

She's silent for a moment, contemplating my words. "But my dad, *Dominic*," she corrects. "He *lied* to me. My whole life."

"Did he ever make you feel like he resented your existence? That you weren't his reason for breathing?"

"No," she concedes quietly.

"Because in his mind, whether biologically you were his or not, you were *his*."

I scrape the last of the ice cream from the tub, smiling at the irritated glare that crosses her face.

"You got good inside you, Codi Rein. That comes from

Dominic, him loving you right. The way a parent should. The way my mom loved Parker and me. The way Mira loved us."

"Truthfully, would you have ever wanted to know?" I push. "That Marcus was biologically your *real* dad? Or would you've preferred to be kept in the dark? Given a choice?"

"In the dark," she speaks without hesitation.

I shrug. "Then you know it's because your dad is your dad, not some asshole that fucked your mom."

She goes quiet again, nodding at my words, hands trapped between her knees.

"Mom gave us a good life. We were happy. We didn't hate the world like we do now. After she died, our dad morphed into someone else entirely. His soul died along with her."

She listens intently as I speak.

"He beat on us. That's when he remembered we existed." I smile regretfully. "Most psychological childhood issues you could imagine, we experienced. Abandonment, death, abuse; physical, verbal, emotional, and mental. You name it. It was rained upon us daily. If it wasn't coming from Kane, Marcus was happy enough to step up and take the reins."

"That's horrible," she whispers, but when I look at her, she's caught in her head, utterly oblivious to the fact that she had spoken, my words no doubt playing on a loop in her mind, imagining the lives we lived.

"Physically, I took most of it on." I wait for her to look at me again. "Parker thinks I'm some hero because I'd let their fists touch me more than him. But after a while, the physical blows you can numb out. Pretend it's someone else beating on your ass and not your own father. Or uncle."

A tear rolls down her cheek, and I pause briefly, letting it slide down off her skin, falling onto her sweater in a silent splash.

"Parker, as much as he'd like to pretend otherwise, he's sensitive. I fight to take control, but he lets himself get lost in here." I tap my temple.

"I did this, Codi. With my stupid plan. We had to find vengeance for our mother. It was all me. I forced it inside of him, and every time I saw him waver off the path, which was all the fucking time, I'd play on his emotions. I'd bring up our mom, what we lost, and what we were forced to live with. I'd fuel his heartbreak. I prolonged it, nurtured it, and when he'd push against my need for revenge, I'd play on his guilt."

"Why me?" She says. "Why not my dad, my mom, my..." She stops herself before her sister's name escapes her lips. "Why me? Why now?" She questions quietly.

I think about the years that passed up until this moment. I guess I owe her this. An explanation of sorts, no matter how empty it might sound to her.

"We were young when our dad died. Far too young to act on his vengeance, *effectively* anyway. Through those first few years, I was so busy trying to survive the nightmare that our life had become, working to keep Mira and Parker safe, avenging my mother had to take a back seat," I admit regretfully.

She watches me intently, searching for answers I'm not really sure she wants to hear.

"When Park and I finally got free from living under Dempsey's thumb, he worked so hard to keep us close, trying in vain to keep the Shay empire alive."

My palm comes up to scratch along my beard, hating having to reminisce about my younger years. "We had no interest in being a part of the world our father was. It took the most important person from our lives. We wanted nothing to do with what our father built. We would've been happy if everything he had burnt to the ground in flames."

She nods in understanding, a sad, sympathetic smile crawling onto her face.

"Marcus eventually gave up trying to pull us into that world. The flames we craved didn't happen, but the Shay empire slowly but surely started cracking, falling away until it no longer existed. Through that, I ensured Parker finished school, and then he came to me with his plans for Ruin. When he was settled and had everything he needed, it gave me the time I needed to focus on the agony inside my heart."

Leaning forward to brace my elbows on my knees, I glance back over my shoulder at her. She's staring right at me, waiting patiently for me to continue.

"I thought about killing your dad," I admit to the concrete stairs, my face trained downward. "Thought about ending it there and being done with it, but I wanted him to hurt. I wanted him to suffer the way I did, the way Parker did. I wanted him to feel as lost and aimless as I have my entire life. Killing him wouldn't have achieved that."

I sigh loudly, pushing myself back, elbows resting on the step behind me. "I watched Sarah for the briefest time, and it didn't take too much to realize her death wouldn't cause him anything but relief. That left you and your sister."

She shifts on her spot, twisting her body toward mine, her knees pulling up to her chest. She likely hasn't noticed the defensive ball she's rolled herself into.

"Your sister caught my attention but not in the way I wanted. There's blackness in her soul. Like mine," I confess. "She's closed off to the world and lives dangerously inside her head."

I swallow deeply. "That left you. You were so fucking happy, and I hated you on sight. You reminded me of my mom." I let her hear the vulnerability in my admission, a truth I've never vocalized until this very moment. "You were happy, carefree, you were *good*. I couldn't stomach it, so I forced Parker's involvement."

She moves to touch me, her hand lifting to grab my arm in reassurance, but she second guesses, her hand balling into a fist and dropping back to her lap.

"You're the sunshine of the Rein family, Codi. I knew they'd drown in darkness if I took you away from them. Just like I did."

Silence falls heavily between us, and she watches me closely as she swallows my words. Finally, she pulls in a large breath. Stretching from her defensive ball, she turns again to face the street.

"I appreciate you telling me all this. I do. But he *deceived* me, Rocco. I get what you're saying, and I understand your want for revenge. I don't actually hate either of you for that. But I fell in love with your brother when I was nothing more than a pawn in a twisted plan for him. Maybe his feelings morphed into something more, but everything we shared was based on something that wasn't *real*, on *hate*."

"The plan was never for him to know you. He was charged with learning your routine, watching you," I confess, and her eyebrows shoot up in interest. "He was drawn to you before he even spoke to you. He chose to continue to spend time with you because he wanted to, not out of loyalty to me."

"He liked the way I looked," she argues.

A grunt of laughter passes my lips. "That too. But that only goes so far. Trust me. Parker fell in love with you all on his honest lonesome."

I stand, jogging down the few steps before turning back to her. "He hates himself right now. I tried to have this conversation with him first, but he doesn't think he deserves you." Her eyes close over in pain, and I shrug. "Maybe he's right, but I hope you think otherwise."

I look down the street, breathing heavily. "Codi, you guys fell in love in a pretty fucking hopeless situation, but still, you fell in love, even with all that clouding you. Surely that's enough to prove that whatever you guys have going on is worth fighting for."

I crack my knuckles in nervous anticipation, waiting for her to give me *anything* to indicate I've gotten through.

"You seem very insightful for an angry person."

"I prefer broody or dark and mysterious." I smile, and she rolls her eyes. "Codi, look at everything I've lost. I've spent my entire life lost in hate, and maybe I'll never escape the destruction of that place. That doesn't mean you and Parker can't."

TWENTY-EIGHT

CODI

I stare at the door, thumbnail caught between my teeth, almost willing it to be locked. God, I never thought I'd actually make it here. I left home intending to seek him out, but honestly, I thought I'd chicken out. I even walked to give myself plenty of opportunities to reconsider, but my focus was absolute. With every step closer to the club, I felt more determined, more convinced of the fact that I *needed* to see him. No matter what the outcome.

Truthfully, I'm unsure what I will say or even my intention in coming here. Reconciliation or closure? I have no clue. I know I need to see him. Talk to him. Based on how easily he looked through me the last time I saw him, I hope he doesn't just turn me away.

Rocco's words haven't moved from my head in days, not since I found him waiting on my stoop.

Firstly, the bastard stole my ice cream. Not cool. I changed into somewhat presentable attire to search down my cookie dough and fudge sauce pint of sugar. Then he devoured more than half of it while he decided to impart his wisdom upon me. Who would've thought Parker's psychotic older brother could be so understanding, so... *insightful?*

But I couldn't fault a single thing he said. So to save myself from waging war inside my head, I focused on what I could handle first.

My dad.

Rocco was right. Genetics be damned. I know who my dad is. I know who loved me throughout my life and who taught me all that is right in the world. The man that kissed my scraped knees and spent hours helping me with homework. The man who scared away my nightmares and held me close whenever I needed to cry. The man who has always made me feel protected and loved.

Dominic Rein. No one else. Only him.

Our apologies were emotional, but I feel closer to him, more than I ever have before. Maybe it's because I know his love is absolute. He *chose* to love me, to claim me as his daughter. There was no obligation or ulterior motive for him doing so. He wanted to be my dad, so as far as I'm concerned. He is. No question. No doubt.

"THAT'S *what you meant when you said she had the ability to crush you,*" *I test, and he ducks his head to hide the emotion disturbing the smooth lines of his face.*

"*I couldn't risk you thinking you weren't mine because you are, Codi. In every way that matters.*" *His open palm patting the part of his chest where his heart beats steadily.*

I nod through my tears.

"*I'd be lying if I said I wasn't frightened you'd want to meet* him. Marcus Dempsey had evil running through his veins. I couldn't let that touch you. Maybe I shouldn't have lied to you, but as long as you know, there was never any malice behind my deceit, that it was all done in love." He shrugs, the hopeful glint in his eyes shining brightly.

"Did you know it was him from the beginning?"

He shakes his head. "No. Not until after Kane died. They became reckless. They knew murder wasn't my style. They didn't care if I knew."

I watch him for a quiet second. "Did it hurt knowing she was cheating?"

He smiles ruefully. "No. I quite enjoyed the days she'd disappear with him. It was just you, me, and Camryn."

"The three amigos," I laugh softly, recalling my childhood.

Wrapping an arm over my shoulders, he pulls me close, kissing my forehead. "The three amigos."

WE WERE GOOD, and that left me all the time in the world to stew about Parker. Rocco was right. We fell hopelessly in love and in love hopelessly. The situation was tangled and thorny. Like Parker's roses, beautiful and flourishing. But in reality, when you looked hard enough and got down to the inner workings, it was barbed and bound to cause pain the harder we tried to hold on.

Swallowing my nerves, I push against the heavy metal door at the side entrance of Ruin, wanting to vomit the moment it inches open. Forcing my doubts aside, I use greater pressure to move the door, cringing when it slams with a loud bang behind me.

I pause briefly, listening for any sound to indicate company, but only silence waves back at me in the darkened space.

It takes me a second to find my bearings, completely turned around by the entrance I took into the club. It's different in the light of day. Still dark, but not enough to cut off my vision. I turn for the main stairs, Parker's office my destination. I went to the loft first, but no one was home. Thank God. Truth be told, I wasn't ready to step foot into the space just yet. Standing on the other side of the closed door, I could visualize it all. Mira's body. Marcus' body. The pools and splatters of blood.

No, I'm happy he wasn't home. Talking this out will be hard enough without Mira and Marcus' ghosts dancing around us. Their presence in our lives is heavy enough.

The door to his office is closed, and I knock softly as I try the handle. It opens without issue, and I slide inside, my back resting against the wood as I lean against it to close it again.

"Roc," he starts, back to me, a sigh long and heavy in his voice. "Told you to leave me be. I don't want to talk about it. Not about what happened, about them, him and I sure as fucking shit don't wanna talk about *her*."

God, I missed the sound of his voice, the thick, rough rasp when he bites out.

"Random fact." I clear my throat, and he whirls around, the drink in his hand spilling along the carpet. "It's too early in the morning to drink."

He watches me cautiously, moving backward, *away* from me to rest his butt against the brick ledge of his window. He twirls his glass in his hand, considering it momentarily before swallowing the contents and discarding the glass on the surface next to him.

"That's an opinion, not a fact. Try again."

I let go of the breath held tightly in my lungs, my eyes scanning over him eagerly.

His jeans are tight along his thick thighs. The material pulled tautly, his legs spread wide, knees slightly bent, pulling at the dark light-washed denim. Inked arms are crossed over his chest, the white shirt stretching over his large frame. The meticulous attention to his hair is lost, no effort having been placed in making it look presentable, it standing on end in every direction. The dark shadows under his eyes are heavy, the glint in his eyes lost, clouded with a cocktail of painful emotions.

God, do I miss him. And I'm mad at myself for needing to admit that.

He lets my gaze drift over him without a single word, waiting patiently for me to speak again.

"My dad's name is Dominic Rein."

An emotion close to relief settles through his body, his eyes closing briefly before landing on me again.

"That's good to hear, Sugar."

My heart twinges at the endearment slipping from his lips. I've missed the coarse gentleness in the way he says it—the emotion behind the simple word.

It's not hard to miss the regret and the remorse in his simple statement. He wasn't there to help me through one of my life's biggest moments of turmoil. He let me wade through it alone, and I can tell now that's eaten away at his conscience. The guilt remains, but still, he's pleased I came through it relatively unscathed.

"I had some assistance from an unexpected source who helped me find reason."

He raises an eyebrow, and I smile unintentionally, shrugging. "Rocco."

He grunts out a silent laugh, the sound showing no inclination of surprise, but maybe it shouldn't. Rocco admitted he tried to talk Parker around. Unsuccessfully, but still, he tried.

"Your turn," I whisper when the quiet expands between us.

He inhales heavily through his nostrils, indecision dancing along his face.

"Fact," he finally speaks. "You shouldn't be here."

My chin wobbles involuntarily, and I bite my bottom lip to stop it, trying in vain to ignore the stabbing pain in my chest.

"That's an opinion. Not a fact. Try again." I stumble over the words, my voice cracking more than once.

He looks away from the challenge, shaking his head and dismissing me. The pulse in his neck ticks, pounding in rhythm with his erratic heartbeat.

After a long, uncomfortable silence, I try again. "Random fact." He turns back to the sound of my voice, a twisted look of appreciation and agony in his eyes. "I feel hate inside me. So much of it. Against Marcus. Against Sarah. Against the circumstances that brought us together. But more than anything, the hate I have that *floods* my insides is for myself."

He looks wounded by my declaration.

"*Sugar,*" he whispers. He didn't mean to speak. He wanted to remain dormant. Silent. He wanted to appear unfeeling, unaffected by my presence, by my words. But his mind and body are working their damnedest to give him away.

"I detest myself because I *should* hate you. I should despise every single thing about you, Parker Shay. I've tried to convince myself that I do. What you did to me is unforgivable, and I have tried so hard to forget you. *So hard.*"

I see the effect of my words, the emotions they stir.

"You should go," he croaks out, denying his feelings. Denying *me.*

I take a step forward, and he stands to full height.

"But I don't," I bite out, demanding he listens. "I don't hate you, not even slightly." I pull at the sleeves of my sweater, nervously playing with the material, working to find comfort in the barrier it's supposed to provide. But it's futile. I feel naked. Open. *Bared.* Standing before him, letting him see my heart struggling to beat without him.

"It's not possible." My voice cracks over the tortured whisper. "How can you despise someone whose love makes you feel *so complete*, you couldn't imagine ever finding happiness without them? How can you hate someone when they're your reason for breathing? The reason that you want to get out of bed in the morning. The reason you smile. The reason you laugh. The reason you wanna live when your life is falling apart around you."

I wait quietly for a single moment, for the slightest indication that he'll give me something. *Anything.* But he doesn't. He only continues to stare at me.

"Random. Fact," I punctuate. "I *trust* that everything you gave me, every small detail of your life you shared, *empty* or not, was real. Everything we felt. Everything we shared. Everything that grew between us. It. Was. *Real.*" I massage the spot my heart beats steadily behind. "I can see it. Even now. My heart is standing right in front of me, the monster in his mind dancing behind his eyes, forcing him to second guess *everything.*"

I see the unintentional tick of his jaw. The thick up and down movement of his Adam's apple. The almost undetectable quiver in this shadowed line of his chin.

"Push it away, Parker," I plead. "*Baby,* please. I'm standing right here, telling you I *love* you."

My declaration swims between us, hanging heavily in the air. He wants to reach out and grab hold of it.

"Maybe I shouldn't." I shrug when he continues to choose

silence. "Maybe it's not typically *right*. But I don't care. I know what I feel."

The inked fingers of one hand rub forcefully against the inked palm of the other, and I watch the violence in the gesture. He's torn between what he thinks is right and what his heart is telling him to trust.

"Tell me you don't feel it back. Tell me you don't love me," I challenge, taking a step forward, but he moves out of my path, forcing the distance between us to remain.

"You asked me if I believe in redemption, and I said it's about perspective. I said that, in the end, you have to find forgiveness in yourself."

His tongue drags along the clean line of his top teeth before he bites down hard. Swallowing deeply, his lips push forward in a grimace, the thought of self-forgiveness coursing distastefully down his throat.

"I don't deserve forgiveness. From anyone."

He won't meet my eyes. His face is turned away, and his stare is focused on the empty wall to his right.

"You're right. You don't."

He startles at the hostility in my agreement. He was expecting me to argue, to dispute him, so the look of complete shock coating his features makes me smirk. He's confused, my behavior throwing a cloud of unease over him, making him shift uncomfortably where he stands.

"I'm not going to disagree with you, Parker. You planned to kill me. Of course, you don't *deserve* my forgiveness.

The self-loathing darkening his person magnifies, and I sigh. Loudly.

"Yet here I am." I shrug in defeat. "Against my better judgment, against what I *know* to be right, I'm giving you mine. Whether you want it or not."

His large, inked hand reaches up, pinching the bridge of his nose before sliding roughly down his unshaven face.

"You just need to forgive yourself," I test, eyes trained at my feet. "It's the least you can do and the only thing I'm asking you for."

Quiet descends, and I let that fire my hope. I let his indecision spike my faith that we'll find our way back to one another.

Parker coughs, clearing his throat, working to pull my attention. I give it to him, my head lifting slowly to let our eyes connect.

"You think you could look at me, for the rest of your life, knowing what I did, what I had planned, and not hate me, worse, be afraid of me?"

I nod well before his sentence has finished, and he shakes his head in disagreement.

"How?" he bites out.

"Because the alternative of living life without you is too painful," I whisper. "Because I know, deep down, you would never have hurt me. I trust what I felt, that what grew between us was, *is,* real."

His hand massages his neck uncomfortably. "Fuck, Codi. You were right to try and hate me. It's more than I deserve."

Silence descends, our eyes connected, and I hate the void he's intentionally building. Physically. Emotionally. He's detaching, fighting to anyway. I see the wall he's struggling to form. But he won't stop. Each time his self-loathing is torn down, he works doubly as hard to replace them with something new. Something darker, more disconnected.

"You think you love me because I was the first guy you let fuck you. Women do that shit all the time." He dismisses me, "They convince themselves it was something more."

I feel as though he's hit me. Thrown the hard brutality of his fist into my stomach, robbing me of air.

"Don't." I shake my head. "Don't you dare turn asshole to push me away."

"News-*fucking*-flash, Codi. I *am* an asshole," he spits, his words spiked in hate. They're directed at himself, saturated in disgust, dripping with contempt. "The sooner you fucking realize that the sooner you'll move on with your life."

"No," I stonewall.

"*No?*" he snarls. "No fucking what? You want a random fact? Here's one for you. *Random. Fucking. Fact,*" he growls, his voice rising with every syllable. "There was no plan for me to actually *know* you. I was doing recon, and I like the *fucking* way you looked. I wanted to *fuck* you, Codi. That's it. I saw you and thought, *fuck*, she'd look nice riding my dick."

My body shakes in anger, but I'm afraid to speak. Petrified that if I attempt words, I'll cry. That I'll beg for him to stop.

"Another one?" he yells, sliding the phone off his desk with excessive force. It's still plugged in, the cord choking its path, causing an almighty bang as it hits the side of his desk, the dull dial tone echoing across the stillness between us. "Random fact. I took your virginity knowing my brother and I would *kill* you."

His eyes challenge me to argue. They dare me to disagree, to dispute his claim. But how can I? There's nothing to argue, to dispute. It's true—every painful word.

"Random fact," he speaks quietly, stepping out from behind his desk and moving toward me, the menace in his voice tickling at the base of my spine and traveling upward. He stops when he's directly in front of me, the hairs on the back of my neck standing on end. "I led you on. I made you fall in love when my goal was always to look you right in your pretty purple eyes and decorate your skull with a bullet hole."

I lift my chin with a confidence I don't feel. Meeting his eyes and hoping he can see the fire burning inside them. More importantly, I'm praying he mistakes that fire for fight and not panic.

"Our relationship was built on deceit. I can't deny that any more than you can. But you've never outwardly lied to me. In fact, you worked your hardest to convince me to remain cautious, to guard myself."

Recollecting on the few months we spent together, in truth, Parker warned me away at any given opportunity. He begged me to remain wary. He used the acid in his personality to hint at the damage he could cause. I chose to push all that away. I made the decision to ignore his warnings and let my heart become tangled with his. I opened myself up in every way possible, and he took it because whether he wants to admit it to me or not, he did the same. He'd argue what he *let* me see was hollow. But the truth is, in every tiny snippet of time we spent together, Parker offered me that little bit *more* of him. And before he knew it, he was lost, tangled, and caught on the thorns of our beautiful disaster just as much as I was.

"Just then, that was the first time you've *lied*. You like to think you've built up this impenetrable wall, but I got through. I. Got. *Through*." I stab a finger at his chest, and he scowls down at me, displeased at being called out.

"And now I'm pushing you back out. I'm sorry I broke your heart, Codi," he speaks, sounding anything but apologetic. He's gone flat. Emotionless. Vacant. "I'm not doing this. Not now. Not ever. I want to be done with all that shit from my past, and that includes you. Maybe in a different life... under different circumstances." He shrugs, taking a loaded step away from me. "You're better off without me. Find someone to fall in love with the right way. Learn from this. Most guys are pricks. Guard your heart. It's precious, Sugar. It just ain't mine."

He turns away from me before he's finished the quiet words that cut into my already damaged soul.

Everything inside of me is screaming to fight. To keep pushing. Everything but my heart. It's endured enough, and right now, it's done with hurting. There's only so much one measly organ can take before it has enough. And this is that time.

So I don't speak another word. I close my eyes, exhale heavily, turn and walk from the club with tears in my eyes and a large part of me still standing in his office.

There's only one place I want to be right now. The one placed I feel most loved. Protected. Cared for and needed. With my dad. He's the only person who, in this horrible mess, can make me see there's always hope.

TWENTY-NINE

PARKER

I lean forward again, pressing play on my laptop before slumping back into my chair. I bring my drink to my lips, tasting the bitterness of my gin slide along my tongue and down my throat. I'm torturing myself, but I can't convince myself to give a shit. This way, I can keep her. Even if it's just within the confines of my fucked-up mind. I can recall every line of her face, every curve of her body, the perfect blonde of her hair, and the creamy tone of her skin. Shit, if I close my eyes and focus hard enough, I can still smell her in my space.

So sweet.

So tempting.

So far from *mine,* the scent burns like acid.

I watch the hurried movements of her legs as she rushes down the stairs, working in haste to put as much distance between us as possible. My doing. Still, it stings like a fucking bitch. The footage ends with the door slamming shut, Codi no longer visible, and I lean forward and press play again.

Twenty-four hours. The length of time my ass has remained

planted in this stifling hell of an office, Codi running away from me on a loop. I've drunk myself sober, worked past inebriated, and moved back into soberness. I'm stuck in a perpetual state of hangover. I'm tired. Weary. Quenching my resounding thirst with more booze. I haven't slept in days. My hand shakes. My head is hazy. I have to blink to remove my double vision.

More than any of that, though. More than the feeling of hopelessness. My heart hurts. It fucking *aches*. I'm working my damnedest to numb it, but it's morphed into a thorned parasite in my chest, ripping my insides open with every tortured beat.

I will it to stop.

Hurting.

Beating.

Yet, the torture continues. Deserved, I know. But I'm weak enough to admit death would be welcome—a sore and sorry wave of relief.

Codi's video stops again, and I reach forward, slamming a finger down to make it play again.

"Self-pity doesn't suit you."

I startle at the masculine voice that sounds further away in my muffled brain. I sit up straighter, coming eye to eye with Dominic Rein, hands in his pockets, standing coolly in the doorway of my office.

Call me fucking crazy, but I breathe a sigh of relief at his presence. I'm relieved. I'm fucking grateful because now it all makes sense. Why he protected Rocco and me. Why he fed us all the timeline of events that unfolded in our apartment.

Dominic Rein wanted to kill us. Himself.

He laughs quietly at what he reads on my face, moving into the room. "Don't look so pleased to see me. I'm not here to hurt you, Parker. You want to die? Sort that shit yourself."

He drops gracefully into the chair across from me, reading

the disappointment in my eyes. His large palm rubs against the strong line of his jaw in thought. He takes his time considering me. His gaze drops to my laptop, reaching out to turn it his way, and I inhale deeply as he taps play, watching his daughter, alone and broken, fleeing my club. The video stops, and he stares at the screen, palm covering his mouth, eyes dancing with fury.

Exhaling heavily, he leans back in his chair before looking at me again. I swallow the remainder of my drink, sliding the glass onto my desk with little finesse.

"You thought I came here to hurt you. Kill you even. Correct?"

I offer a single nod in confirmation.

"Contrary to popular belief, I tend to keep away from murder. It's messy." He scowls. "Not to mention, it's not always friendly to the conscience."

Readjusting the cuffs of his dress shirt and pulling at the sleeves, he exudes the authority of a man not to be fucked with. One not to cross.

"*Obviously,* I'm more than unimpressed that your plan for revenge included my daughter," he pauses, his attention dragging across the room in bored curiosity. "But, I get it." He shocks the shit out of me by admitting.

He sees the surprise on my face and laughs. "What I *don't* get," he continues, eyeing me intently, "is how you can love my daughter but be okay with breaking her heart."

I shift uncomfortably in my seat, swallowing deeply. Out of nowhere, I feel stone-cold fucking sober. My mouth opens to speak, but nothing comes out. I clear my throat, trying uselessly to find anything worthy to say. But the truth is, he's right. I broke Codi's heart. I'm a piece of shit. Worthless.

"I don't deserve Codi. Better yet, she deserves someone

better than me." I settle on the truth, the only viable reason for causing her pain.

"Agreed." He nods, and I scowl heavily in his direction. Not at *him,* just at his support of the pitiful truth that I'll never be good enough to claim the heart of the only person I want.

Silence descends between us. It's awkward and uncomfortable as fuck, and I'm tempted to ask him to leave, but that just leaves me alone once again, suffocating in my self-pity. That, and in all honesty, I don't think he'd listen.

"My marriage turned sour relatively early on." One leg crosses over the other, and his attention is focused on readjusting his pants as he speaks. "We fell pregnant with Camryn at the beginning of our relationship, and our parents convinced us that marriage was our only option. Sarah resented me, and she resented Camryn, but I couldn't find it in myself to return her feelings of anger. I had Camryn. How can hate be born from the birth of your child?" It's a rhetorical question, and he shrugs, exhaling heavily.

"I always thought she'd move past it all and learn to love the life we'd started to build." He rolls his eyes, his head shaking in irritation. "When information started filtering itself to your father's ears, after careful consideration and investigation, I knew it had to be her, but I had no clue who she was metaphorically in bed with. I assumed it was unintentional, that she was an unknowing party in the arrangement. So, I ignored the gravity of the situation. Then she got pregnant."

He stands then, moving towards my booze, pouring himself a sizeable whiskey. The tension in his body has him coiled tight, rehashing painful moments from his life that stir emotions inside of him that he's not comfortable with. Yet, he continues, turning and leaning against my liquor cabinet, one hand tucked casually in his pants pocket, the other holding the tumbler in his hand.

"Experience would now tell me that I'm a fucking idiot and never once considered the baby wasn't mine. Shit, even Sarah seemed more excited by this pregnancy than the last. Hindsight is a wonderful thing. It's obvious now her joy stemmed from the fact that this baby wasn't mine."

His neck tips back, the amber liquid in his glass disappearing down his throat in one swallow.

"Camryn looked so much like me when she was born. Codi, on the other hand, looked like neither of us. It happens, though, throwbacks from family genes. As my trust for Sarah dissipated, I became more aware, and as Codi grew, it became more and more obvious. Her skin tone, the color of her hair, and her eyes were *so* different. I gave into temptation, into my curiosity. She has a completely different blood type. To both Sarah and I."

His fist clenches. Unravels and clenches again. "I was so fucking mad. I wanted to kill her," he admits, moving to sit across from me again. "How could she betray me so forcefully? I arrived home with a fire in my soul, with hate in my heart, but as soon as I stepped through our front door, Codi launched herself into my arms, kissed my face, giggled, and said, '*I missed you, Daddy.*'"

Men like Dominic Rein don't show vulnerability, but in this private moment, with tears in his eyes, he's shown me his.

"My blood might not run through her veins, but my *blood* runs through her veins."

"She's yours," I agree, the roughly spoken words giving away my emotion.

"She's mine," he concurs, sniffing thickly and swallowing deeply. "In every way that matters. Fuck, biology."

Clearing his throat, he shifts in his seat. "The kind of better that Codi deserves doesn't exist in this world. I've come to accept that. I just want her to find love with someone who'd lay down their life for hers. A man whose heart is overflowing with the love he'll offer her. The same way hers will spill over in love for him. It seems you're that man for her. Is she that woman for you?"

He takes my long, drawn-out blink as confirmation. "Well, I suggest you spend the rest of your life loving her greater than your fullest potential. Fiercely. Without quandary. You're right if you think someone else can love her harder or more completely than you. You *don't* deserve her. But if you know that *no one* will love her the way you do, then you make this right."

I turn my head away, tears stinging my eyes. "What I did," I croak, and his sigh is heavy enough to grab my attention.

"We all make mistakes, Parker. If you let them define you, you'll live a life like the one you have been these last twenty-four hours. If you choose to *learn* from them," he implores, leaning forward in his chair. "This gigantic, fucked-up mess brought you love. If you let your mistakes swallow you, it was all for *nothing*. Make it mean something, Parker. Grab onto the positive in this shitty situation, and don't fucking let go."

My head drops into my hands, and I take my first full breath in months. Years, even.

"What if she won't—" I lift my head to an empty office, Dominic having left without a sound.

I throw my chair back, standing in haste as I rush from my office and down the stairs. The exact path Codi took when I crushed the last shreds of her heart.

Throwing open the door of Ruin with excessive force, I come face to face with Dominic, leaning casually against his car, a satisfied smirk dancing along his face.

"Good. You're ready," he announces. "Let's go." He taps the

passenger door, indicating I get inside, and walks around the car to jump in the driver's seat.

The guy was either talking out of his ass, and I was about to meet a bloody and painful death, or he was taking me to find my heart. The promise of the latter is too much to pass up, so I climb in his Audi without regret.

"Where are we going?"

"Dinner." He smiles, pulling onto the street.

THIRTY

CODI

"Did Dad say why he wanted us for dinner so last minute?"

Camryn glances at me and then back to the road. "Nope. He said it was important, though." She leans forward, turning the radio off with an irritated grunt. "Fucking hate that song. *Wait.* You don't think mom's back?"

I didn't even contemplate that as a possibility. Sarah fled the day I went to dad with Parker's story, heartbroken and disbelieving. I understand why she ran. She knew her secret was out. Her lifelong trail of deceit was about to unravel, and she knew she'd be left with no shield of protection.

"Do you think Dad will kill her? If she does come back?" My voice is soft as I vocalize the thought as soon as it pops into my mind. I'm not saddened or frightened by the idea. More curious about Camryn's thoughts and maybe my lack of emotion or turmoil attached to the possibility.

Camryn's quiet as she considers my words, but when she finally speaks, it's confident. "No."

"*No?*"

"Uh-uh." She shakes her head, eyes darting to me and then back to the road. "No matter how much he hates her. She still gave him the two of us. He'll let her live."

I surmise she's right. It's crazy to think that only a few months ago, talking about death, about taking the life of another, would have been met with shock and disgust on my behalf. Yet here, driving to our family home for dinner, Camryn and I are discussing these exact points like it's nothing more than a conversation about the weather. About our mother, no less.

There's no denying that I've changed. How could I not? My life up until Parker was quiet, undisturbed, and *straightforward*. Now darkness has been let into my life, irrevocably changing how I view the world. I'm still me. Codi Rein; sweet like sugar, but inexperienced is no longer a word I feel associated with. My naivety is gone, having disappeared in a puff of smoke the moment I saw two people die right before my eyes.

"Well, I can't see her car." Camryn pulls me from my thoughts, and I glance around the driveway.

"You don't think dad has pulled us here to tell us he's going to prison? For killing Marcus?" I hate speaking his name. I hate thinking about him. I hate knowing that we're genetically linked, whether I admit it or not. A shiver runs along my spine, and I shake it off, my mouth twisting horribly in distaste.

"Did you see those fucking cops?" Camryn barks out a laugh. "I get they're on Dad's payroll, but could they be any more obvious? The lead detective turned his back to stare at a wall while dad fed us *what happened*." She finishes her sentence in quotation marks, her eyes wide with disbelief. "Not to mention you and Parker were showering, washing *evidence* from your skin, and not one of them blinked an eyelid."

I don't let my thoughts return to that emotionally charged moment with Parker. Both of us breaking at the seams, our grief and anguish leaking from our eyes. The rough, stuttered sound of his cries still haunts my dreams. If I let my mind go there, I can still feel them echoing into my neck, kissing along my skin. All I could do was stand there and hold on, knowing that no matter what had happened between us, he had me to lean on.

I rub my eyes. There are no tears. Jesus, there'd be none left in my body. I'm all dried out. My eyes feel like sandpaper in my skull. I've cried too much. So much so that my body has now refused to cooperate with my need to rid my rollercoaster emotions from my body with thick, ugly tears.

Camryn touches my arm, and I startle.

"Babe. Dad's fine. He's not in trouble." She has misread my dilemma, but I'm okay with that. If she knew my thoughts were on Parker and not Dad, she'd want to talk about him, and I don't want to do that. Not now. Not ever.

"Yeah." I force a weak smile, moving from her car without another word.

The smell of rich tomato sauce hits us as soon as we enter the house, and Camryn inhales happily.

"Spaghetti. Fuck yeah."

Her footsteps are close behind mine as she follows me toward the kitchen, babbling about garlic bread and parmesan cheese.

Parker stands as soon as I step into the room, and my feet cease their ability to move. My body locks rock solid, from the tips of my toes to the hair follicles on the top of my head. Everything pauses, and my capacity to pull in a breath seems to be lost.

Camryn slams into me, yet, my body doesn't move an inch.

"Fuck, Codi. What the hell?" She growls, pushing at my back in irritation. "*Oh,*" she adds, finally noticing our unexpected dinner guest standing awkwardly at our dining table.

She moves toward him without fanfare, hugging her body around his while standing on tiptoes to whisper in his ear.

A small smile plays on his lips, and he nods down at her when she pulls back. "Noted."

She winks, tapping his arm before kissing our dad's cheek and sitting at the table.

"Codi." My dad speaks, but I can't move my eyes away. They're glued to him, standing in my family home, looking undeniably awkward yet heartbreakingly hopeful. "You remember—"

"Bob." Parker cuts him off, the word a little louder than necessary.

Biting my lip, I hide the smile threatening to creep onto my face. Our eyes remain glued on one another, a smile stretching his lips. It's genuine, and my heart spasms in my chest, kick-starting itself back to life.

"Come. Sit. Eat," my dad instructs, and without warning, my feet concede to his direction, moving me to my seat across from Parker.

Neither of us eats, too caught up with watching one another. He looks healthier or at least showered. His hair is styled like I'm used to, and while the shadows under his eyes are hollow and dark, his eyes hold a spark I was convinced had died only twenty-four hours ago.

I should probably speak. Let him know that I'm happy he's here, but my vocal cords seem to have seized. He's much the same, watching quietly for long, drawn-out minutes.

The only sound in the room is the clatter of cutlery along Camryn and dad's plates, my heavy breathing echoing in my ears.

Without warning, Parker stands, and Dad and Camryn stop,

food halfway to their mouths as their eyes settle on his shaking frame.

"Excuse us," Parker speaks, eyes still focused on me, and without looking at my family, I stand too.

Parker follows me from the dining room, up the stairs, and into my childhood bedroom. The door closes softly behind him, and I stand awkwardly in the middle of the space, waiting.

"Thank you for coming to Mira's funeral," he starts, rolling his shoulders in discomfort. I hear the sadness in his voice as her name leaves his mouth. His tongue catches on his lips, his eyes glimmering with emotion.

"I wasn't sure I was welcome. I... When you finally saw me, you looked at me so vacantly."

A bark of laughter escapes his closed mouth, eyes tipping to the ceiling and back to me.

"I clocked your car the moment you pulled up. I was too scared to look you in the eye. Selfish reasons." He smiles sadly. "I didn't want to see how I felt painted clear as day on you. More than that, I feared seeing the hate in your eyes. Before you walked out of my life, your eyes were shooting daggers of hate at me. I wasn't ready for that to pierce me again."

I remain quiet, his words drowning me in sadness. Maybe relief. Solace in knowing I wasn't fighting this tsunami of heartbreak alone, barely holding on as wave after wave of misery and pain crashed against us, making it impossible to fight.

"In the end, I couldn't help myself," he continues, eyes scanning teenage Codi's bedroom. "I threw up every last defense I had left, which was next to nothing, and I looked." He finally settles his stare back on me. "Your chaotic eyes were as uncertain and sad as you were. I'm asshole enough to admit all I could feel was relief. Because, although I deserve it, you hating me was enough to make me want to die."

He lets that filter between us, and I continue to choose my silence. For no other reason than he seems hell-bent on needing to speak.

"I'm sorry," he starts again, licking his lips and coughing to clear his throat. "I'm so fucking sorry, Sugar. For everything—"

"Parker," I cut him off. "I told you, I get it."

He nods, shifting uncomfortably on his feet. "I know that. I appreciate that you do not hate on me for what I did and that you're working to understand the place I was in. Still, I'm sorry, baby. For everything. For the stupid fucking plan in the first place, for pulling you in, for deceiving you, for taking shit from you that shouldn't have been mine to take, not when I was living a lie. I'm sorry for taking your love and throwing it away. I'm fucking sorry."

He looks equal parts defeated and relieved by his apology, and I step toward him, needing to touch him. But he stops me with a quick shake of his head, a palm held up in a gesture to wait.

"Let me get all this out first. I need... I never told you the most fucking important thing about me. I should've. Instead, I held it in here." He taps a fist against his large chest, his Adam's apple bobbing with the effort against the thickness of his throat. "Without knowing it, I let what I felt for you fire my hope, and I know I shouldn't have held onto it without shouting to anyone who would fucking listen, but I held it tight, Codi. Fuck, did I hold on. I let it keep me alive. Even when I sank into the depths of hell, you kept me breathing."

Inhaling heavily through his nostrils, he clears his throat, his eyes fixated on mine, boring into me with an intensity that makes my cheeks burn.

"I think you know how I feel about you, but you deserve to hear me say the words. Because, fuck, Sugar, hearing you tell me you loved me is the greatest fucking memory I have to hold onto. People talk about *showing* someone you love them, that love is in actions, not words. It makes sense, but it doesn't hurt hearing the person that makes your heart beat tell you that you're that person for them too."

My face softens. I feel it. The gentleness in my eyes, the emotionally clogged happiness drifting along my face.

"I love you, Codi," he confesses quietly. "First moment you smiled at me, I knew I was fucked," he barks out a soft laugh. "You kick-started something in here." He beats a fist against his chest. "I tried so hard to hold onto my resentment, my hate, but it didn't stand a chance, not against what I felt for you."

He steps closer, the swirling storm in his gray eyes gliding over my face. "You consume me. Body, mind, fucking soul. You're all that's real in my life. You put me back together. Before I even knew I wanted to feel whole again."

The tears I thought had emptied from my body rush out of my eyes and down my cheeks. I brush them away, but they reappear just as fast, and then he's standing in front of me, his large, inked hand sliding across my face to wipe away my tears.

"I love you," he repeats. "No one in this world can love you as hard as I do. My love for you is everything that's important in my life. Maybe I don't deserve you, but that doesn't mean that I'm not going to try my fucking hardest to make you believe I do."

He tucks a lock of hair behind my ear, his fingers trailing down my jaw, his thumb pulling across my bottom lip. We stand there in silence, his declaration dancing in the breath of space between us, letting our hearts heal with the reality that we found our way back to one another. In this tangled, hopeless mess, we found something worth fighting for. Something worthy. Something unique.

Each other.

"Random fact," I whisper, and he smiles at my lips. "I'm ready for you to kiss me now."

The fire in his eyes spikes, skating over my face as his large hand holds my jaw, tilting it upward.

I've missed this. His rough and needy touches. The dominant way his body directs mine.

Leaning down, his bottom lip pulls against mine, a tease of a touch making my lips part on a shaky exhale.

"Tell me you still love me and that I didn't fuck everything by being a fucking coward," he murmurs against my lips.

"I love you," I respond without hesitation, the declaration kissed across his lips the way it should've been from the very beginning.

He growls his approval, finally sinking his mouth against mine. His lips are soft, but his kiss is not. His lips feel like safety, yet his kiss is anything but innocent. It's sinful and immoral in the best possible way. We've been through hell and back, and it's not surprising our kiss is a wicked form of worship.

Parker's tongue strokes dominantly against mine, and I moan into his mouth, finding my ability to breathe again after too long without his oxygen. My tongue meets his eagerly, and I know he feels the same way, his rough growl sounding right from the back of his throat and down my spine.

We lose ourselves in our kiss, or more, we find one another. All the hurt, all the pain we've endured, we let this single moment of intimacy swallow it whole. We want it gone from our life. Extinct, without the ability to find traction ever again. We let our love conquer everything we've lost, together and apart. Until it's just Parker and me, lost in a kiss shared by two people who love one another. Nothing less, but a whole lot more.

He pulls away first, his rough groan vibrating against my

mouth as his teeth graze my bottom lip. He kisses the spot softly, hand still grasping my jaw tightly as he meets my eyes.

"First time you smiled at me, I knew I was fucked. Our first kiss sealed my fate. I never stood a fucking chance against you, Sugar." He leans down, his swollen lips finding the shell of my ear. "Really fucking glad I didn't," he whispers, and I pull him closer, relishing in the feeling of being wrapped around him the way I long to.

"Random fact." He pulls back, his dirty smirk playing along the bruised color of his lips. "I want you so fucking bad it hurts. But let's take this slow. I want you to know I want more than a knee to the junk." He winks, and I laugh softly.

"A headbutt could also be arranged."

His hand drops away from my chin, pulling me into his body and hugging me close.

"More importantly," I continue, tipping my head back to catch his eyes. "There will be no taking of anything slow. I waited twenty-five years to have sex. You are not holding back on me now I've had my taste."

"Thank fuck," he groans, planting his lips against my forehead. "Come. Let's eat. The sooner we're finished, the sooner we're out of here."

We're at the door when he stops, looking down at me. "I think my mom would've fucking loved that I found you, better, that I somehow convinced you to fall in love with me."

DINNER FINISHED, Camryn stands, moving to clear her plate. "You guys head off. I might crash here tonight," she announces unceremoniously.

My cheeks shade involuntarily, and I scowl over at her. "Subtle, Ryn."

She only shrugs, moving from the dining room. "Have fun," she sings.

Parker moves toward my dad, their hands connecting in a tight handshake, quiet words whispered between them.

It's nice to see acceptance from my father for the man I love. I don't know what happened between them, and I likely never will. I'm okay with that. All I know is that twenty-four hours ago, Parker had shunned me and turned me away without hope of reconciliation. The next thing I knew, he was sitting at my dinner table with my father's blessing. I'm just happy it worked out.

WALKING THROUGH MY FRONT DOOR, a buzz of nervous excitement vibrates through my veins. Parker is fast on my heels, barely a step between us as he trails me into my bedroom. We're alone, but he still closes the door, shutting us away in our private space.

"I need to shower. My wallowing may or may not have interfered with my want to bathe over the last twenty-four hours."

He stalks towards me, starvation in his eyes. Yanking his shirt over his head, he throws it to the floor, his abs contracting with every step closer to me he takes.

"*Oh,*" I stutter, feeling hunted in the same way I feel desired.

Yanking me toward his body, I hit his solid frame, and he lifts me effortlessly, slamming my back against the closest wall.

"Parker, I—"

He cuts off my words with his mouth, tongue slicing between my lips, massaging mine. His kiss swallows my surprised gasp while his hands move into my underwear, grabbing my ass.

His hands knead, his tongue massages, and I whimper. I claw to get closer.

Pinning me against the wall with his frame, he uses one hand to rip at the scrap of material covering me. Breaking our kiss, my head slams against the wall, eyes drunk with want, chest heaving with unrivaled need. His eyes meet mine, the gray storm drunk like mine, and his dark lips are swollen from our harsh kiss.

Undoing his pants, he keeps my eyes, his face dipping forward, to kiss my lips before pulling back.

My body is on fire. Burning. Hot. Flames scorched over my skin with my unforgiving need for his touch.

His chest meets mine, his lips falling to my neck as the thick head of his cock teases my entrance.

I cry out.

I beg.

I moan.

I plead.

And finally, when I think I'll die without feeling him inside my body, he surges forward, burying himself entirely in one swift thrust.

Neck tipped back, I scream.

In pleasure.

In pain.

In *relief.*

"Oh. Parker."

"Feels so fucking good," he mumbles into my neck, pausing, his chest pushing against mine with every labored breath.

This is what my body craved. Don't get me wrong, reaching your peak, your body exploding in a powerful, mind-blowing orgasm, is like nothing else. You disconnect from your body, from the unrivaled pleasure coursing through you. The way you *lose* control, your body convulsing, shaking, arching, *moving* as *it* needs to, to ride you through your pleasure. It's like nothing else. *Nothing.* But this, right here, the moment of penetration, is a close, *close* second for me. My God. The way Parker stretches me, *forcing* me to feel every strong, powerful inch of him. Every nerve in my body pulsates in an almost unsatisfied need. *So* good, but I need *more.* So much more. The anticipation is at its highest because I know what's coming. I know how incredible he can make me feel. Where he can take my body. To the peak I'm chasing. That moment of pleasure that possesses my body until I'm no longer me. Codi doesn't exist. In her place is just an explosive ball of energy, readying itself to detonate into an abyss. A soul-shattering, mind-blowing, body-quaking abyss.

Parker's teeth bite into my neck, and I groan, undulating my hips to find relief.

He growls, licking up the column of my neck. Ever so slowly, he pulls from my body, and I shiver.

"Fuck, I love you." He meets my eyes, leaning forward to kiss me.

"Codi. Baby. The shit you do to my heart, to my body... I can't explain it. I... I love you," he breathes out desperately. "I love you."

Cupping his jaw with my hands, I scan my eyes over his. "Parker. You own me. Mind. Body. Soul. Everything in here." I drop a hand to my heart, palm open wide over the spot. "It's yours. Only yours. Forever. I love you, too."

His lips smash down on mine, and we lose ourselves in the manic way our bodies need to touch. Parker thrusts heavily in and out of my body, his kiss never ceasing, wanting me to feel him love me.

I feel it.

I live it.

I reciprocate.

It's crazy to think how far we've come from that moment he walked into my shop until now, and what we've each endured. It's incredible to realize that such a fierce love could grow in such a twisted mess of hate, revenge, deceit, and sorrow.

But it did.

It fucking flourished.

I have to believe that we would've always found one another. Or maybe we were always supposed to meet the way we did. Maybe it was our test. And we more than passed. We *aced* it because people search their lives for what Parker and I share, and we found it. In hopeless circumstances, we held on. We held on as tight as possible, and our tangled love prevailed.

EPILOGUE

PARKER

"Sugar, fuck, if you could see my view," I groan, skating my hand down the back of her naked thigh. It's fucking pathetic how desperate the words sound, but Jesus, nothing, and I mean fucking *nothing,* has ever looked this good.

Codi looks over the naked shoulder at me, sweet lips lightly parted, purple eyes drunk with need.

She's naked. On all fours. Knees far apart.

"Fuck, baby, I need a picture." I stand, eyes scanning her room for my phone.

"*What?*" she gasps, her knees drawing together before I scowl down at her. She stops but stares at me with beautiful wide eyes.

"Trust me. I'll show you, and if you hate it, I'll delete it."

She swallows deeply. "Promise?"

"Sugar, I don't need to promise that. When you see what I'm seeing, you'll be turned on knowing I have it on my phone. It'll turn you on to know I can stroke my cock while staring at my favorite fucking place on earth."

That gets her, her hips pushing backward ever so slightly, searching for relief. She cries out softly when she hears the tell-tale click of the camera on my phone, and I smile to myself.

Codi Rein. My sweet fucking dirty, Sugar.

Sliding my phone up beside her, I put the image in front of her eyes, watching them dilate with wild lust.

"See," I whisper. "This is heaven on fucking earth, Sugar. Look at your creamy thighs, spread wide for me." I trail a finger along the image like I would her skin, and she bites her bottom lip.

"Look at your perfect fucking ass cheeks, round and ready for my mouth, for my hands."

Her breathing stutters, and I know if I reach my hand back to find her sweet spot, she'd be drenched, clenching, and greedy for my fingers.

But I refrain. For now. Enjoying my form of torture.

"Your arched back," I continue, touching the photo. "All the way down to your tight little asshole, begging for attention. Almost ready for my cock, don't you think, baby? So greedy whenever I touch you there, clenching down on my fingers as I let them fuck your ass."

Her neck tips back, an audible whimper escaping her throat.

"Then there's your pretty pink pussy. Look at her. Glistening. Wet. For me," I whisper against her ear. "All. Fucking. Mine."

Biting her earlobe, I pull back. I leave my phone against her pillows so she can see. "I'm gonna leave this here and let you see what I see while my tongue's teasing that sweet little cunt of yours."

I groan when I move back to my position at the back of her bed. Fuck. I'll never tire of this. Of her. She's perfection. In every possible way.

I waste no time feasting on her pussy. Gliding my tongue back and forth over her slit in thick, broad strokes. She pushes back eagerly, trying to fuck my face.

Palms on her ass cheeks, I grab hold, pulling her back and giving her what she wants.

I eat her. Messy. Greedy. Feral.

She's so close. I can feel her throbbing against my tongue.

I stop, and she cries out.

"No. No, don't stop. Baby, please." Her forehead hits the mattress, and she groans in frustration. "I was right there."

"Mmm…" I agree, standing to a full height behind her and yanking her hips backward. "Wanted to feel you come on my dick, though."

Looking over her shoulder, her cheeks flushed, eyes wild with her impending orgasm, she runs her tongue along her teeth. "Hard."

Gliding my head along her clit over and over again, I frown. "Huh? Sorry, I couldn't quite hear that."

"Hard," she grits out, her body shaking every time the head of my cock hits where she needs it.

"*Sugar*," I tsk. "Give it to me how I want it, then you'll get what you need."

She exhales heavily, pushing her tits down into the mattress to arch her back more. "Fuck me hard, Parker."

Lining up at the heat engulfing the head of my dick, I push forward only slightly. "You didn't say please."

She glares at me over her shoulder, purple eyes shooting sparks in my direction, and I laugh loudly but give her what she wants.

I slam forward and pull out fast, just to do it again.

She comes. Like I knew she would. Her body was already

there, just needing that last push over the cliff to fall into the sweet pleasure of nothing.

The slap of skin echoes the loud and incoherent cries of her orgasm as I fuck her. *Hard.* Like she wanted.

It still blows my mind that we made it here. Together. That her love for me was strong enough for her to forgive all the shitty things I've done. I don't deserve her. I know that. That doesn't mean I'm ever giving her up. Not a fucking chance. She's mine. And for some warped reason, she thinks I'm worthy of her. I'm not idiotic enough to convince her otherwise.

She pushes up from the bed, her back hitting my chest, and I hold her there, large palm squeezing her tit as I move in and out of her body.

The back of her head rests on my shoulder, her matted hair slick against her forehead. I kiss her.

"I need you to be my wife." I pull back, my words humming softly against the stuttered sounds of her breathing.

"Wha—"

I kiss her again, cutting off her question and letting my tongue dance in her mouth, cutting off her ability for coherent thought.

Fuck she feels good. My neck tips back, leg muscles straining as I bury myself deep inside one last time as I come on a long, satisfied groan.

"Fuck, Codi."

Her arm twists upward, cupping my head and bringing my mouth down to hers. Our kiss is slow and unhurried. We spend minutes lost in the intimacy of the moment.

"People think a proposal should be a huge fucking deal; flowers and champagne, me on one knee. I disagree. What we just shared is as intimate and emotional as anyone can get. Lost in one another the way I'm lost in you."

Her purple eyes blink softly, and I exhale.

"I don't wanna ask you to marry me because it doesn't feel like that measly question is enough to show you how much I want this. I *need* you to be my wife, Codi. Like I need my next fucking breath."

I swallow down my nerves, not wanting her to see how fucking anxious I am that she'll say no. "You put me back together and showed me life was worth living. I don't want to waste another second of this life without you. I *need* you to be my wife, so every day, I get to see your purple eyes and the realness in your smile, knowing I make you happy. I *need* you to be my wife so we can start planning our life together; travel, kids, whatever the fuck you want, Codi. I *need* you to be my wife so I can call myself your husband. I fucking *need* you to be my wife so I know I can love you forever. And that you'll love me back for just as long."

She spins in my arms, throwing her arms around my neck. "I want all that and more. I love you, Parker Shay. I need to be your wife just as much as you need me to be. Maybe more."

My lips grow into a wide smile, peace filtering into my soul. "Random fact, you've just made me the happiest motherfucker on the face of this earth."

She smiles, sighing dreamily. "Random fact, we're naming our first baby Bob."

I laugh. Loudly. The sound making her smile grow.

"That's an opinion, not a fact. Try again." I push her back onto the bed, pinning her beneath me.

"Random fact, I never thought a man would be my reason for breathing. I was wrong." The words are whispered, her eyes lost in mine.

Leaning down, I kiss her. I have to, she's just given me the world, and I plan on spending the rest of my life showing her how grateful I am.

Codi Rein may have started as a means to an end, but that was lost the moment I laid eyes on her.

She was supposed to be a no-one but quickly became my everything.

She wasn't supposed to make me smile, and she wasn't supposed to make me laugh. But she ignited happiness in my soul when I thought it no longer existed in the bleak darkness of my world.

She wasn't supposed to make me love her, but I was a fool to think I stood a chance.

Codi Rein controls my heart. It's hers. She may have started as a means to an end, but she quickly became my happily ever after.

Thank you for reading TANGLED LOVE.
We hope you enjoyed Codi and Parker's chaotic love story.

Intrigued to find out who claims Rocco's misguided heart?
Read Reining Devotion now....

Rocco Shay is unhinged.
He had plans to kill my sister.
I hate him. But he's the only person I feel at peace with.
Does that make me a monster?
One-click REINING DEVOTION now.

If you enjoyed Tangled Love, you'll love our mafia-inspired
series, Lies of the Underworld.
Start with book one, VIRTUOUS LIES, today.

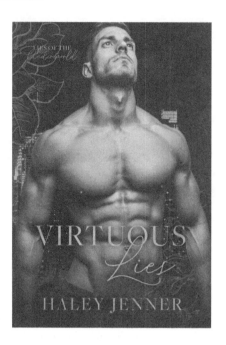

To keep up-to-date with our new books, sign up for our newsletter: www.authorhaleyjenner.com

PARKER & CODI'S PLAYLIST

Way Down We Go, Kaleo
Good As You Were Bad, Jana Kramer
Goodbye In Her Eyes, Zac Brown Band
We Found Love (Acoustic), Tyler Ward
I Never Told You, Colbie Cailat
I Have Questions, Camila Cabello
Forever Young, Louisa
I Love You, Alex & Sierra
Too Good At Goodbyes, Sam Smith
Whiskey, Maroon 5 (feat A$AP Rocky)
Tragic Endings, Eminem (feat Skylar Grey)
Stupid Love, Jason Derulo
You Ruin Me, The Veronicas
Please Don't Say You Love Me, Gabrielle Aplin
Missed, Ella Henderson
The Devil's Tears, Angus & Julia Stone

You can find this playlist on Spotify:
Tangled Love

ACKNOWLEDGMENTS

Ellie. We're running out of ways to say thank you. We'll never stop, but that just means you'll have to hear us bowing down at your feet for eternity. You make us better writers and not just through your editing, but because you make us more conscious of who we are as authors now. So, maybe here, we'd like to thank Instagram for bringing you to us. Thank the holy fucking greatness of memes that kick-started our appreciation for you as a person. You're our Yoda, our Sorting Hat, our Three-eyed raven. Anyway, this is getting weirdly long. You're our form of a bible; let's break bread and drink wine (eat pizza and get drunk).

Can we double-paragraph you, ellie? Or is that weird? Too bad. Special mention needs to be made about this cover. HOLY. MOTHERFUCKING. SHIT. Thank you for securing this image of Warren for us. Writing Tangled, we had a picture in our mind, and you made that happen. We don't even know how to say thank you for that. We heart you. Big time.

Stacey, Sarah, and Samara. Your names are like a solid fixture in our books now, and we LOVE that; a forever part of the HJ family. The time you take to read our books and offer us feedback before we let them out into the big, wide world means everything to us. Truly. You ladies take away the crippling nerves of release week. We love you, you know this, but it doesn't hurt to be told a million times more.

To the amazing group of people that make up our Group Therapy reader's group. We hope you know how much we appreciate each and every one of you. Group Therapy is one of our favorite places, and you bring smiles to our faces every day.

To our readers. We're still constantly blown away by the love and support shown to us in this amazing community of book lovers. We feel so blessed to be a part of this ridiculously beautiful collection of people. There are no words to describe how grateful we feel every time you engage in our posts, every time you share something of ours, and every time we read a review. It's overwhelming, and it's humbling. Each and every one of you holds a special place in our hearts (like double the love because there are two of us). Thank you for continuing to read our words to let yourself be consumed in our stories. We hope you love them as much as we love you. Kisses. (And hugs from J. H *would* hug you, but she's kinda weirdly uncomfortable with physical affection. She still loves you, though.)

We hope you enjoy Parker and Codi's tangled love story. These characters hold a special place in our hearts, and we hope we've done their chaotic story justice.

Much love, as always, H and J x

ABOUT THE AUTHOR

A blonde. A brunette. A tea lover. A coffee addict. Two people. One pen name. Haley Jenner is made up of friends, H and J. They're pals, besties if you will, maybe even soulmates. Consider them the ultimate in split personality, exactly the same, but completely different.

They reside on the Gold Coast in Australia's sunshine state, Queensland. They lead ultra-busy lives as working mums, but wouldn't want it any other way.

Books are a large part of their lives. Always have been and they're firm believers that reading is an essential part of living. Escaping with a good story is one of their most favorite things, even to the detriment of sleep.

They love a good laugh, a strong, dominating alpha, but most importantly, know that friendships, the fierce ones, are the key to lifelong sanity and fulfillment.

facebook.com/authorhaleyjenner
instagram.com/authorhaleyjenner
amazon.com/Haley-Jenner/e/B0758DDWDX
bookbub.com/authors/haley-jenner
tiktok.com/@haleyjennerauthor

OTHER BOOKS BY HALEY JENNER

Please visit your favorite eBook retailer to discover other books by Haley Jenner:

Lies of the Underworld

Virtuous Lies (#1)

Fractured Secrets (#2)

The Chaotic Rein Series

Tangled Love (#1)

Reining Devotion (#2)

<u>Stand-alone</u>

Impact

Impact

Cross your Heart

Cross your Heart

FOR KEEPS. FOR ALWAYS.

For Keeps. For Always.

UNTAMED (a short story)

Untamed

Made in United States
Cleveland, OH
08 May 2025

16739891R00197